BOOKS BY BRAD MAGNARELLA

THE PROF CROFT SERIES
Book of Souls
Demon Moon
Blood Deal
Purge City
Death Mage

THE XGENERATION SERIES
You Don't Know Me
The Watchers
Silent Generation
Pressure Drop
Cry Little Sister
Greatest Good
Dead Hand

THE PRISONER AND THE SUN
Escape
Lights and Shadows
Final Passage

BLOOD DEAL

A Prof Croft Novel

by

Brad Magnarella

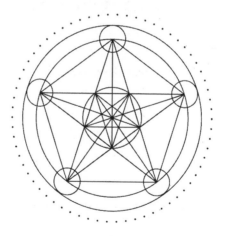

Blood Deal

A Prof Croft Novel

ISBN-13: 978-153977-572-0
ISBN-10: 1-539-77572-0

Cover art by Damon Freeman
www.damonza.com

First Edition

Printed in the U.S.A.

For my parents

1

"*Vigore!*" I shouted, my cane aimed at the lock.

In a burst of beveled wood, the lock exploded. Shouldering through the door, I stumbled into a living room. The ivory-white carpet and crowd of expensive décor gave me pause. Most amateurs were either those with a genuine interest in the esoteric or those who believed magic would pave the way to wealth and power. The already wealthy tended not to dabble. And yet, from down a corridor lined with gilded wine racks, the screaming picked up again, becoming a woman's pleas.

"For God's sake, do something, Morty! *Do* something!"

"Christ, Gert, can't you see I'm trying?" Morty's muffled response sounded more fed up than fearful.

I checked my hunting spell. *Did* I have the right apartment?

At the end of the corridor, I poked my head into a dining room. An aging woman who I took to be Gert was standing on a dining room table that would seat ten, white pumps kicking around a mess of books and casting items. She had both hands buried inside her frizz of dyed-black hair, startled eyes fixed on a kitchen to my right. With grunted curses, a balding man in a camelhair sweater was jabbing a broom between a counter and fridge.

"It's going up the wall, Morty! There it is! Swat it!" Gert could have been talking about a mouse, but the spell paraphernalia, now spilling from the table, suggested otherwise.

I craned my neck for a better view. Beside the stainless-steel fridge, I glimpsed a scurry of legs that looked like human fingers. The crab-sized creature flattened itself to the wall and squeezed behind a row of ceiling-mounted cabinets. A whipcord tail disappeared last.

Crap. A riddler.

"It's getting into the family china!" Gert cried. "Stop it! Get it out!"

"What's it look like I'm doing?"

"Don't," I warned Morty, who had curled his thick fingers around the cabinet door. "Back away. Now."

He and Gert turned toward me, Morty's jowly face tilting in confusion. These were probably my least favorite moments as a wizard garbage collector, an informal title I still held. Or that held me. Never mind that I'd banished a demon lord in October. The feat had restored my good—or at least tolerable—standing with the Order, but six months later, and here I was, having to bail out a pair of amateurs who didn't know toadstool from Toledo.

"That thing in there is dangerous," I said, which was a bit understated. A riddler's tail carried a razor-sharp ridge on the underside. One slash, and Morty would be looking at a severed broom and a fingerless hand—if he was lucky. Dangerous? Try lethal.

"Who are *you* supposed to be?" Gert asked in a New York-sharp accent, giving me a quick up and down. "Bruce Wayne?"

"Huh?" *Oh, the tuxedo.* "My name's Everson Croft. I heard screaming and came to investigate. You're in luck, I've dealt with these creatures before. I work in, um, extermination."

Morty backed from the kitchen, gripping the broom in both hands. He looked from the sound of rattling plates to me and back. "I don't even know where the thing came from."

"What do you mean you don't know where it came from?" Gert took my offered hand as she stepped carefully from the table to one of the chair seats, then down to the floor. She carried the powdered air of someone accustomed to being waited on and didn't thank me. "It came from those silly books. I told you they were trouble. I told you not to fool with them."

"You were the one who said we needed to start thinking outside the box."

"Starting a home business, Morty. Selling some of our assets, Morty. That's what I was talking about. Not whatever all of *this* is." She threw her arms toward the table. "And now we have something crawling willy-nilly over the family china that Emerson says is dangerous."

"It's Everson, actually," I said, eyeing the cabinets.

"And as an exterminator, *he* would know," Gert finished.

"Well, you're impossible to please," Morty grumbled.

"I'm impossible? *I'm* impossible?" Gert hooked an arm around one of mine to get my attention. "I hired a designer last month, one of the Upper West Side's best. She completely overhauled the apartment—I mean, completely. Did a *wonderful* job. Positive colors, feng shui, the whole shebang. Do you think Morty noticed? Do you think he voiced a single word of appreciation?"

Morty pulled on my other arm until I met his aggrieved eyes. "That was after I told her the apartment was fine as is, that we couldn't afford a designer. Do you think she listened to me?"

They began raising their voices over one another, even as something in the kitchen shattered.

"Listen," I said, freeing my arms and placing my hands on their backs. "I'd love to stand here and play Dr. Phil, but I have a job to do. I'm going to need some space." They were too engrossed in their argument to respond, but they let me guide them into the hallway, where they continued firing cannonballs.

"I kill myself trying to make you happy," came Morty's fading voice, "and all I hear from you is how bad I'm screwing up."

"Well, you *are* screwing up," Gert assured him.

I closed a swinging door behind them and turned to the dining room table. I immediately spied the black book he had cast from and groaned. Translated from Sanskrit, the book promised the caster the ability to summon a wish-granting genie. But without a magical bloodline, the best an amateur could hope for was a bug from a shallow nether realm—which was just as well. The bugs could be deadly, but the so-called genies could be downright apocalyptic.

I stepped into the kitchen, drawing my cane into sword and staff. Another piece of dishware broke as the riddler scuttled inside the cabinets. I tracked the sound with my eyes, right to left.

"Come out, come out, wherever you are," I whispered.

In the cabinet above an eight-range stove, the clattering ceased. I took another step forward, a Word of Power on the tip of my tongue.

The cabinet door flew wide. In a pale flash, the riddler was launching toward my face, tail lashing, fleshy mouth slurping at the air.

I threw my staff and sword into an X in front of my face and shouted, *"Protezione!"*

A light shield crackled into being, sparking with the riddler's impact. When something hot bit my neck, I realized the riddler had whipped its tail around. The creature was clinging to my spreading shield, mini plungers on its knuckled legs suckling for purchase.

"Respingere," I cried, before it could lash me again. A force pulsed from the shield, blowing the creature back into the cabinets. Doors clapped, and several plates crash-landed to the tiled floor. The riddler ended up on the stovetop, legs kicking air before the tail popped it upright again.

I was preparing another blast when I felt blood welling from my neck wound, threatening to spill onto the tuxedo. "C'mon, this is a rental," I cried. The last thing I needed was to lose my frigging deposit.

I entrapped the riddler in a dome of light and then grabbed a monogrammed kitchen towel from beside the sink. After sponging the laceration, I pinned the balled-up towel in place with a shoulder. *Yeah, this isn't going to make fighting awkward or anything.* I wheeled around in time to see the riddler lash free of the light cage and scrabble behind the fridge.

"Oh, no you didn't."

Aiming my sword toward the space between counter and fridge, I cast a low-level force, hoping to push the riddler out the other side, where I had my staff aimed and a shield invocation waiting. A scraping sound told me the riddler was anchoring itself to the condenser tubing in back. Increasing my force only succeeded in shoving the fridge out at an angle.

I sighed. "You're just not gonna make this easy, are you?"

I sheathed my sword and dug into my jacket pockets. My taboo-magic alarm had sounded after I had already left my apartment, so I was only carrying the bare minimum: a vial of copper filings and a couple of odd items. *But what's this?* I pulled out another vial. *Ahh, now dragon sand I can use.*

I poured a tiny mound into the palm of my hand. More scraping among the fridge's tubing—and now scrabbling. As the riddler's finger-like legs wrapped around the side of the fridge, I shouted, *"Fuoco!"* and gave the granules a hard blow.

Fire spewed from my palm, enveloping the riddler in a dark-red plume that washed around the fridge. The creature recoiled with a cry—a horrid, high-pitched sound, like air being forced through wet flaps of flesh. I backed from the eye-stinging heat and waited. A moment later, the riddler emerged from the other side of the fridge in a smoking stagger.

"Don't take this personally, little guy," I said, aiming my cane at it. "Just doing my job."

I enclosed the riddler in a light dome. This time, I pushed more energy into the spell, shrinking the dome like a fist, increasing the pressure—something new I'd been working on. The riddler twitched and began to bulge in places. In a final fit, it raced in a tight circle, tail whipping, before dispersing in a burst of phlegm.

One less hole in our world. One less creature that didn't belong.

"Hallelujah," I muttered.

As I inspected the towel that had staunched my bleeding, voices grew in the corridor. I turned at the same moment Gert appeared through the swinging door. She and her husband were still pitched in argument, but when she glanced up, she stopped, her narrow jaw dropping.

"Morton, come here! Look at our kitchen!"

Admittedly, the kitchen looked like the site of a small bomb blast: fractured cabinet doors, spilled and smashed plates, a singed refrigerator. What mattered most, though, was the lack of human blood—better yet, the lack of a human body. I was about to point that out when Morty came up beside her.

"This some kinda joke?" he asked. "First the front door, now this?"

"Excuse me?" I said.

Gert threw her arms up. "And he's going around calling himself an expert!"

"I'm right here, you know," I told Gert, who clopped past me.

"Doesn't he know this stuff costs money?" Morty plodded after her. "What'd he say his name was?"

"Edgar something," Gert replied distractedly.

"Well, if he thinks he's getting any more of our business, he's got another thing coming," Morty decided.

Man, I really was ready for another level of wizarding.

As Morty and Gert fussed over the damage, I turned to the offending spell book. Using the copper filings, I created a casting circle around the book, then dusted its black cover with dragon sand. I closed the circle and whispered, *"Fuoco."*

A controlled fire hissed up, consuming the tome. It would be ashes inside of thirty seconds, whereupon the fire would safely self-extinguish, but I couldn't wait. A glance at my watch told me what I'd feared. I was running late, and this one was a biggie: a date with my colleague Caroline Reid.

I was almost to the destroyed front door when Gert unleashed a scream. "He's set fire to the table, Morty! He's trying to burn down our apartment!"

I shook my head. "Yeah, you're welcome."

2

I almost forgot to tip the elevator man before hurrying into the crowded reception hall. Fortunately, the address had only been a short cab ride from Morty and Gert's place, but I was still twenty minutes late. Not terrible for me, but terrible under the circumstances. This was to have been Caroline's and my first date. A trial date, we decided—or rather she decided. Caroline had been skeptical over the whole idea. As I rose onto my tiptoes and searched the formal crowd, I had the sinking feeling I'd just given her plenty of reason.

"Don't strain yourself," a voice said near my ear.

I turned to see a woman I almost didn't recognize. Her golden hair, usually worn down in waves, had been straightened and parted across her brow, then knotted into an elegant pattern behind her head. Her dress was no less stunning. The lace over her shoulders joined a mauve bodice that opened at the waist into slender, stylish folds to complete the floor-length gown.

My stagger was no performance. "Wow."

Caroline stepped forward and kissed my cheek. "Looking sharp yourself, Professor." The scent of her perfumed skin made the room waver. I planted my cane and returned the kiss.

"Listen, sorry I'm—"

"What's this?" she cut in. Her blue-green eyes were studying the spot on my neck where the riddler had lashed me. The wound had stopped bleeding, and I'd put healing magic to it on the way over, but judging by Caroline's attention it must have still looked angry.

"Oh, shaving error," I said, faking an embarrassed laugh.

"Nice try, Everson, but that didn't come from a Gillette."

"Straight razor, actually. Nothing like the original, until it decides to slice you open. I couldn't get the gash to stop bleeding, which is why I'm running late. I'm really sorry about that. I should've called."

Lies on top of lies. Great way to kick off a relationship.

"I'm just glad you made it." Caroline relaxed her scrutiny of the wound and took my arm. Together we surveyed the ultra-wealthy crowd. "I always feel like a fish out of water at these things."

"I thought these were your people," I teased.

"By proxy," she replied. "But if I have to listen to one more person rue the tax burden of owning a second home in the Hamptons or, God forbid, an Italian villa, I'm going to gouge out my eardrums with a caviar spoon."

"Ouch."

I took two flutes of champagne from a passing tray and handed one to Caroline. With a smile that relaxed her shoulders, she clinked my glass, and we sipped. The venue was the penthouse of an affluent New York developer, the event a fundraiser for Mayor Lowder—or "Budge" to most New Yorkers—who was seeking reelection in the fall. Caroline didn't belong to the affluent or political classes. Her father worked as an attorney for the mayor's office, and she was here tonight in his absence—though probably also to freshen up her own contacts. I supposed that went with being the city's preeminent expert on urban affairs.

When I looked over, she had polished off her champagne, surrendering the glass to a white-jacketed server. She seemed to steel herself before turning to face me.

"The secret to mingling," she counseled, "is to keep moving, like you have someplace you're determined to get to."

"And where's that?" I asked.

I followed her raised eyes to a second-story gallery. "If we can make it upstairs, there's a balcony with an incredible view of Central Park. We'll step out to catch our breath."

"Sounds like a plan."

And that was where I would tell her the truth about who I was, I decided. I couldn't keep holding a curtain up over the other half of my life. *Nope, nothing to see back here.* There was a good chance she would reject the truth—reject me—but I wasn't going to lie to her anymore.

"Ready?" she asked after I'd relinquished my glass.

My heart beat like a bass drum. "Let's mingle."

Caroline nodded and wheeled toward the crowd. I followed, a hand on her low back. Despite her just-voiced reluctance to play socialite, Caroline was a natural. Her face glowed as she exchanged greetings and kisses, turned to introduce me, clasped hands with women, joked with men, closed with vague promises to get together soon, and then proceeded to the next group.

I leaned toward her ear as we edged deeper into the crowd. "Sure *you're* not running for mayor?"

She turned just enough to give me an eye roll.

"Caroline," a gravely voice called from our left. It took me a moment to place the aging man with the iron-colored hair and bushy black eyebrows. Constantine Moretti, head of New York's last Italian crime family. He stepped forward in a striped charcoal suit, a woman with lush auburn hair on his arm.

"Mr. Moretti," Caroline said, a smile dying on her face. "What a surprise."

"For a second there, I thought you were gonna walk right past. Like father, like daughter, I guess." His grin didn't reach his black eyes. "You remember my wife, don't you?"

Caroline turned toward the middle-aged woman who, despite her formal black dress, possessed an aura that felt feral. She appraised Caroline with orange-tinted irises before offering her hand.

"It's good to see you again, Anita," Caroline said.

Anita nodded and accepted Caroline's hand, her nostrils opening out.

"So what's it gonna take to get your old man to return my calls?" Mr. Moretti asked.

Caroline's neck stiffened. "You're asking the wrong person."

Mr. Moretti peered around. "Is he here?"

"No. He ... he wasn't feeling well."

"Maybe you can give him a message."

"I'm not his answering service."

Mr. Moretti flashed another hard grin. "Relax. I was just gonna say, if he needs anything to be sure to let me know. We grew up in the same neighborhood, your old man and me. He ever mention that? There's no reason why old neighbors can't give each other a boost now and again, right?"

"I can think of a few," Caroline muttered.

"Tell him hello in any case," Mr. Moretti said. "I'll try him again this week."

"Have a good night," Caroline said, and moved away from him.

"What was that all about?" I asked when we were out of earshot.

"Oh, Moretti refuses to accept that the old days are gone. His family used to control construction and trucking in the city. That's how they built their empire. But as City Hall severed those connections, and other crime families moved in to dominate the vice trades, Moretti's revenue dried up."

I nodded in understanding. "And he wants access to the mayor's office to try to resurrect his old businesses."

"Exactly, but he's barking up the wrong tree. My father would never work with his kind." Her gaze moved past me and hardened. She changed course, as though trying to disappear from someone's view.

I peeked back, expecting to find Moretti tailing us. Instead, another man stood out, mostly for his tall, broad-shouldered build—and yeah, stellar looks. His copper hair and stone-hewn face belonged in a men's fitness magazine. Though engaged in conversation, he was clearly watching us, or at least Caroline.

Old flame? I wondered, a knot of jealousy hardening my gut.

Caroline squeezed my wrist. "This is Everson Croft," she said.

I turned distractedly and then nearly dropped my cane. I was standing in front of a smiling Mayor Budge Lowder and his wife, Penelope. I'd seen both on TV and in the papers, of course, but never in person.

Budge seized my hand and began pumping away. "What do you say there, Everson?"

Despite being on the far side of fifty, Budge Lowder had a boyish look. It was a combination of his baggy tuxedo, chubby face, and the dark cowlick he kept finger-combing to keep from spilling over a pair of round glasses. The look was almost comical, but I remembered Caroline once saying that only a fool would judge the man on appearances.

"It's an honor to meet you," I said.

"Hey, when you show up with a knockout like this," the mayor replied, cocking his head toward Caroline, "the honor's all mine." He clapped my shoulder and broke into hearty laughter that put me at immediate ease.

"Behave yourself," Caroline told the mayor, frowning in disapproval. "Everson's a colleague."

"Oh, yeah? Over at Midtown College?" Like a switch had been flipped, Budge went from being a barroom pal to a sober uncle, his large brown eyes turning soft with interest. As Caroline fell into conversation with the mayor's wife, the mayor edged closer to me. "What do you teach?"

"Ancient mythology and lore," I replied.

"Yeah? I've got a small collection of the Greek myths."

I raised my eyebrows. That was farther than I got with most laypeople on the topic.

"I devoured those stories as a kid," he went on. "All those heroes and creatures. But the human condition's in there too, isn't it? The good, the bad, the absurd." He gave a sad laugh as he peered around. "I should know. I live it every day."

Even though he was a political personality and no doubt working me for a vote, I caught myself nodding sympathetically. Stuck between the developers, debt-collectors, mob bosses, vampire bankers, and six million mostly-struggling New Yorkers, I would never want the man's job.

"Oh, hey." Budge perked up. "I haven't introduced you to my better half." He placed his arm around his wife and, without asking, pulled her from her conversation with Caroline. "Penny? This is Everson Croft. He's an expert in mythology over at Midtown College."

I noticed that he'd upgraded me to expert. This guy was good.

Penny's handshake was soft, almost apologetic. Indeed, with her pretty, pale features and quiet voice, she seemed Budge's polar opposite. I found my sympathies shifting to her.

"Pleased to meet you," she said.

"Oh, and he and Caroline are tying the knot," the mayor added with a prankish grin. He flinched when Caroline swatted his shoulder. "Hey, I can foresee these things!" he protested.

"Do you have any advice for us?" I asked, giving him a conspiratorial wink.

The mayor straightened and cleared his throat as though he were about to deliver an important speech, then relaxed with a smile. "It's pretty simple, kids. Know when to agree, when to disagree, and when to agree to disagree." He looked over at his wife. "Isn't that right, honey?"

She gave a forbearing smile. "Whatever you say, Budge."

The mayor laughed and hugged her to his side. "That works too."

"Well, if you'll excuse us." Caroline took my arm. "My fiancé and I have a wedding to plan."

That got the mayor slapping a thigh. "Hey, we expect an invite!" he called after us.

The men and women who had been waiting for an audience with the mayor shoved into our wake.

"He's fun," I said.

"Yeah, until he's not," Caroline replied thinly.

I waited for her to explain, but we had arrived at a spiral staircase that she seemed determined to climb. Two twists later, and we were on the gallery level. A comma formed between Caroline's eyebrows as she scanned the sea of guests below, probably looking for the man who had been tracking her. I followed her gaze, but couldn't spot him.

We continued along the gallery, passed through a set of glass doors that opened onto a balcony, and stepped outside. A cool breeze ruffled Caroline's gown. I removed my tuxedo jacket and draped it over her shoulders.

"You're a gentleman," she said.

"I try," I answered.

"You *are* trying, aren't you."

"What do you mean?"

"Well, for starters, you're getting to your classes on time. I can't remember the last time I had to cover for you. You've been attending all of the faculty meetings. You've upgraded your wardrobe. You even smell nicer." A small smile played at the corners of her lips. "If I didn't know better, Everson, I'd say you were trying to impress someone."

I felt my face flush. "Or trying to keep Snodgrass off my back."

She made a skeptical sound. "Well, *I'm* impressed, anyway."

Impressed enough to accept what I'm about to tell you?

We were leaning our elbows on the east-facing rail, taking in the dark expanse of Central Park. From our high vantage, its dangerous wilds and moonlit reservoir held a certain romance.

Now was the time to make my bold confession about wizarding, about what I felt for her. My heart slammed harder as I opened my mouth. But when I turned, Caroline's brows were bent in distraction.

"Is, ah, everything all right?" I asked.

"Hm? Oh, fine." She was holding my jacket closed at her neck. "These kinds of events tend to overwhelm me. It might not look it, but I prefer observation to participation. Probably why I'm a researcher."

Nice try. But you're trying to bullshit a bullshitter.

"Are you sure that's all it is?"

"Yes, Everson."

Despite our flirtatious banter of only moments before—and that we still had the balcony to ourselves—a formality had grown between us, hardening the air. And I knew it had everything to do with the man she'd spotted inside. I turned so my body was facing hers.

"If you ever need help with anything," I said, "you only have to ask."

She gave a ghost of a smile. "I know, Everson. Thank you."

All right, that went nowhere.

I was debating whether to ask her pointblank about the mystery man, when I realized we were no longer alone. Someone was standing just outside the glass doors, about ten feet behind us.

"Caroline?" a voice said.

I turned to find tall, dark blond and handsome stepping toward us. He moved with the purpose and elegance of young royalty, but there was something else going on with him. Something I hadn't picked up in the crowded reception hall. The man's aura. He wasn't human, but a full-blooded faerie.

3

I moved in front of Caroline, my grip tightening around my cane. New York's fae were among the oldest families in the city. Lords of great wealth, they operated on the periphery, their motives alien. They also wielded magic, including glamours to appear human. That made me feel a little better about the man's divine looks, but if that magic was a threat to Caroline...

"It's all right." She rubbed my back. "Everson, this is Angelus," she said coolly.

Geez, even his name sounded divine.

The fae crossed the remaining distance in three easy strides and offered his hand. He had a good four inches on my six-foot frame, and I had to look up a little to meet his slate-blue eyes. His shake was sturdy and polite but hummed with energy. A small head tilt told me he felt my energy, as well.

Neither of us said anything, as though reaching a silent accord between extraordinary gentlemen.

After another moment the fae being released my hand and turned to Caroline. "I hope I'm not interrupting."

"You are, actually," Caroline said.

"If I could just speak with you for a few minutes."

"I already told you we had nothing to discuss."

My gaze moved between them, wondering what in the hell kind of relationship Caroline could have with a full-blooded fae.

"You'll want to hear what I have to say," Angelus said, his handsome eyes steady on hers. "It involves your father."

That seemed to give Caroline pause. She sighed as she turned to face me, her set expression letting out a little. "Would you mind if I stepped inside for just a moment?"

"As long as you're okay," I said.

"I'll be fine. We're not going far."

Not wanting to appear the insecure date, I nodded my assent.

She gave my hand a squeeze, then passed through the door Angelus had opened for her, my jacket still over her shoulders. As Angelus closed the door, our eyes met briefly. I could read nothing in his.

He and Caroline took up a position along the rail of the gallery, visible beyond the diaphanous curtains covering the doors. I turned back toward the Park, but kept the two in my peripheral vision. The fae's distance from Caroline appeared respectful as he began to talk, Caroline facing him with crossed arms.

I was speculating on what they could be discussing—something about her father?—when a series of high-pitched beeps sounded. I looked around in confusion before realizing the sound had come from my pants pocket.

The pager.

I drew it out, its cold-iron case doing the job of protecting its circuitry from my magical aura. (I'd tried the same with a cell phone, but no dice—a lot of smoke, though.) I recognized the number flashing on the display. Detective Vega had been working doggedly for the last several months to set up her unit in homicide, crimes that didn't fit the usual mold. She had also been holding me to my agreement to act as a consultant.

I looked from the pager to Caroline and back.

"Crap," I whispered.

I opened the glass doors and poked my head inside. Angelus, who had been saying something about a "fair exchange," stopped as he and Caroline noticed my presence.

"Sorry," I said to Caroline. "I just received a page I need to return. Do you know if there's a telephone around here?"

"You can use mine." She began to unsnap her small purse.

"No, no, I've, ah, never been able to figure those things out," I stammered, which was to say I didn't want to explode her three-hundred-dollar device. "I was thinking of a landline."

"There's one in the guest bedroom," Angelus said. "Through that door." He aimed his gaze past me, toward the far end of the gallery, and took a half step back, as though my presence were making him uncomfortable. I looked at Caroline, who gave a small nod: *I'm all right.*

"Okay," I replied, in a tone I hoped sounded like a warning to Angelus.

I noticed that he waited until I reached the indicated door before he resumed speaking. Though I tried, I couldn't make out anything said above the steady swell of conversation coming from the lower level.

Caroline's a tough cookie, I reminded myself.

Yeah, but did she know who she was dealing with? Not everyone was willing, or able, to see the supernatural dimension of the city. And in the years I'd known Caroline, she had never brought it up herself, always hewing to the rational, the mundane. No, I was all but certain Caroline didn't know who he really was. Furthermore, I was certain this *Angelus*—if that was even a real name—was deceiving her, something the fae were known for.

I flipped a light switch in the elegant suite and spotted the phone on an antique desk to my right. To reach it, I passed the foot of a sumptuous king bed that reminded me of something else the fae were known for. Seduction.

I left the door open a crack, and then moved the phone to the desk's end, where I could still see a thin slice of Caroline and Angelus down the gallery.

Consulting my pager, I dialed.

"Vega," she answered after one ring.

"Are congratulations in order, Detective?" The last time we'd talked, a month earlier, her new unit had been far from a sure thing.

She ignored my question, posing her own. "Where are you?"

"At a fancy little gala on the Upper West Side," I replied, then mumbled, "watching my date being hijacked by a being who shouldn't exist." I leaned over to see them better through the door.

"Give me an address and I'll have someone pick you up."

"Why?" I asked. "What's going on?"

"What do you think?"

"Homicide?"

"Plural, and they're unusual. I need you to take a look." She wasn't asking.

I craned my neck until it started to stiffen. Caroline was gesturing in what appeared frustration while Angelus listened with small nods, hands behind his back. I didn't like the idea of leaving Caroline alone with him, though whether out of concern now or jealousy, I couldn't say.

"Croft," Vega snapped.

Through the fuzzy connection, I made out the chatter of a police-radio and the rise and fall of sirens. It sounded serious. I pivoted the phone from my mouth to exhale in frustration, then dug for the slip of paper onto which Caroline had jotted down the address for the gala.

"You ready?" I asked, and read it to her.

4

"**Y**ou're leaving?" Caroline asked.

"Yeah, an emergency came up." I flashed the pager as though offering proof. I glanced over at Angelus, who had stepped back to give us space, and moved closer to Caroline. "I'll explain later," I told her.

And maybe you'll return the favor.

"Well, all right," she said, eyes dark with disappointment. "Oh, your jacket." She removed it from her shoulders and helped me into it, making me feel like even more of a dipshit.

"I'll give you a call tomorrow," I said, "make sure you got home okay." I kissed her cheek. As I stepped past Angelus, I shot him a look that said, *If you lay a finger on her, so help me God, I will hunt you to the ends of this world and any others you try to hide in and gut you like a goblin.*

He responded with a vague nod.

Outside, I paced the front of the building, cursing the timing of Vega's page. I had just walked out on a first date with Caroline Reid—the woman I'd been pining after for two years—and left her with an immortal. Whatever Vega was calling me to had better be good.

It wasn't long before a dark blue sedan pulled up, the driver side window sliding down. I groaned. The hefty man with a wreath of tight brown curls was an associate of Vega's. He had been a little too eager to deliver my pencil for a bite-mark analysis in the fall, I remembered.

"You gonna make me idle here all night?" Hoffman asked in a brusque New York accent.

I dropped into the passenger seat and slammed the door, inhaling a stale fusion of coffee and baked-in cigarette smoke. I kicked around some fast-food bags until I had enough foot room, then buckled in and peered over at Hoffman. "So where are we headed?"

He ignored my question and circled the block. "For the record, I don't agree with this thing here." He gestured between us, though I knew he meant the NYPD contracting me as a consultant. "Ask me, you're a con man, and the worst kind."

"Tell me what you really think."

"Demons and hocus pocus?" He snorted. "You lifted that straight from television."

"I read too, you know."

"Twenty years I've been out here, and I haven't seen anything that couldn't be explained by common sense and good policing."

"Maybe that's why you're taking orders from a fourth-year detective," I suggested.

The balls of Hoffman's greasy cheeks turned red. "And hey, I know that was you who called, trying to get Vega's address and number. Think I'm stupid?" He was referring to the night in October when I'd tried to warn her about an imminent shrieker attack. "You impersonated a police detective," he went on. "That shoulda got you five years, right there."

"Instead, I got the rest of my probation wiped." I smiled with as many teeth as I could. "Funny how that worked out."

"Look, I don't know what kind of swindle you pulled to get Vega on your side, but it's not gonna fly with me. Try another stunt like that phone call, and I'm putting you in bracelets. We clear?"

"Tell me, Hoffman, are you always such a flirt?"

"Screw you," he said. "You're the one who looks like a fruit."

I followed his glance down at my rented tuxedo, complete with cummerbund. He might have had a point.

Hoffman coughed into a thick fist, as though clearing the final bits of rant from his chest. "All right, so here's what we're looking at. Double homicide at Ferguson Towers."

"*That's* where we're going?" A sprawling housing project between the Brooklyn and Manhattan bridges, Ferguson Towers was notorious for all manner of illicit activities—from sophisticated drug operations to contract killings. To say they had a crime problem was like calling someone with stage four cancer "under the weather."

"Yeah, don't know why we're wasting our time," Hoffman said. "The stiffs are a pair of junkies. They were probably knocked off for getting behind on payments or something. Or maybe another junkie had his eyes on their stash. But Vega don't like something."

"What's that?"

"The pair of them had their necks torn open," he said.

In post-Crash New York that wasn't exactly jarring. "Is there a 'but' in there?"

Hoffman looked at me sidelong. "There wasn't enough of a mess."

"A bloodsucker?"

"Maybe, but that don't mean a vampire," he said quickly, eyebrows raised. "Plenty of sickos in this city to go around. Who knows? Maybe one of 'em has a chronic iron deficiency."

"Maybe," I agreed. But we weren't talking about a human.

Ten minutes later, we heaved onto a curb and passed through an open chain-link gate. Ahead, a handful of police vehicles and an ambulance huddled in the gathering night fog, lights strobing. Grim towers took shape around us. Hoffman parked among the vehicles on the project's central plaza.

"Piece of advice?" he said, killing the engine. "Watch your head when we go in. Just last week an officer had a brick dropped on him from an upper story. We're not exactly celebrities around here."

"No catching bricks with my head," I replied. "Got it."

"I know you can't shed your outfit, but you might want to lose the dandy bits. That's likely to earn you a cinderblock." He gave a guffaw before radioing to Vega that we'd arrived.

I unknotted my bowtie and stuffed it into a pocket, wishing I'd worn my trench coat. As I leaned forward to unclasp my cummerbund, I examined the forbidding towers. There were six of them, three clustered on one side of the plaza and three on the other, a half-mile of chain-link fencing surrounding them.

Geez, I thought, grabbing my cane. *What kind of supernatural would want to mess with this place?*

"Stay close," Hoffman said.

We left the sanctuary of his car, Hoffman hustling toward the nearest tower, sidearm readied. I whispered a Word as I followed. Light from my cane slid into an umbrella-shaped shield. Peering through it, I half expected to see bricks dangling over the sills up and down the steep columns of windows. Instead, I made out silhouetted heads behind security bars. Despite what Hoffman had said, I sensed more fear in their blacked-out gazes than malice.

We stepped into a dingy lobby of caged ceiling bulbs, and I dispersed my shield. Ambulance attendants idled around a pair of empty gurneys. A pair of officers emerged from a stairwell.

"Any witnesses?" Hoffman asked the officers.

"If so, no one's talking."

"They're not even opening their doors," the other one said. "We did an entire vertical tour. The whole tower looks like a frigging ghost town."

"Damn Stiles," Hoffman muttered. "Well, go on and check out the other towers."

The officers glanced at each other nervously before pacing out the front door.

"Who's Stiles?" I asked.

"Runs the east towers."

"Is he the manager?"

"Don't worry about it," Hoffman said. "Victims are down here."

"Down, you said?"

"Got a problem with that, Merlin?"

A nauseating blend of heat and cold broke out across my face as pressure began to build against my chest. *Other than my major phobia of being underground?*

"No," I wheezed.

5

I followed Hoffman's wide frame and wavering flashlight down two flights to a littered landing. A stench of stale urine pervaded the space, undercut by the ripeness of recent death.

"Down here," Detective Vega called from beyond a propped-open door.

Hoffman and I descended another short flight of steps, arriving in a boiler room fit for an eighties slasher film. A convolution of old pipes and valves ran around the cold, damp space. We stepped over soiled clothes and brown drug envelopes until we arrived in a back room.

Vega, in her black suit and blouse, was talking to a member of what appeared to be a forensic team. A crime-scene light glared hot over a pair of draped bodies. I couldn't imagine the heat was helping the smell.

Vega finished her conversation with the technician and turned toward us.

"So what's going on?" I asked, my throat tight around my words.

Vega trained her dark eyes on the bodies. "The victims were killed sometime last night. Maintenance man found them a couple hours ago."

"Hoffman said the cause of death was torn jugulars?"

Hoffman was grunting goodbye to the forensic team as they began to file out around us. "We won't know until the autopsy," Vega replied. "But it's the most visible sign of trauma."

"And no blood?"

"Not *enough* blood. I've seen opened throats before. They leave small ponds."

I tucked my cane under an arm and accepted the pair of latex gloves she handed me. As I donned the gloves, I made a cursory assessment of the covered bodies. The two were sitting side by side against the opposite wall, only their ratty shoes showing. "Could their throats have been slashed *after* they were dead?" I asked. "Maybe they OD'd."

Hoffman huffed, but didn't say anything. He seemed better behaved around Vega.

"Some drug stuff *was* found on them," Vega allowed. "But the attack would had to have happened after the blood started to thicken and settle, and that takes about eight, ten hours."

"But you don't think that's what happened."

Light gleamed from her pulled-back hair as she shook her head. She led me to the closer body and lowered the sheet from his face.

His youth struck me first. A white male, he couldn't have been older than twenty, twenty-one. A tousle of rust-colored hair topped a gaunt, rigid face. His gaping eyes were dilated, either from death or fear.

"Ready for the rest?" Vega asked.

"I think so."

She dropped the drape to his chest, exposing the man's throat. Or what was left of it. His trachea had been cracked in two and forced aside. Rags of flesh and gray vessels hung from the gaping wound, as though powerful jaws had clamped down and shaken violently.

I glanced over the young man's sweatshirt and faded denim jacket. "I see what you mean about the blood," I said. With the condition of his throat, the man's clothes should have been painted black. But except for a few flecks, they could have been fresh off the Salvation Army rack.

"Take a look at the skin around the wound," Vega said.

I leaned closer until I recognized a pattern. Like a dinner plate that had been licked clean, only a few thin, rust-colored streaks remained. Whatever had killed this young man had sucked out his blood, then lapped up the stray splashes with its tongue.

I swallowed hard against a tide of bile. "And the other victim?"

"Same," Vega said.

I stood back to indicate I'd seen enough.

"Forensics took saliva samples," she said, replacing the drape over the victim's face. "Also picked up some potential trace evidence, including fresh bullet casings. But with the backlog and that we're dealing with junkies..."

"It's going to take weeks," I finished for her.

"Try months. I was lucky to get forensics to even come down here. So, what could we be looking at?"

I pulled off my gloves, remembering to pocket them. The last time I'd left gloves at a crime scene, a demon had cast from the sweat inside them. "Well, not your garden-variety killer, that's for sure."

"You hired him for that?" Hoffman said.

Vega turned her back on him. "Reminds me a little of the disembowelment cases."

"There are similarities," I said. "But lower demons wouldn't have stopped with blood. They would've cleaned out the vital organs, derived as much sustenance from the victims as they could."

"What about a greater demon?" Vega asked.

I suppressed a proud smile. Vega had made a radical transition in her thinking that few could have managed without heavy meds. But we weren't talking about a greater demon either—the Order would have picked up its presence. Sure, they had missed Sathanas, but he'd been partially hidden by the powerful energy that flowed around St. Martin's Cathedral. No such energy existed around Ferguson Towers.

In response to Vega's question, I shook my head.

Her brows folded in. "Well, what does that leave?"

I flipped through a mental reference of supernatural beasties in greater New York. Werewolves had crossed my mind when I first saw the throat—the moon cycle was right—but while werewolves were maulers, they weren't bloodsuckers. Ditto ghouls and trolls, who left very little of their victims intact, gnawing down to bones, and often eating those, too.

Conversely, vampires would do a great job of explaining the lack of blood, but not the torn-up throat. They tended to be precise in their blood draws. Unless it was...

"A blood slave," I mumbled.

"A blood what?" Vega said.

"Sorry." I blinked up at her. "I've told you about the vampires in the city, right?"

"You mean Wall Street?" Though Vega's acceptance of the supernatural had come around in a big way, it seemed she still carried an edge of skepticism sometimes. Like now.

"Well, the heads of the big investment banks," I said. "Arnaud Thorne at Chillington Capital is the oldest and most powerful. He and his fellow vampires control a lot of things in the city, including small armies of blood slaves. Humans who were vampire-bitten."

"I thought they became vampires, too," Vega said.

"Not always. That process involves the vampire giving some of its own essence back to the victim, but in the case of blood slaves, the vampire mostly takes—blood, emotions, identity. The vampire hollows the person out, essentially."

"And then controls him," Vega said.

"Exactly. As long as the blood slave *remains* under the vampire's control."

"Oh, this is ridiculous," Hoffman complained. "Vampires? Blood slaves?" He waved a hand at the whole idea and left the crime scene, his heavy shoes pounding up the steps. "Load of crap."

Vega rolled her eyes. "He'll come around."

"I'm not holding my breath."

"What did you mean by *as long as the blood slave remains under control?*" she asked.

"Well, history is dotted with legends of blood slaves breaking their masters' hold. Without a mind of their own, and deprived of their own blood—for centuries, in some cases—the blood slaves go on a bit of a rampage. Tearing open throats, drinking down all they can."

"What about the size of the wound?" Vega's gaze had shifted to the covered victims.

"A slave's jaw can unhinge. Combine that with their superhuman strength..."

"But how can we be *sure?*"

"We find him," I said.

"Super. How?"

I pulled a folded kerchief from my pocket and opened it beneath a steady drip of water falling from one of the pipes.

"What the hell are you doing?"

"Preparing a spell." I returned to the first victim and, wincing, exposed his torn-open neck again. With a finger tenting the kerchief's damp center, I ran it along an area of intact skin where the creature had licked. "A hunting spell. With the saliva, I should be able to lock onto the creature's location. Would it be a problem if I set up a casting circle down here?"

"If you promise not to shove me inside."

"Heh. Special circumstances, Detective. Won't happen again."

Vega backed up a safe distance anyway as I hunkered down and began to sprinkle out a circle of copper filings.

"I have a question," I said, "and don't take this the wrong way, but when did the NYPD start caring about drug addicts? I mean, some would say the killer did the city a favor. And with all the homicides out there... I guess what I'm asking is why do *you* care?"

"I'm trying to prevent a war."

I stopped and looked up at her. "A war?"

At that moment, a riot of angry shouts sounded from upstairs. Vega drew her sidearm and broke into a run. I left my copper circle half finished and followed, cane pulled into sword and staff.

6

We arrived upstairs to find Hoffman and four NYPD officers shouting down their aimed firearms at three men across the lobby, two of whom were aiming assault rifles and shouting back. The third, a shaven-headed black man, stood between his armed associates in a pair of aviator sunglasses, arms crossed. Between his lips, a toothpick slid back and forth.

In the confusion and close acoustics, I couldn't make out a word being shouted, but something told me the lobby was one slammed door from becoming a shooting gallery. I readied my staff for a shield spell.

Before I realized she'd left my side, Vega was marching into the middle of the mayhem. My heart leapt into my throat. She was putting herself right in the potential crossfire.

Vega waved her arms overhead. "Everyone shut the fuck up!"

Within seconds, the shouts wound down, giving way to ringing echoes.

Vega looked sharply from one side to the other. "Now lower your weapons." She holstered her own pistol, which seemed either incredibly bold or stupid. When no one complied, Vega stepped up to the man with the shades and toothpick. His lean leather coat rippled around his boots.

"Stiles," she said sternly.

It was the man Hoffman had mentioned, the one in charge of the east towers. The toothpick between Stiles's lips stopped moving, and he said something over a shoulder. His men eased back and lowered their assault rifles.

After another tense moment, the police responded in kind. My own shoulders let out as I sheathed my sword into my staff.

"Now, do you want to tell me what this is all about?" Vega demanded.

Hoffman jutted his chin toward Stiles. "Scumbag put a gag order on the towers. No one's talking, meaning we can't do our jobs."

Vega turned to Stiles. "Is there a reason for that?"

"Maintenance shouldn't have called you," he replied, his voice deep and even. "We manage our own affairs."

"Oh yeah?" Hoffman challenged. "So what are two stiffs doing down in your boiler room?"

"We'll take care of that," Stiles said.

"I bet you will," Hoffman muttered.

"Let me guess," Vega said. "Revenge hits?" When Stiles remained silent, Vega nodded. "One of Kahn's dealers showed up at Manhattan General last week with a stump for a right hand. Which means he was caught selling in your towers, right? And now you think what happened downstairs is Kahn's retribution—taking out two of your clients, sending a message. Well, I've got a news flash for you. You're not as smart as you think."

The toothpick paused for a moment before resuming its back-and-forth slide. My gaze moved to Stiles's henchmen. The one to his left had the lumped-up face of an NFL lineman, while his partner looked like he was on leave from the Mexican wrestling circuit for unnecessary roughness. Though they aimed their weapons floor-ward, their thick fingers remained tense on the triggers.

I hope to hell you know what you're doing, Detective.

"We have a lead on someone," she continued, "and it's not any of Kahn's people. If you'll let us do our job, we'll bring the perp to justice, and you and Kahn can carry on, business as usual."

"Business as usual," Stiles said, "is cops not invading my buildings."

"Oh, you think this is an invasion?" Hoffman gave a hard laugh. "We'll show you an invasion, buddy. Got a list of crimes a mile long we could nail you for."

"Then why haven't you?" Stiles asked.

Hoffman's red cheeks balled up. "Smartass sonofa..."

Vega showed him a staying hand before training her gaze back on Stiles—a man whose illicit profits probably paid officials and crack lawyers to keep him in business. Vega was up against someone she couldn't strong-arm, and I could see in her eyes she hated that.

"Look, we get that these are your towers." She swallowed as though the words were leaving a bitter residue. "Just let us do our jobs here, and I'll keep you up to date on the investigation. Tell you about any arrests. But you're gonna do a couple of things for me."

"Really," he said evenly.

"First, you're gonna put out the word that anyone who saw something can talk to us."

His shades remained fixed on her face. "And...?"

She drew up her five-foot frame. "And you're not gonna act on what you *think* happened downstairs."

"I can't promise that."

Vega's anger broke its dam. "Where do you think this is gonna lead, huh? You kill two of his, he kills four of yours, you turn around and kill eight, and pretty soon this place is ground zero." She drew in a hard breath and pushed it out through her nose. "You've got three thousand people in your towers, more than half of them children. Same for Kahn and the west towers. Think, for God's sake!"

So this is the war she's trying to prevent, I thought. *Two drug lords ruling opposite sides of the same project, and the police can't lay a finger on either one.* I remembered the silhouetted heads I'd seen peering down from the caged windows like frightened prisoners.

"Just..." Vega forced another breath. "Just give us time. A month, at least."

Stiles's toothpick journeyed back and forth for several more rounds. "A week."

"Get real," Vega said.

Stiles muttered something over his shoulder, prompting NFL to step forward and punch the button for the elevator. As the three moved past Vega, the Mexican wrestler dug into his pants pocket and handed her what looked like a business card. Vega begrudgingly gave him one of hers.

"Fine, a week," she said as the three boarded the elevator. "But we have a deal, right? No retribution."

The flaps of Stiles's coat billowed as he turned, his henchmen flanking him, their assault rifles at opposite shoulders.

"We have an understanding," Stiles said. "But only because it's you." Though I couldn't see his eyes, I felt them looking over the rest of us in contempt. "Now take the bodies and get out of here. I don't want to see another blue uniform or flashing light tonight." Though he spoke evenly, his words carried the promise of real violence. He inclined his head forward. "And Ricki." The barest smile lifted his lips. "Welcome home."

The elevator door rattled closed.

I stood over the casting circle, aiming the opal end of my cane at the kerchief with the swabbed-up saliva. Though the confrontation upstairs had been heart-pounding, I wasn't as concerned as Vega over the one-week deadline. Chances were good we'd find the bloodsucker tonight.

I spoke an incantation and white light swelled from the gem, absorbing essence from the steaming fabric. "That's right, my homicidal friend," I whispered. "You can run, but you can't—"

Without warning, the light sputtered and went dim. The cane took on weight as the power rushed out of it.

What?

I looked from the opal to the kerchief before pushing more energy into the incantation. The kerchief smoked, then broke into flames.

"*Crap*," I spat, stomping out the fire.

I retreated from the smoking casting circle and examined my cane, which remained heavy and dull. Something was blocking the spell. I circled the room, head bowed low, until I saw what. At the angle between the wall and floor, the thin trail went all the way around the room.

"Well that's just flipping *fantastic*."

"What's going on?"

I turned to find Vega entering the room. "The killer covered his tracks. Made it so any part of himself he left behind—hair, skin cells, saliva—couldn't be connected back to him. At least not energetically."

"How?"

"Salt." I scuffed my shoe over the barrier. Power left the room in a soft whoosh. "It's often used as an energy container, less often as a disrupter, but it gets the job done. Magic that tries to push past it sort of craps out." I shook my cane as one might a faulty electrical appliance.

Vega stooped over the salt. "The techs thought it was boric acid, for pests. Guess you can't blame them for not thinking magically." She straightened again. "Can't you just do the spell in another room?"

I shook my head. "Once the connection's broken, it's broken. The killer knew what he was doing."

"Pretty clear thinking for a mindless blood slave."

"Yeah," I grumbled, "that's bothering me, too."

Vega paced the room, swearing under her breath. Her anger wasn't hard to translate. Unless she caught the killer, Ferguson Towers was going to erupt.

She stooped beside a grate in the floor, opened it on a rusty hinge, and shone her flashlight down. Apparently deciding the pipe was too narrow for someone to have climbed, she huffed and kicked the grate closed.

"If we can't track it," she said, "what does that leave?"

I swept a shoe over my casting circle. "Stiles is going to allow witnesses to talk to you, right? Maybe someone saw something. And then there's forensics. If you can make this a priority case—"

"You're telling me my job, Croft. I'm asking what *you* can do."

I scratched the back of my neck. The truth was, my specialty was nether creatures, not vampiric beings. Meaning if I was going to help Vega, I needed to study the crap out of them.

"I'll look into it," I said at last.

"Look into it?" Her eyebrows collapsed down. "We only have a week, Croft."

"I'll have something before then. I promise."

"Yeah," she said thinly. "I know about you and deadlines."

I held up three fingers of my right hand to form a W. "Wizard's honor."

Vega shook her head. "Come on. I'll give you a ride."

7

Detective Vega and I left the tower together and hurried toward the cruisers. When we were safely in her sedan, I remembered something. "Hey, what did Stiles mean when he said, 'Welcome home'?"

She yanked the gearshift into drive. The sedan jerked forward, scraping a neighboring cruiser. "What do you think?"

I looked from Vega to the grim towers and back. "You lived here?"

"Tower two. Room twelve thirteen." She peeled from the plaza. "Six of us in a one-bedroom."

"So you have three siblings?"

"Four. All brothers. Our dad raised us."

That went a long way toward explaining her take-no-crap attitude.

"For how long?" I asked.

"Till I was twelve. Our dad got us into a subsidized home in the Bronx. More room, safer neighborhood, though both were sort of relative."

As she jounced the sedan off the curb, I craned my neck around at the towers. "And you knew Stiles back then?"

She hesitated before answering. "He was my first boyfriend."

I looked back at her with a surprised laugh. "What?"

She shrugged. "I was young and dumb."

I'd picked up on some sort of familiarity between Vega and Stiles, but wow. That gave the standoff in the lobby a whole new context.

I searched for something to say. "So ... were you able to stay friends?"

"Where am I dropping you off?" she asked abruptly, glancing over at my tux. "The Copacabana?"

I was surprised she'd tolerated my prying into her past for as long as she had, but with my concerns shifting back to Caroline, it was just as well. I dug out the address for the gala.

"Upper West Side," I said. "One Hundred Fourth Street."

Fifteen minutes later, we pulled in front of the crenellated apartment building.

Vega's dark eyes glinted over at me. "Look, Stiles might play the cool cat, but he's got a quarter-inch fuse. That much hasn't changed. He says he'll stomach us for a week, but if the creature strikes there again, forget it. Which means we can't let that happen. I need you to commit to this, Croft."

"I'm committed, I'm committed," I said, my gaze wandering to the front doors. I hoped I hadn't missed Caroline, especially if she'd left with—

Vega's hand clamped my jaw and squeezed.

"Ow!" I cried through smooshed-together lips.

"I'm serious, Croft. No crapping around or getting pulled into other things. Not until we find the killer." She released my jaw, the place where her fingers had pressed still throbbing.

"Yeah, yeah, it's a deal." I worked my jaw around. "Geez."

"I'll check in with you tomorrow."

Before she could decide to grab my jaw again, I backed out the passenger side door. Vega watched me, concern for the residents of the Towers anchoring her stare.

"It's my spring break this week," I said. "No teaching duties. I'll give it my full attention."

"Good."

As the sedan sped away, I paced to the front doors of the building. The concierge, a pleasantly plump man with an obvious toupee, opened the door a couple of inches and raised his thick eyebrows.

"Yes?" he asked, pronouncing it *jes?*

I read his glinting nametag. "Hi, Javier. I was here a little earlier, for the gala?"

"Jes, Mr. Croft. I remember you from check in."

"Good memory. Is it still going on?"

"Oh, no-o-o," he said. "Gala over. Everyone leave."

Damn. "Did you happen to see a young woman with blond hair done up in back? Light purple gown with lace up here? She would have been carrying a small white purse."

"Beautiful woman?"

"A stunner, Javier. An absolute knockout."

"Ahh, jes, I remember. Your date?"

"I ... yeah, I think so. And you saw her leave?"

"Oh, jes. I see."

"Did she leave with..." I swallowed. "...with someone else?"

The man's face tilted in what appeared confusion. "What you mean, Mr. Croft?"

"I mean, did a man escort her out?"

"You mean someone else?"

I squinted at him. *That was what I just asked, wasn't it?*

"That's right, someone else."

"No-o-o-o?"

"Look, just dish it to me straight, Javier. Yes or no?"

"Beautiful woman leave with someone else?" He shook his head. But he was still giving me that *the fuck?* look, meaning something wasn't quite translating. I peeked past him to the concierge desk, where I could make out the top of a telephone. Probably easier to get the answer from the source.

"Would you mind if I made a call?"

"Oh, no-o-o, Mr. Croft. Only I can use. Building rule."

"All right, fine." Exhaling, I looked around. "Do you know if there's a payphone close by?"

He pointed past me. "Two block. But you should not be out at night."

Thanks for the public safety tip, pops, but you're not leaving me much choice. I nodded and wheeled to leave, but then turned back. "Tell you what, Javier. While I find that phone, would you mind calling me a cab?"

"Jes. Can do."

"Great, have him swing by the payphone." I was about to leave again, when I noticed Javier holding out a hand, palm up. "Oh, right."

I pulled out my wallet and flicked through the nest of small bills until I found a five. I handed it to him, stuffed my wallet away, and set out at a fast walk, hoping there was enough left for the taxi. Though I earned a decent salary through the College, the costs of wizarding remained just shy of prohibitive. Another reason to log some hours with the NYPD.

But first I needed to contact Caroline, make sure she'd arrived home safely. Leaving her with a full-blooded fae was feeling more and more careless, especially with Javier's odd responses now clunking around my stomach.

I was halfway down the block when I heard footsteps. I drew my cane apart and wheeled, but not fast enough. A force rammed me in the jaw. When my knee banged into something hard, I realized I'd dropped to the sidewalk, sword and staff clattering from my grip. A throbbing pain spread from my right cheek, its epicenter the size of a fist.

I blinked up as I pawed the sidewalk for my weapons. A short distance away, three men stood in dark suits. Rising to my feet, I turned and hawked a rag of blood.

"Excuse me," I said woozily. "Think I just ran into one of your fists."

"Everson Croft," the blond-haired one said.

A bone-deep chill radiated from him. Coupled with the hollow voice, I knew why. Arnaud Thorne's blood slaves. I glanced down at my naked ring finger. Wonderful. This *would* be the one night I'd remove Grandpa's ring and leave it on the dresser because it didn't go with the tuxedo. The same ring that just happened to protect me from Arnaud and his vampire ilk. But maybe that was a good thing.

"Sorry, fellas, but if you're here for the ring, you're out of luck." I held up my fingers. "See?"

In dark slashes of motion, the three surrounded me. "We have a message for you," Blondie said.

I looked from one circling set of hollow eyes to the next. Eyes at odds with their smooth, youthful faces and tailored suits, but a chilling reminder of their preternatural strength, speed, and blood lust. Silently, I called power to my casting prism, grip tight around my weapons.

"A message?" I said.

Blondie, the designated speaker, pressed closer. "Stay away from Ferguson Towers. It's not your concern."

Though my mind was still foggy from the blow, it wasn't hard to work backwards. If Arnaud had blood slaves watching the crime scene and tailing wizards-for-hire, he had some sort of interest in the crime itself. Which seemed to fit with the theory I'd floated to Vega.

"Aww, what happened?" I asked. "Did one of your pals wander off the reservation?"

A blow collapsed my stomach, the sick pain folding me over.

"Do you understand?" Blondie asked.

I gasped for air. Okay, maybe popping off smart to one of Arnaud's undead had been a bad idea, but I had this thing about being muscled around—which seemed to happen an awful lot.

"Understood," I whispered. "Just do me a favor and tell Arnaud..." I gathered my breath as the blood slaves leaned nearer. "...*respingere!*"

My staff crackled with light and an orb-shaped shield exploded from its white opal. The force blasted the blood slaves up and back a good twenty feet. All three landed on their feet, however, stunned but not hurt. Maintaining my shield, I turned in a slow circle, sword held out.

The slaves started forward. A single blood slave I could probably handle. But three? I swallowed hard, the taste of copper slick on my palate. This could get really ugly really fast.

"Hey!" A sharp whistle. "You the one that called a cab?"

I turned to find a taxi idling at the corner. I started to wave him to safety, but when I peeked back, the sidewalk was empty, shadows of buildings where the blood slaves had once stood. I sheathed my sword and limped toward the cab, jaw aching, a nauseous stone in my stomach. There was a reason I had stayed out of the Financial District for the past six months.

Behind me, a cold voice cut through the wind: "You've been warned."

8

It was after midnight when I stepped over my threshold and into my West Village apartment, locking the door's three bolts behind me. I stood for a moment in the dark, the tension easing from my neck, my shoulders. It had been a hell of a night, and to be back in a familiar, protected space, remnants of my own magic charging the air, comforted me. Until my cat spoke.

"You look like shit, darling."

I found Tabitha's ochre-green eyes hovering above the divan beneath the west-facing window. I sighed and turned on the floodlights. "You know, a simple 'welcome home' would be nice now and then."

"Why does your face look like a catcher's mitt?"

I touched the hard knot on my jaw where the blood slave had

driven his fist. "Here again, starting with 'Are you all right?' would be the polite approach. Then you could bring up the mitt."

I paced over to the kitchen, dug an old bag of peas from the back of the freezer, and pressed it to my throbbing jaw. No sense wasting healing magic on a little swelling.

Tabitha shifted her forty-pound pile of fur so she could watch me without lifting her head. "Any luck with what's-her-name?"

"Who?" I asked, knowing full well she meant Caroline. I did my best to keep Tabitha out of my personal life. She approved of roughly zero of the women I had dated, and wasn't shy about telling me. I suspected at least some jealousy at play, not to mention frustration. Tabitha was a succubus spirit trapped in a cat's body. Her days of seducing and consuming men were long past.

"Oh, don't play coy with me," she said. "I heard you on the phone earlier."

I eyed the rotary behemoth on the kitchen counter, the need to call Caroline burning inside me. But I wasn't going to call her in front of Tabitha.

"Have you done your tours tonight?"

"Oh, not this again," she moaned.

"A deal's a deal. Food and five-star accommodations in exchange for a tour of the ledge every two hours."

"Five-star? This place?" She snorted and closed her eyes. "No one's interested enough in your dump—or *you*—to be watching."

"Excuse me. Were you not here this past fall? What were those creatures called that came and attacked us? Oh, right—*demons*."

"Old news." She paused to stretch, a yawn revealing her mouth of impressive teeth. "The six months since have been an absolute bore."

"Well, cheer up. That's probably about to change," I said, thinking of Arnaud's warning. "Out. Now." When she didn't move, I exercised the nuclear option. "No more goat's milk until you do."

She sighed and heaved up her bulk. Only after staring daggers at me did she drop from the divan. "You're such a brute sometimes."

"Anything out of the ordinary," I reminded her. "Or anyone watching. Especially if they're young men in expensive suits."

She muttered something I probably didn't want to hear and squeezed through the cat door. With Tabitha out of the way, I swapped the bag of peas against my face for the phone receiver and dialed Caroline's number. Just hearing her voice would do wonders for my anxiety.

I got her recorded voice instead. Nuts.

"Hey, Caroline," I said, trying to sound casual. "Just wanted to check in and see how the rest of your night went. Make sure you made it home all right. I'm sorry again for ducking out like that. There was a good reason, actually. I was hoping I could tell you about it over breakfast. Or brunch, whichever. My treat. Anyway, if you could give me a call when—"

The voice mail cut me off with an abrasive beep.

"—you get this."

I hung up, feeling like a bumbling fifteen-year-old. Good thing Tabitha hadn't been around—I would never have heard the end of it.

All right, so either Caroline's phone was out of service range, which would never happen in the city, or she had shut it off for the night to sleep. Alone, I hoped.

Tabitha reappeared just as I was placing the frozen peas back against my jaw.

"Anything?" I asked.

"No male models in suits." She hopped up on her divan and collapsed onto her side. "Sorry to disappoint you."

Arnaud must have figured he'd made his point. Meaning I was now stuck between his warning and my pledge to help Detective Vega.

I prepared Tabitha a bowl of warm goat's milk, fixed myself a pot of Colombian dark roast, and climbed the ladder to my library/lab. It was late, my face and stomach hurt, my ego was bruised, and I wanted nothing more than to crawl into bed and shut off my brain, but I had work to do. Stepping past my hologram of the city—dim, thank God—I stopped and faced the wall of mundane books.

"Svelare," I said in a low, thrumming voice.

A ripple moved across the spines. In the next moment, encyclopedias and classical titles became magical tomes and grimoires. I retrieved a thick black book from the bottom shelf, a tome on the undead. At my desk, I took my first sip of coffee and opened the book to a section concerning vampires—blood slaves, in particular. I jotted down notes on a yellow legal pad as I read.

An hour later, I closed the book and reviewed my notes, pen tapping between my teeth. It was looking like a good news, bad news scenario—and unfortunately, more of the second.

Good news: being unsophisticated creatures, blood slaves tended to lair in the same proximity to where they fed. That narrowed our search radius considerably. Bad news: that small radius also meant that if we failed to find the creature before he fed again, Ferguson Towers could be looking at body number three—and if Vega was right, at an all-out war between Stiles and this person Kahn in the west towers.

That was bad news item number one.

Bad news item number two was the blood slave itself. I hadn't needed to read up on them to appreciate their speed, strength, and lethality. A blood slave, especially one without a master, would tear through Detective Vega and her squad like lunch meat. I would need to be physically involved, not only in the search, but in the creature's eventual execution. Thanks to my research, I had plenty of material to work with in that second department—silver through the heart being the most surefire way of doing the deed.

But the fact that my direct involvement *was* needed led to bad news item number three: Arnaud Thorne.

The vampire had warned me off the case. If I ignored his warning, his slaves would be back, this time to deliver more than a stiff jaw. I had Grandpa's ring now, sure, but we weren't talking about a showdown at the O.K. Corral. Arnaud would pick the time and place, and not by mutual consent. I probably wouldn't even see his slaves before I was missing limbs.

I stood with my cup of coffee and paced the length of the bookshelves. Though hard to understand at times, vampires had their own code of decorum. For an eminent vampire like Arnaud, losing control of a blood slave and having it run amok was tantamount to weakness, profoundly embarrassing. He probably wanted me off the case so he could take care of the errant slave without anyone knowing. Maybe all I had to do was back off for a couple of days. Let Arnaud's blood slaves snatch up the killer and sweep him under the rug.

I returned to my desk and penned a report to the Order on the night's riddler banishment. I had already asked for, and received, permission to work with Detective Vega, but I included a reminder anyway. When dealing with the Order, it was always better to err on the side of caution.

The message sent, I cut the lights and headed down to bed. Despite my exhaustion, I tossed and turned, seeing the disappointment in Caroline's eyes when I told her I was leaving, remembering Angelus's subtle possessiveness. I couldn't shake the feeling I'd lost her, somehow.

Eventually, I fell into a dark and troubled sleep.

9

Though I had set my alarm, it was the ringing telephone that woke me the next morning. I held my wind-up clock to my face—*eleven?*—and thrashed out of bed. The phone rang again, hopefully Caroline responding to my message left last night. I reached the telephone on the fourth ring, clearing the sleep from my throat, and lifted the receiver.

"Hello?"

"Sleeping in, Croft?"

"Oh." My heart sank. "Hi, Detective."

"What do you have for me?" she asked.

"Well, I had an interesting encounter last night," I said, carrying the telephone over to my reading chair and plopping down. Tabitha regarded me dully before closing her eyes again. "After you dropped me off."

"Related to the case?"

"Three of Arnaud's blood slaves jumped me, warned me to stay away from Ferguson Towers."

"Did they say why?"

"I'm fine, by the way. Thanks for asking." I moved my jaw around. The knot was gone but the right hinge remained sore. "They didn't say much other than that it was none of my business."

"Good work, Croft. Be sure to turn in your hours. We'll take it from here."

I sat up. "Wait a minute. What are you talking about?"

"If Arnaud's involved, the killer's probably one of his."

"Yeah, but you can't just take an elevator up to his office and ask him."

"Why not? He's made himself a person of interest."

I remembered my meeting with the vampire back in October, one that saw me offering Arnaud my throat before Grandpa's ring blew him off me. "I can't let you do that."

"Why not?"

"I've told you what he is, but you can't possibly understand."

"What the hell are you talking about?"

"He's dangerous, Vega. Like, *super* dangerous."

"Right, and you said the vampires have survived by keeping a low profile. Offing an NYPD detective doesn't strike me as fitting that M.O."

She had a point—under normal circumstances. But if Arnaud was as desperate to make this go away as I suspected, the normal rules might not apply.

"Well, give it a couple of days," I tried. "Maybe he'll take care of the matter himself."

"We don't *have* a couple of days," she cut in. I didn't have to see her face to know her brows were crushing together. And it was my fault for telling her about last night's encounter, dammit. In my just-woken state, I hadn't been thinking clearly. I should have kept the run-in to myself.

"Why don't..." I couldn't believe what I was about to say. "Why don't you let me talk to him?"

"One, you're a consultant, not an investigator," Vega replied. "And two, how would you even get downtown?"

Good question. The last time I'd made it past the wall that fortified the Financial District, I'd very nearly gotten shot. Scratch that—the last *two* times. A third run at the Wall would be testing fate.

"Then let me come with you," I said.

"You're still on the forbidden entry list. *I* can't even get you through."

An idea hit me. "I might be able to do something about that." I carried the phone into my bedroom and over to where I'd thrown my tuxedo onto the back of a chair. I stooped toward the jacket, inspecting the fabric closely.

"Are you gonna clue me in?" Vega asked impatiently.

"Aha!" I plucked out a curly brown hair and held it up in triumph. "Just be here in an hour."

"I don't like surprises, Croft."

"Oh, and grab me an ID."

"What?"

I hung up and tried Caroline. Voice mail again.

I set the phone on the counter and held the hair I'd plucked closer to my eyes. I would have to put my concerns for Caroline aside for the moment.

I had a potion to cook.

"You've got to be kidding," Vega said, staring over at me.

"Hey, watch where you're going!" I shrank against the passenger seat as Vega jerked the steering wheel, narrowly missing the back of a stopping bus. We shot into the center lane of Broadway, Saturday morning traffic honking and hooking from our path. Vega swore and laid on her own horn. After seconds that felt like minutes, the view outside the windows stopped wobbling. "Sweet Jesus," I sighed, releasing my death grip on the door handle.

She glanced over at me. "A little warning next time?"

I looked down, smoothing the tie over my now-ample paunch, and tugged my brown polyester jacket straight, part of the suit I'd picked up at the corner consignment store while my potion was cooking. "I warned you the copycat potion could take effect any minute."

"Yeah, but I didn't think you'd look just like him."

I swung down the visor until my reflection was looking back at me. Detective Hoffman's reflection, actually. I studied his damp red face, then turned my head slightly, combing thick fingers through the wreath of curly hair. The same hair my tuxedo jacket had picked up in his car last night.

"Well, I'm not sure how long it's going to last," I said. "I didn't have a lot of his material to work with. Meaning we're going to have to get through pretty damned fast."

I watched the approaching Wall, a giant concrete barrier that fortified the Financial District from the rest of Manhattan. Sweat was already soaking through the back of my shirt as Vega slowed toward the short line for official vehicles. Ever since I'd climbed into the car, my wizard's intuition had been tingling in the bad way.

"Be cool," she said.

"And you be careful," I replied.

The car ahead of us pulled through, and a pair of armored guards waved us forward with automatic rifles.

"ID," the one on Vega's side said.

The guard on my side tapped my window. I powered it down and squinted up at him. Though the private security guards all looked like steroid-infused clones, I recognized this one's square jaw. He was the same guard who had tried to wrench Grandpa's ring from my finger in the fall.

He caught me staring. "You got a problem?"

"No, no problem. ID's right here." I pulled it up by the cord around my neck.

He aimed his shield sunglasses at the card, then at my face. "What's your business down here?"

Vega ducked to peer past me. "We're following up on an investigation."

"I asked Porky here," the guard growled.

Though it was actually Hoffman he'd insulted, the muscles in my jaw bunched up anyway. I forced a deep breath. "Yeah, we're following up on something," I said as sedately as I could.

"With who?"

"Arnaud Thorne," I said. "If he'll see us."

According to Vega, ever since I had used her car to leap the checkpoint, security at the Wall had become more stringent. If a vehicle, even an official one, didn't proceed straight to the stated destination, the private guards would swarm.

Square Jaw remained staring at me. A tiny camera in the corner of his glasses clicked and whirred. By his silence, I guessed someone was speaking into his earpiece.

After a moment he opened the car door. "Out of the vehicle."

My heart lurched. "What do you mean?"

"You deaf?" He took the rifle strapped around his torso into both of his hands. "I said out of the vehicle."

"You too," the guard on the other side ordered.

I peered over at Vega, the skin of her brow taut. I remembered her telling me these guys could turn an NYPD officer into Swiss cheese without fear of repercussion. All thanks to the vampires holding the city's purse strings. Vega gave me a single nod before stepping out on her side.

"What's this about?" I asked in a tone of professional impatience.

Square Jaw used his rifle barrel to jab me around. "Hands on the hood." He spoke over the car to Vega. "You. Open the trunk."

Fear and humiliation burned over my face as I splayed my hands against the sedan's warm metal. A moment later, hands pummeled my pockets and slapped up and down my legs. I'd left my cane and necklace at home and secured Grandpa's ring behind the metal button of my pants. The guard missed the last, no doubt because he wasn't looking for it. I widened my stance to hold up my slipping waistband. The potion in my system was starting to thin.

"Where's your piece?"

"I'm not carrying one today," I said.

He called to the back of the vehicle. "Anything?"

I turned but couldn't see Vega or the other guard behind the raised trunk door.

"Vehicle's clean," the other guard said. "Her piece is standard."

Square Jaw pulled me from the hood and shoved me toward the car door. "You're clear to pass."

The trunk door slammed closed and Vega got in on her side, brows angled sharply down. I was ducking my head to join her, relieved the enhanced screening was over, when Square Jaw seized the scruff of my jacket and yanked me back.

"Hey," I cried. "What do you think—"

He spun me around against the car, looking me up and down.

"What's your problem?" I demanded.

But I knew. The firming of my face, the thinning of my body, the itch of hair growing back atop my head—my potion was running on fumes. I was changing before the man's eyes.

"Hey, Parker," the guard called to his partner. "Come take a look at this shit."

Parker sauntered around the vehicle, rifle in his grip. He snorted. "Magic user. I've been itching to bag one of these freaks."

"That's not all," Square Jaw said, a hard grin pulling his mouth to one side. "It's the same guy who gave us shit about the ring, remember?"

Parker nodded slowly, then ducked to look into the sedan. "And isn't that the broad who pulled her piece on us?"

"Sure is," Square Jaw said. "Close the line."

10

The hydraulic-powered gate whirred closed behind us, clunking into the cement wall and sealing us inside an area the size of a large garage. Bollards blocked our way forward. Parker trained his rifle on Vega, while Square Jaw moved his own rifle around to his back. He pushed his sleeves up.

"C'mon, guys," I said, one hand held out, the other balling up the side of my pants to keep them from puddling around my ankles. "I'm sure we can work something out. I'm decent with love potions if you guys are having any trouble in that department."

Square Jaw snarled.

"N-no," I stammered, "I didn't mean with each other."

The fist Square Jaw drove into my chest stunned my heart. I pawed toward him, mouth gaping, no air going in or out. His other fist came up beneath my chin, slamming my mouth closed with a bloody clack. I landed against the car, my head thrown back on the roof.

"Not such a smart ass now, are you?" he said.

"I don't know," I answered blearily, buildings whirling overhead. "My reserves are pretty impressive."

I straightened and stared around. I could hear Parker behind me, shouting for Vega to drop her weapon and get out of the car. But the more immediate danger was Square Jaw, who was moving in with both hands as though to throttle me. I jacked my right knee up and caught him square in the jewels.

Square Jaw's hands changed course, diving for his groin as he grunted and collapsed to his knees. Behind me Parker's shouting rose in treble before getting drowned out by the sedan's engine.

What the...?

I skipped back as rubber screamed over road top, foul smoke billowing from the rear tires. The sedan began to spin, slamming into walls. The front fender came around and clunked Square Jaw in the helmet, dropping him like a sack of bricks. Parker opened fire, bullets pinging off metal and reinforced glass.

I called power to my casting prism. Aiming a hand at Parker, I shouted, *"Vigore!"*

Without my sword to concentrate and direct the force, it burst from my palm like branch lightning. Launched from his feet, Parker slammed into a wall, his weapon and pieces of gear clattering around him. He landed face first, like a flipped pancake. But my force had also caught the rear of the sedan, pushing it sideways so that its front end was now aimed at me.

I could see by Vega's startled expression that she'd lost control.

She wasn't going to be able to stop the car. And I wasn't going to have time to cast.

I stumbled back against the steel door. The sedan fishtailed, Vega's side plowing toward me—and then stopped with three feet to spare.

I looked from Vega, who had thrown her arms up, to either side of me. I was no longer alone. I recognized the blood slave to my right from last night, Blondie's hands clutching the side of the hood. He and the other blood slave shoved the car away, the heels of their patent leather shoes braced against the metal gate. They looked at me dispassionately.

"Thanks?" I said.

"Mr. Thorne will see you," Blondie said.

The other blood slave stepped over to Square Jaw, who was groaning on the pavement, and shoved him with a foot. "Let them through," he ordered.

Vega killed the engine and peered past me to a pair of blood slaves in brass-button suits.

"Think it's some kind of trap?" she asked.

I studied the doormen and then ran my gaze up Arnaud's landmark skyscraper. "You can never tell with a vampire. But that we're here at his invitation tells me no. It's considered impolite for a vampire to tear apart his guests. That doesn't mean we can relax our guard, though."

"So why invite us?"

"Good question." I began working to untie the thread I had

used to secure Grandpa's ring to the inside of my pants. "Either he wants to send a sterner warning or he wants something else entirely."

"Like what?"

"No telling." I freed the ring and slipped it onto my third finger. "Just stay close."

"You think he's going to let you in wearing that? Didn't you say it burned him or something?"

At Vega's question, the ring grasped the base of my finger more tightly. "Short of severing my finger, I don't see how he's going to get it off me. But I don't think that's his concern right now or else his blood slaves would've shaken me down back there. I think we're good on the ring."

"Fine, but this is still an official investigation. I'm asking the questions."

I showed my palms—*no argument here*—and we got out of the car. The copycat potion spent, I cinched my belt around my too-large pants and followed Vega toward the front entrance. As the blood slaves opened the glass doors, Grandpa's ring began to pulse with the enchantment of the Brasov Pact, the centuries-old truce between European wizards and vampires.

"Welcome," a lilting voice called from across the chilly lobby. As my eyes adjusted to the gloom, I made out the pretty face and white-blond hair of the undead receptionist. "Mr. Thorne is expecting you."

"Thanks," I muttered, then signaled for Vega to follow me to the elevators, where two more blood slaves stood.

"I'm sorry," the receptionist said pleasantly. "Not her."

I stopped. "What?"

The receptionist tilted her head in a show of apology. "Mr. Thorne has requested to meet with you alone, Mr. Croft." She nodded at Detective Vega. "She can wait down here."

Vega's hands balled into fists as she stalked toward the desk. "Excuse me, *Miss*, but I'm an NYPD detective on official business. I need to speak to Mr. Thorne as part of an investigation."

The receptionist's smile conveyed coldness now rather than empathy. "His lawyers are off today. If you'd like to make an appointment, Mr. Thorne may agree to see you next week."

"Listen to me, you little—"

"We understand," I interrupted, gripping Vega's upper arm. I whispered into her ear as I turned her away, "I've been through this song and dance with them before. It's pointless. I say you let me go up there, see what I can get him to tell me about Ferguson Towers."

"I don't care what he is," Vega seethed. "This is *bullshit*."

"Yeah, I know."

Vega was having a bad run, from her confrontation with Stiles to the checkpoint guards and now this. But I was relieved, to be honest. I'd seen Vega in action enough times to know she only knew one speed—full throttle. If she went into Arnaud's office, jabbing him with questions and accusations, he would grin, fold his hands, and tell us nothing.

"Thinks he's above the law," Vega went on, her accent regressing to her housing-project roots. "I don't care what City Hall says. I'll take the pale son of a bitch down myself."

"Now, now." As I steered her toward a sitting area, I noted several blood slaves watching us. "Let's keep that kind of talk to ourselves, hmm?"

Vega looked around, seeming to pick up on the attention, too. She straightened, as though to re-professionalize, and looked me straight in the eyes. "Get me a name, a location, something we can use."

"I'll do my best."

Before Vega could change her mind about letting me go up alone, I hurried toward the elevators.

I shifted my weight on the swift ride up, wondering what in the hell I was getting myself into. After the St. Martin's case, I had resolved never to return to the Financial District. And now here I was—not only in Arnaud's territory, but en route to his executive office. I shuddered at the memory of the vampire's fangs and cold breath against my throat.

The elevator door slid open on the top floor, and the blood slaves escorted me down a long hallway of dark carpet and oiled wood. The tantalizing scent of Arnaud's office, a mixture of leather and musk, seemed to beckon. Arnaud's head blood slave received me at the tall doors of the office. I recognized him by his almond-shaped eyes and short monk's bangs.

"How nice to see you again," Zarko said in a mocking voice.

"I can't say the feeling's mutual," I replied. I wasn't being smart. The last time we'd seen one another, his right hand was wrapped around my throat, and he was holding me two feet in the air.

He opened the right door, grinning as he bowed.

The strong scent of Arnaud's office enveloped me and penetrated my thoughts. I struggled to hold them together—I needed to be coherent to face Arnaud—but the soft carpet underfoot told me I had already entered his lair.

Through a pool of tannic brown light, I made out a lean figure, a pale mane of hair falling to his shoulders. The mane shook with soft laughter.

"Oh, my poor boy," came Arnaud's silky voice. "You have really gotten yourself into a pickle this time."

11

I squinted through the distorting light, forcing Arnaud into focus. He was wearing one of his patent silk suits, light-colored, loose around the arms and legs, a scarf draping his shoulders, open shirt underneath. His dark eyes sparkled as he looked me over, a smile forking his thin lips.

"And just when I'd begun to forget about our unpleasant encounter last fall," Arnaud said. "You were very nearly in the clear, my boy."

Though he spoke with an edge of menace, he wasn't trying to incite fear. Not like the last time. On the contrary, he was layering the atmosphere with an opiate mist. Whether as insurance against my trying to use the ring or as a simple demonstration of his power, I couldn't say.

"What do you want?" I asked, correcting my sagging posture.

He chuckled. "I'm not the one who came seeking you, Mr. Croft."

"Would've made things easier," I grumbled, rubbing my swollen jaw.

"Would that have been your preference? To sit and talk at your place? Next time, perhaps."

"Yeah, sure," I said, waving a hand. Before my weakening legs could give out, I made my way to his arrangement of oxblood leather chairs and sat. "Do you mind?"

I caught a subtle tensing in Arnaud. I was being a poor guest.

"Zarko," he called. "Be a dear and prepare Mr. Croft and me a couple of Scotch on the rocks. The vintage '32 would be nice."

"Depression-era?" I said. "Wow, that makes me all warm inside."

"This is an *eighteen* thirty-two," Arnaud corrected me.

"Oh."

The vampire took a seat opposite me, folding his legs neatly. He studied me for a long moment before opening a hand of slender fingers. "Well?"

"Fine, we'll start with why I came, and then you can tell me why you agreed to meet." I blinked against the blearing effect of the opiate and cleared my throat. "I received a visit from three of yours last night. Why?"

"Oh, were they not clear? I shall have to speak to them about that."

"Cut the crap," I said. "You know what I'm talking about. Why warn me away from Ferguson Towers?"

With the ring to protect me, I felt I could be a little more forward. Especially since I didn't know how long I could hold out.

Seeming to understand time was on his side, Arnaud accepted his drink from Zarko, sniffed it, and then swirled it several times. At last he took a small sip and sat back, pale tongue slipping across his lips. "You cannot beat a good Scotch," he said. "Distilled right here in New York, in fact, shortly before the Great Fire of '35. Very tragic. So many fine buildings lost. Well, go on." He nodded toward the glass Zarko had set on my end table. "That's a small fortune you're neglecting."

"I didn't come here for the spirits," I said. "What's your interest in Ferguson Towers?"

He waved a hand dismissively. "As an investor, I have interests throughout the city."

"A housing project? Please. Let's walk through it, shall we? Two junkies are found murdered in a boiler room yesterday, their throats ripped open. Someone pours salt around the site to prevent magic from connecting the evidence to the murderer. And shortly after a wizard leaves the crime scene, three more someones shove him around and tell him to get off the case. Seems like an awful lot of trouble to protect a killer. One of yours, I assume?"

"Oh, assumptions are such dangerous things."

"If you're willing to spell out an alternate theory, I'm all ears."

"Mr. Croft," he said, swirling his glass lightly. "Do you know how many people I employ here?"

"Oh, they're people now?"

"Hundreds. And of those, do you know how many have resigned without my consent?" He leaned toward me. "Exactly none."

I struggled to hold his blurring face in focus. "There's a first time for everything."

"Not in this case, Mr. Croft."

"Then the creature belongs to one of your banking buddies, and you're trying to corral it before it can draw a spotlight on what you really are."

Arnaud sat back with a chuckle. "There you go again, Mr. Croft. Assumptions, assumptions. What makes you think the killer is one of ours?"

"Oh, I don't know—that the victims are all blood drained."

"Ours isn't the only kind with a taste for blood, you know. And was it merely blood the *creature*, as you call it, was after?"

My head dipped, and I jerked it back up. I wasn't going to be able to hold out much longer. "Look, whatever we're dealing with, do I at least have your assurance that you're going to take care of it? I get that this has to be an embarrassment for you."

"How I choose to act is none of your concern."

"Well, maybe it concerns the six thousand people living in those towers." In my drug-hazed state, the silhouetted faces I'd seen in the windows seemed to be moving around me.

"Ah, you humans and your sentimentalities," Arnaud said. "You could accomplish so much more without them."

I nearly swooned again. When I righted myself and blinked, it felt as though the skin around my eyes had puckered. And what had I accomplished here? Denials from Arnaud that the killer was one of his. Another warning to stay away from the case. Vega wasn't going to be happy.

"You brought me up here to tell me something," I managed. "So tell me."

He drained the rest of his glass and set it on his oiled end table. "I can keep eyes on you, Mr. Croft, but not at all hours. It seems your domicile is rather well protected, and you have that exquisite feline watching the street. After observing the dramatic lengths you and your partner just undertook in attempting to bypass the Wall, it occurred to me that you might agree to stay away from Ferguson Towers but still advise the detective from afar. And with that bit of insight, a more superior solution came to my mind."

"Oh, and what's that?" I asked, not sure I wanted to know.

"Put my last warning out of your head. You're back on the case."

"Huh?"

"However." Arnaud held up a finger. "Your instructions are now to mislead the detective." I was already shaking my head when he added, "Send her on a wild goose chase."

"Forget it."

"The alternative is to have her removed from the investigation. And though I suppose I could tug certain strings to make that happen, someone would just step into her place." Arnaud seemed to be talking to himself before redirecting his voice back at me. "And then we'd be back to square one, wouldn't we? Frankly, Mr. Croft, I'm too busy to meddle in such matters."

The thought of misleading Vega struck me as wrong in so many ways. "I'm not doing that."

"Oh, I think you will, Mr. Croft," Arnaud said.

"And why's that?"

"Because Detective Vega has a young child. And your humanity will prevent you from carrying out any foolishness that would lead to his disappearance. Such as contradicting my directive."

His words hit me like a fist in the face. "You wouldn't," I growled.

He smiled.

"You son of a bitch."

"Oh, come now," Arnaud said, eyes gleaming. "We were getting along so pleasantly."

"I'll... I'll..." But in the muddy atmosphere of the room, I couldn't complete the sentence, much less the thought.

"It seems you need some fresh air, Mr. Croft. But before you return outside, do we have an agreement? Or would you rather have to explain to the detective why her son is imperiled?"

That was the reason for the opiate. To make an impossible offer and then prevent me from thinking clearly enough to see my way through it. Blasting him with the ring was out of the question, though I was damn sure tempted. That would only earn me—and probably Vega—a bloody date with Death.

"What am I supposed to tell her?" I asked.

Without taking his eyes from mine, Arnaud said, "Zarko, I've written something on the blotter on my desk. Could you bring it here?" A moment later, he reached back and accepted a folded piece of paper from his head blood slave. "You will begin by telling the detective that I warned you away last night out of concern for your safety. After all, your grandfather and I go back many centuries, and I feel a certain *tenderness* toward his descendants." He grinned as though at a clever joke, then rattled the paper softly. "I have here a name and an address. Someone who, you will tell the detective, I feel may have information as to the killer's identity and whereabouts. I want you to visit him together. I am supplying this information in exchange for the assurance that I will no longer be questioned on the matter." He raised his pale eyebrows. "Are we agreed, Mr. Croft?"

Though I'd been beating my thoughts around for the last minute, trying to resuscitate them, they would only coalesce around the photo on Detective Vega's desk of her and her young son.

"Mr. Croft?" Arnaud said.

"Just give it to me."

"I'll take that as a *yes*." Arnaud placed the paper into my groping hand. "I will be watching to ensure you share this information post haste. And if you tip the detective off to our agreement, I will know that as well."

"How?" I challenged.

"Changes in the detective's behavior, the patterns she sets for her son, extra protection, so forth and so on. I have little patience for such duplicity and will show even less mercy. Do not test me there, Mr. Croft. Keep the detective occupied with what I have given you. If there is any additional information I wish to impart, I will have one of my men deliver it to you. Are we on the same page?"

I couldn't take the atmosphere any longer. My head was dizzy and pounding. I stood, the paper clutched in one hand, and staggered toward the door.

"And Mr. Croft," he called after me. I turned at the doorway to find Arnaud standing from his chair. "I like to think I can offer treats and not merely threats, so I'll say something else. Should this..." He circled a hand as though in search of the right word. "... *arrangement* conclude to the satisfaction of all concerned, there may be something in it for you."

"I don't want your stinking money," I mumbled.

"Money?" He chuckled. "Oh, no. I'm talking about something far more valuable, Mr. Croft. Information."

The angle of his voice made me hesitate. "Such as…?"

"Such as what became of your dear mother."

I stopped breathing. "What?"

"That will be waiting for you on the other side. Consider it a blood deal."

I took two heavy steps toward Arnaud before Zarko gripped my arm and steered me toward the door. Though I struggled, I was no match for his strength. A moment later I stumbled into the hallway, the slaves who had brought me up already steering me toward the elevator.

I looked at the folded-over piece of paper, then back at Arnaud's closed door, feeling like I'd been offered a deal by the devil himself.

And goddammit, I knew I had to take it.

12

I rooted around in Vega's glove compartment until I found the aspirin bottle. My head hurt like hell, and it wasn't only from the toxicity of Arnaud's office. It was from just feeding Vega the crap about the person on the piece of paper, Sonny Shoat, being a potential lead. It was from not being able to tell her about the threat to her son, or about the promise Arnaud had made to tell me what had happened to my mother, who had died when I was one.

I shook two bitter tablets into my mouth, chewed and swallowed them dry, and then leaned my head back against the rest.

"Why is he insisting you come with me?" Vega asked.

"I don't know," I said, eyes closed. I couldn't look her in the face. "It was just one of his conditions for doling out information."

"He has more?"

Yeah, more to mislead you. "He suggested he might."

"What the hell? Does he think this is some kind of game?"

"Probably."

Vega cussed again, and I felt the car cut hard in and out of several lanes before she turned left. "I have some things to do at the office, including finding out what I can about this Sonny Shoat, and then I need to talk to Stiles, make sure he's still good on our deal. I'll drop you at your place and call you later."

"Fine by me."

Besides needing to sort out my thoughts, I wanted to get a hold of Caroline. With the vampire's opiate leaving my system, my wizard's intuition was tapping the base of my skull again, telling me something was off.

"There were no calls," Tabitha said languidly from her divan.

I shushed her as I finished dialing my voice mail service. But she was right. Zero messages.

I thumbed the switch hook for a fresh dial tone and then spun Caroline's number. As had happened last night and this morning, the call went straight to her recorded voice: *"Hi, you've reached Caroline Reid. I'm sorry I'm not here to take your call..."*

I waited out the rest of the message, then cleared my throat.

"Hey, Caroline. It's Everson again. Look, I'm getting a little worried here, so if you could call me as soon as you get this, I'd really appreciate it." I could understand her turning her phone off for the night, but it was two in the afternoon.

I leaned my arms against the kitchen counter, my sternum and jaw aching from my encounter at the checkpoint, my head pounding from my meeting with Arnaud, and now my stomach in nervous knots for Caroline. And I had been planning to spend my spring-break week in a bathrobe and furry slippers, catching up on some arcane reading while sipping artisan coffee.

A bout of hard knocking shook the door.

I raised my head. Did I even want to answer that?

"Oh, I forgot to mention," Tabitha said. "I caught a couple of men watching the building. They disappeared when you showed up with the detective."

"You know, that probably should have been the first thing you told me when I came through the door."

"No-o-o, I was supposed to say 'welcome home,' which I did. I then started to ask why your face looked like a walnut, but I caught myself and asked if you were all right. Also like you told me. The information about the men watching the building must have gotten lost in your labyrinth of etiquette."

"Never mind." I pushed myself from the counter and walked warily toward the door. The men were probably blood slaves sent by Arnaud, maybe to ensure I was fulfilling my end of the bargain. As long as I remained on my side of the threshold, I was safe. The power of my wards, which I had spent the last six months rebuilding, would keep them out.

"Were they dressed in suits?" I asked.

"Long coats and hats," Tabitha replied. "But they didn't look like male models."

I lifted my cane from the coat rack beside the door and peered through the peep hole. I saw what Tabitha meant. The men in the hallway weren't blood slaves. If anything, they looked like something out of 1920s New York, in their Homburg hats and knee-length wool coats.

The two men glanced around impatiently. The larger one in the fore knocked again.

I twisted the three bolts open and cracked the door. "Yes?"

"You Everson Croft?" the knocker asked.

"And you are...?"

"I'm Floyd and this is Whitey, my associate. We'd like to ask you a few questions."

I studied Floyd, with his stout frame and dark eyes that moved back and forth over mine. Whitey was much thinner, with white hair and pale eyes that looked everywhere but at me.

"Can we come in?" When Floyd saw my hesitation, he added, "It's about your friend, Caroline."

A charge went through my chest. "What's going on? Has something happened?"

"That's what we're trying to find out."

"Yeah, yeah, of course," I said quickly, opening the door and gesturing toward the sitting area.

In the shock of hearing Caroline's name, I hadn't thought to ask who they were. Some part of my mind had slotted "Detective" before their names, but the men hadn't flashed badges. And why would they have hidden from Vega when we pulled up? Then the familiar-sounding names clicked.

Oh, crap.

I wheeled in time for a brass-knuckled fist to plow into my jaw. Already weakened from my sparring session at the checkpoint, my chin crumpled in a rude spear of light, and I dropped straight down. Floyd and Whitey were members of the city's Italian crime syndicate. Moretti's men.

I went to raise my cane, but it had tumbled from my grasp. And my casting prism was shot.

Floyd squatted beside me, near enough that I could smell his cold aftershave. "Now that I've got your attention," he said in a whisper that managed to sound intimate and menacing at the same time, "you want to tell me where she is?"

Beyond him, Whitey had closed the door and drawn a vintage Colt pistol, his pale eyes flicking around the apartment. I couldn't see Tabitha, but I hoped she had enough sense to keep her head down.

"What are you talking about?" I asked, blood trickling into my throat.

"Caroline was your date last night, wasn't she?"

How did he know that? "A provisional date. It was something we were trying out." When Floyd's face wrinkled in confusion, I started again. "Yeah, yeah, we met up at a fundraiser for the mayor."

"So where'd you take her after?"

"After? I didn't."

Floyd peered up at Whitey as if to say, "Can you believe this guy?" then turned and cracked his brass-knuckled fist against my face again. A flash lit up my right eye and spread into a bruising throb. But Caroline's wellbeing was my immediate concern, not the state of my face.

"Eyewitnesses saw you leave with her," Floyd said.

"What?" I felt like I was in a Twilight Zone episode. Then I remembered the apartment building's concierge, Javier. "Wait, wait, ask the guy who works the door. He saw her leave."

"He was one of the witnesses," Floyd said from over me.

"The hell he was. When I talked to him last night, he told me she left alone..." My counterargument trailed off as I realized that's not what Javier had said. Not exactly. I replayed the odd exchange in my mind.

Did she leave with someone else?

What you mean, Mr. Croft?

I mean, did a man escort her out?

You mean someone else?

That's right, someone else.

No-o-o-o?

Christ. Javier's confusion hadn't stemmed from a language barrier, but from the belief he'd seen her leave with *me*. I thought of Angelus and fae powers, namely glamours. The son of a bitch could have assumed my likeness for others to see, but without Caroline necessarily knowing. Hot anger broke through me at the idea. I would find her, but first I had to get rid of these guys.

"I have an alibi," I said.

"Oh, yeah?" Floyd's lips tightened into a smile. "Hear that, Whitey? Lover boy here's got an alibi."

"Homicide," I said. "I was consulting on a case for the NYPD. I left the party around 9:30 and didn't get back until after it was over. Detective Vega will confirm that. I believe you just saw her outside?"

That seemed to give Floyd pause.

"Look," I said. "When I left, Caroline was talking to a guy named Angelus. Six foot five or so, dark blond hair, a face you want to smash, it's so damn perfect."

"That don't sound like someone who would be mistaken for you," Floyd said.

"Yeah, no kidding."

Floyd sighed from his haunches and looked up at Whitey. Some sort of nonverbal communication seemed to pass between them. At last, Floyd nodded and straightened. "We're gonna look into your alibi," he said, staring down at me. "But I'm gonna tell you something right now: we find out you're fibbing, and what happened here today's gonna seem like a beach vacation. And don't even think about running. Not unless you want both your legs broken."

"Great," I said. "You enjoy the rest of your day, too."

Floyd shook his head and followed Whitey out. I gained my feet and locked the door behind them.

"And that's exactly why I have you tour the ledge," I called back to Tabitha.

"Did you say something, darling?" When I turned, Tabitha was lifting her head from her paws, blinking slowly. "What did those men want?"

"You slept through all of that?"

"It didn't sound like it was going to be very interesting." Tabitha yawned. "Is that blood on your mouth?"

I wiped my bottom lip with the back of a hand and retrieved my cane. "Forget it."

I wasn't going to get into it with my cat. Touching my cane to my hurt places, I uttered healing incantations. I needed to be at full strength. Caroline was missing, and the Italian mob was interested for some reason. Which meant it was time to dial up some magic.

In my library/lab, I took the slip of paper onto which Caroline had written the address for last night's gala, aimed my cane at it, and spoke an incantation. White light bloomed from the opal, absorbing Caroline's essence from her writing.

Without warning, the cane kicked in my hand. It spun me in a complete three-hundred-sixty-degree circle before the opal's light faltered and went dim. The cane took on a ponderous weight.

"Again?" I groaned.

I pushed more energy into the incantation, already knowing it was a lost cause. Like the salt barrier, something was coming between the item and my target. But in this case I suspected fae magic.

I didn't know where in the city the fae lived. They were secretive, like I'd said. But I knew someone who might be able to point me in the right direction.

Even if she was a night hag.

13

"*Soglia,*" I whispered, aligning my mind with my apartment's defenses—defenses designed to keep out nasty supernaturals. But now I needed to let one in. Not only that, I would be setting out the equivalent of a piece of cheese as bait. I shuddered at the thought, but if I was going to learn anything about the fae in the city, and fast, I had little choice.

From my pocket, I pulled out a piece of black lava rock—an element to which night hags had an affinity—uttered "*Aprire,*" and set the rock on the floor before the door. The threshold's energy hit the stone's shadowy aura and coursed over it, creating a small hole in my home's defenses.

In the back of the fridge, I found an expired carton of milk. I counted to three, then glugged it down. My stomach shook and burbled, drowning in the spoiled milk. I needed to make my sleep as unpleasant as possible—more night hag bait.

"I'm going to sack out for a bit," I told Tabitha when my stomach had settled to a dull nausea. "If you hear me moaning or thrashing around for more than a few minutes, could you come and wake me?"

"Sure, darling."

As if she would be staying awake herself.

I closed the shades and crawled into bed, lying down on my back. Not wanting my protective necklace to act as a deterrent, I turned it around so that the coin hung between my shoulder blades. I then straightened my arms and legs and tried to clear my thoughts. After a few moments, my awareness began to crumble and break apart.

I was in a forest of tall trees, a child, and I was lost. I peered around, frightened by the sameness. Moving in any direction would only plunge me deeper into the forest, to a place no one would find me. And then night would fall, and the creatures would come out.

"Mom!" I cried in a thin, straining voice.

I had never called to her before. Nana, the woman who had raised me, had always been the soother of my scraped knees and hurt feelings. But I had a clear image of my mother, a photo in our old living room of her standing beside a window, light paling one half of her face, lost in thought. Now, an urgent tugging on my heart told me she was the only one who could lead me from here.

"Mom! Help me!"

Footsteps approached from behind. I turned and beheld the beautiful woman from the photo. Same light-brown hair brushed over one shoulder, same sad smile, same soft eyes. Only now they were looking at me.

"Mom!" I ran forward and threw my arms around her leg, pressing my cheek to the pleasant-smelling fabric of her slacks.

Her hand brushed my hair. "What's wrong, Everson?"

I sniffled. "I was lost."

She laughed softly. "Well, I found you, didn't I? I'll always find you."

"How do we get out of here?"

"I can point the way, but I'm going to need you to be a brave boy and make the journey yourself. Can you do that?"

I clung to her more tightly. But a chill wind cut through me, and her slacks suddenly turned ragged and rancid. Her thigh, so soft a moment ago, became a bony ridge, hard against my cheek. The hand stroking my hair began to hook and pull. I leaned my face back and let out a hoarse scream. My mother was gone, replaced by an old woman with a long, crooked nose and wild shocks of gray hair.

"What's wrong, Everson?" she cackled.

"No!" I wheeled to run, but the woman caught my wrist in a withered hand and yanked me back.

"Leaving so soon?" she said. "I wouldn't think of it, a handsome young boy like you."

"Stop!" I beat at her hand. "Let me go!"

When the necklace that hung between the woman's baggy breasts shook with delighted laughter, I saw that it was made of small bones. Children's bones.

"Let you go?" she asked. "Like this?"

I had been leaning back, and when she released my wrist I fell onto the rotten leaves. As I kicked myself away, the old woman lit up with more cackles, her mouth a graveyard of broken teeth.

"Stop," I pled. "Leave me alone."

"But don't you want to play with the other children?" she asked, stalking after me. She pulled a dripping leather bag from a cord that cinched her waist and opened it toward me. From deep inside came a chorus of screams, the sound drawing ice-cold nails across my soul. "There are so many, Everson. And they're always anxious for new playmates. Jump inside. Don't be shy."

This was a night hag, I realized. They visited their victims in nightmares, torturing their dream forms before stuffing them into a bag made out of stitched human skin. With enough visits, the sleeping victim would die.

And with that, I realized *I* was dreaming.

I fought to remember the chain of events that had delivered me here: creating a seam for the hag, calling her to my space with the lava rock, drinking sour milk to invoke the nightmare.

"Back off," I said in a voice that sounded more adult. But I was still scared witless. I struggled through the wet leaves, away from the nightmare creature bearing down on me with that awful sack. And then I felt the hard edges of something between my shoulder blades.

My necklace!

I dove a dream hand behind my neck. But before I could claim the powerful charm, the night hag took a giant leap. Her gnarly feet landed on my torso, pinning my arm beneath me. With a snarl, she crawled her hooked toes forward, the horny black nails gouging the skin of my chest.

"You're going to join the other children," she said, "and you're going to enjoy yourself."

I tried to worm my fingers farther down my back—I was only inches from the coin—but they wouldn't budge. I tried to buck my body and shove the hag off me, but I couldn't move. The hag's weight on my chest had paralyzed me. Her eyes, once rolling with delight, sharpened to the malevolent blades of the criminally insane.

I listened for Tabitha, hoping she had heard me scream.

"Such a handsome-looking nose." The night hag licked her sore-riddled lips with a black tongue. "I don't suppose a little taste would hurt, hmm?"

She leaned lower, teeth drawing apart. A smell of bloating and decomposition broke against my face.

Might not be able to seize my charmed coin, I thought, *but I can still cast through it.*

I stopped struggling and focused on the coin's symbol, squares offset to create a star-like pattern, lines to channel and focus energy. It pulsed like a warming ember beneath my back.

"So delicious." Her tongue scraped along the bridge of my nose.

"Respingere," I mumbled.

The force discharged with enough force to propagate through my dream body and throw the hag off me. The paralysis broken, I sat up and pulled my necklace over my head, the heavy coin clenched in my palm.

The hag let out a withering scream. "You little bastard!"

She jerked the dripping sack from her belt and charged, fresh screams rising from the sack's mouth. She opened the sack wider until it looked large enough to swallow me.

I held out the glowing coin and bellowed, *"Intrappolare."*

A shaft of blue light slammed into the onrushing creature. She screamed as the force knocked her from her feet. I advanced, angling the amulet to direct the light over her, pinning her to the forest floor.

I had my night hag.

"Release me!" she screamed. "Release me, curse you!"

"I have a few questions first."

She writhed against the force, spitting and wringing her sack.

I channeled more energy through the coin. "I can do this all day, you know."

She relented suddenly, her voice becoming a frail whimper. "You would torment an old woman?"

"You mean the one who just tried to eat my nose?"

Her face curled up again. "What do you want?" she spat.

"You're not a faerie, but you roam the wilds of their realm. You're aware of their comings and goings."

"What of it!"

"I'm looking for a particular fae. He goes by the name Angelus."

Her eyes showed a brief glint of recognition. "I know no one by that name."

I shrugged and leaned against a tree. "How long we do this is up to you."

"No, mortal." Her lips wrinkled into a grin. "I have only to wait for you to awaken."

"I'll destroy you before that happens."

She cackled. "You haven't the power."

"Oh?" I pushed more energy through the charmed coin. The shaft of light pinning the hag turned bright.

"Owww!" she howled, covering her head with her bony arms.

I backed off. "That's just a taste," I lied. I had pushed hard enough to make Thelonious stir. "Now tell me about Angelus."

She lowered her arms with a scowl. "What about him?"

"First, who is he?"

"He's a *prince*." Her lips puckered around the word.

"In the faerie realm?" I thought about that. The fae didn't carry royal titles in the city. They were more like the Vanderbilts and Rockefellers: old, wealthy families, but without the name recognition, which was how they seemed to like it. "What does he do in the city? Where does he live?"

"How should I know?"

"I've seen you pushing your shopping cart up and down the sidewalks. How many centuries have you been in New York? And you're going to sit there and tell me you have no idea what a prince from your realm does in the city or where he lives?"

"I don't know what he does."

I upped the energy until her warts began to sizzle and burst.

"I don't!" she insisted. "But he lives near the Park."

"Where near the Park?"

"East Side! Seventieth Street! Now release me!"

I eyed the hideous creature. Stealer of souls, robber of cradles. I *could* try to destroy her, but that would mean expending energy that might not even be sufficient to the task. And if Thelonious made a visit, things would go from very bad to much worse. No, I couldn't risk it.

"Fine," I said, pulling power from the coin. "I release you."

The hag growled and gained her feet. I eyed her loose grip on her sack.

"Liberare!" I cried, thrusting the coin toward it. The force tore the sack from her grasp and flipped it, releasing the trapped souls. They streamed away, like celestial eels into a great ocean.

"Nooo!" the night hag shrieked. "Come back! Don't run away!"

The night hag grabbed her sack and ran after the streaming souls, leaping up in fruitless attempts to reclaim them. She soon became lost among the trees, her wretched cries trailing after her.

14

For the duration of the cab ride, I clutched my cane in both hands, my nerves taut in the beating middle and frayed at both ends. Fortunately, the cabbie wasn't a talker. I had him drop me off where Seventieth Street met Central Park.

The day was cool and brisk, the sidewalks dotted with New Yorkers in hats and scarves. The street the night hag had given me was in one of the city's wealthier pockets, though something told me I wouldn't find the fae in any of the ornate towers facing the Park. That would be too obvious.

Opening my senses, I headed east at a fast walk, eyeing the passing buildings. Though none featured ethereal auras, I began to pick up a low white noise after several blocks, like soft static. The static grew as I hastened my pace—then it receded. I backed up until I was standing where the static was at its peak. I found myself beside a stone staircase leading up to an emerald-green door. Somehow I had missed both just a few seconds before.

A subtle, intricate magic was at play, blending the edifice with the buildings on either side so it wouldn't stand out. Only a steady eye brought the door into full focus. I moved my gaze up the narrow townhouse, counting four floors, each with a window and simple decorative balcony.

Yes, this was the place.

I climbed the steps. Finding no bell, I knocked on the door, the dense wood seeming to swallow the sound. But a moment later, the door opened onto a slight man in traditional butler's attire, silver hair combed to one side. Though he appeared fully human, I immediately recognized him as a fae. His aura was calmer than Angel's, tempered by age, but not weaker.

Definitely not weaker.

If he was surprised to see me—or anyone—at his door, the emotion remained folded in a drawer behind his placid face. I tried to peer past him, but against the light from outside, the space registered dimly, perhaps from another veiling. All I could make out was the beginning of parquet hallway, too wide, it seemed, to fit inside the narrow building.

The butler cleared his throat. "Yes?"

I decided to forego etiquette. "Where's Angelus?"

"I'm afraid he's not in, sir."

"Where is he?"

"I couldn't tell you." His gray eyes, which seemed to eddy at their depths with ancient knowledge, gave up nothing.

"I need to talk to him."

"It would appear so."

"Listen," I said, fighting to control my voice, "Angelus left a party with a friend of mine last night, and no one's seen her since. Do you know anything about that?"

"Angelus isn't in, sir," he repeated.

His head turned slightly. Somewhere behind him a door opened, and an impossible number of voices spilled into the hallway before the door closed again. How many people were back there? Was Caroline among them?

"I'm sorry, sir," the butler said, "but I must return to my duties."

"No, wait." I went to jam a foot against the closing door, but a force kicked it back out. A threshold.

"Good day, sir." He closed the door.

I tried the knob then pounded on the door. When it didn't open again, I descended to the sidewalk and peered up at the townhouse. If Caroline was inside, it would explain why my tracking spell had fizzled out as well as why her phone couldn't receive a signal, the protective energies of the building breaking apart both.

I balled my hands into helpless fists. The defenses here were too complex for someone of my wizarding grade. Even the butler seemed to know this, regarding me more as a minor nuisance than a threat. I considered appealing to the Order to intervene, but I knew that had about as high a probability of getting a response as winning the New York lottery.

The pager in my pocket began to vibrate. Vega was probably ready to follow up on Arnaud's bogus lead. I left the townhouse in search of a payphone, eventually finding one on Third Avenue.

"What's up?" I asked when Vega answered.

"There's a diner two blocks from Ferguson Towers called Firpo's. How soon can you be here?"

"Why? What's going on?"

"We have some new information."

My heart sped up as I thought of Arnaud's threat against her son. Neither Vega nor I could be seen poking around Ferguson Towers. "Well, ah, what about our interview with Sonny?" I stammered.

"That can wait."

I looked around desperately, torn between keeping Vega and her son safe and finding Caroline.

"Croft," Vega said sternly.

"Uh, fine. I'll catch a cab here in a minute."

She hung up.

I wheeled from the phone booth and found myself face to face with the blond blood slave. "Geez." I pressed my hand to my slamming heart. "Do you have to sneak up on me like that?"

"Get her away from the Towers," he said.

I was preparing to play dumb before realizing that, with his preternatural hearing, Blondie had heard every word on Vega's end of the conversation. He reached into a jacket pocket and held up a smartphone, the crisp image of a young boy at play on its screen: Vega's son.

"That was taken two minutes ago in a Brooklyn park," Blondie said. "I hear his sitter has a bad habit of texting when she should be keeping an eye on him. All I have to do is give the word."

I shouldered him aside and waved for a taxi.

"Don't," I said. "I'll get her out of there."

I found Vega in a booth in the back corner of the dimly-lit diner. She was talking to someone across from her, the back of the booth blocking the person from view. As I approached, a pair of wringing hands slid into my line of sight, then thick arms, and at last a hulking body, the squat head swiveling to face me. I pulled up short. What in the hell was one of Stiles's henchmen doing here?

"Thanks for coming," Vega said. "This is Rancho."

When my eyes slid back to the henchman, the one whom I'd dubbed the Mexican Wrestler, I half expected him to be reaching for a weapon. Instead, Rancho offered his right hand, his expression either fearful or earnest, I couldn't tell. His palm was damp when we shook. Vega scooted over to make room for me, and I joined her opposite Rancho.

"So what's up?" I asked, looking between them.

"Rancho has something to share," Vega said. "Go on, tell him what you told me."

"I'm not supposed to be talking," Rancho said in a half-whisper, peering around the side of the booth. Besides being dimly lit, the hazy diner was empty. "If Stiles finds out..."

"Everything you say is confidential," Vega said impatiently. "And I'm telling you that as an old friend."

Rancho hunched his shoulders and pushed around his coffee mug with a finger. "I'm Stiles's number two. I run security in the east towers and have a dozen guys patrolling for me. Every night around midnight, I do my own patrol. Make sure no one's where they shouldn't be, you know?" He wasn't talking about the security of the residents, I understood, but the security of Stiles's drug operation. His job was to keep Kahn's sellers out of the east towers. "Anyway, I'm doing the tour of the lower levels. Pit Stop and Bones are down there."

"The victims," Vega told me. "Before they became victims."

"Yeah, they're not supposed to be down there," Rancho went on, "but they're whacked out pretty good, and I'm not gonna pick 'em up and carry 'em out, you know? So I keep going, and I'm getting this feeling like someone's watching me. And I'm hearing things. Breathing. Something moving. But too big to be a rat, you know? And it's bothering me, 'cause except for where my flashlight's pointing it's pitch black down there. So I give the room a sweep, and I swear to God, something's moving just outside of my light, quick as fuck."

"Did you get a look at what?" I asked.

"For a blink, yeah," Rancho whispered. "Cause when my light forced it into a corner, the thing came at me. I mean, one second it's back behind the pipes, and the next it's almost on top of me. I caught a face, white as this coffee mug, and wild hair, and a mouthful of teeth." Rancho arranged his shaking hands so he was holding an invisible gun. "I squeezed twice—bam! bam!—and got the fuck out of there."

"Those bullet casings we found?" Vega said to me, raising an eyebrow.

"And he didn't come after you?" I asked, the fact striking me as unusual.

"He?" Rancho shook his head. "That was no dude."

"What do you mean?"

"That's why Stiles thinks it's one of Kahn's," Rancho said. "Some of his runners are women. Stiles ordered me to go back down, to make sure I'd finished her off. But there was no way I was gonna have that thing come at me again. And just so you know," he said, leaning forward to look me in the eyes, "I've dealt with some of the baddest mothers out there. Been stabbed, shot, bottles broken over my head—shit don't scare me. But that thing in the basement..." His next breath rattled out of him. "I'm telling you, she wasn't one of Kahn's. She wasn't even a person."

Vega nudged my leg twice under the table, as though to say *blood slave.*

"So you lied to Stiles about going back down?" I said.

"Yeah, and the next day Pit Stop and Bones are torn to shit."

I chewed on that for a moment. "Did any of your people see her come or go?"

"No one saw nothing," Rancho said. "And we keep eyes on our doors twenty-four seven."

I remembered the drain Vega had checked out in the boiler room and thought back to what I'd read about blood slaves lairing near their prey.

"I talked with Stiles earlier," Vega said to me. "Son of a bitch is on a power trip. Isn't going to let us take another look at the crime scene. Doesn't want us anywhere near *his* towers, as he calls them."

I felt the tension ease out of my shoulders. *That's a relief.*

"But I sent Hoffman out to track down the plans for the buildings," she said. "See if there are any other access points to the lower level."

"While Hoffman is working on that," I said quickly, "maybe we should head over to that interview in midtown." *And get both of us far, far away from Ferguson Towers.*

"Wait," Vega said. "Rancho's got something else."

The hulking man peeked around the edge of the booth again, then hunched his head even lower. "Stiles isn't going to give you a week. He just wanted to let that get around so Kahn would lower his guard."

"He's planning something?" I asked.

"Yeah, and it ain't gonna be a tit for tat. He's going big."

"How big?"

"Taking out Kahn big."

"When?" I asked.

"Two nights from now. Man, if he knows I'm telling you this, he'll waste me. But I've got a family in there. I've got kids to look out for. My baby girl just turned two. You should see her face when I walk in the door. Just lights right up. No judgment or nothing." A softness took hold in Rancho's coal-black eyes. "I'd die before I let her catch a stray bullet—or missile."

I tried to picture the three-hundred pound monstrosity tossing a little girl up and down and blowing raspberries against her belly.

"Thanks, Rancho," Vega said, setting a few twenties in front of him, probably out of her own pocket.

"I didn't talk for the money," Rancho said. "I'm talking because I need you guys' help. I'm asking you to catch whatever the fuck that thing is and show it to Stiles. You know what he's like, Ricki. Once he gets a notion, God and Satan can't knock it out of his head."

"We're doing everything we can," Vega said, her hip-check my cue to slide from the booth. "But keep the money. Buy something for your little girl. We may need you for more than just info next time."

15

"Something wrong?" Vega asked from behind the wheel.

As we'd left the diner, I had caught two of Arnaud's blood slaves watching from down the street. I had no idea whether I'd gotten Vega out of there fast enough. For all I knew, her son was now missing, his sitter searching the playground, calling his name in ever-growing distress. That would be on me. I let myself become too interested in Rancho's story when I should have been urging Vega to leave. I guess my face looked as stricken as I felt.

"Just thinking about a friend," I said, switching from one track of worry to another. "She left a party last night with someone, and no one's seen her since. I can't get her on the phone."

"Maybe she doesn't want to be found," Vega said.

I'd thought about that, especially with the Italian mob looking for her. "Maybe," I agreed. "But could you check and see if anyone's filled out a missing persons report on her?"

"What's the name?"

"Caroline Reid."

She pulled out her smartphone, making her steering more haphazard. After a few queries, much of it in police jargon, she said, "Thanks," and hung up. "A report went out around noon," she told me.

"Who filed the report?"

"Didn't say."

Probably her father. I considered having Vega relay the info about the fae house on East Seventieth Street to Missing Persons, then decided against it, my brain a switchboard of conflicting signals.

I massaged my aching temples.

"Goddamn Stiles," Vega seethed. I turned to find her white-knuckling the steering wheel, eyes staring spears at the road ahead. "I knew he was gonna pull some kind of shit, but saying he'd give us time just so he could give himself an advantage against Kahn?" She faced me, a pair of fingers held up. "Two nights, Croft. We've got two nights to wrap this up."

"Maybe this lead will turn into something."

"Coming from Arnaud?" Vega snorted. "I may not know any vampires, but I know the type."

"What do you mean?"

"A person of interest wanting to aim the spotlight anywhere but at himself. They give us bad info all the time. I'm much more interested in the building plans for the Towers, learning how that thing got in and out."

"Were you able to find out anything about Sonny Shoat?"

"Yeah, the man's a real prince." She gave me a sidelong look. "For the last thirty years he's been running a club near Times Square. A seedy joint called *Seductions*. Man's been in and out of custody, mostly for drugs and beating up on his girls."

I felt my jaw steeling. I could forgive a lot, but not preying on women or children.

"So we'll go in there," Vega said, "let him deny knowing anything, and then we'll get back to figuring out how that blood slave accessed the tower."

I was trying to come up with something to divert Vega from her plan when her phone beeped. She looked at a text message on the display, typed something back, and returned the phone to her jacket pocket.

"Everything all right?" I asked.

"Just my sitter saying they're back at the apartment."

Kid's safe, I thought, relaxing into the seat. *But for how much longer?*

Sonny's graying hair hung like damp drapes around a gaunt, predatory face. Underneath a leather vest, he went shirtless, like the women he employed.

"A murder, you say?" He set a booted foot against his metal desk and tipped himself back, hands clasped behind his head. I could just make out his rat-like eyes studying us from behind a pair of sunglasses, his left lid jittering up and down. But it was his canines I was more interested in. Arnaud had sent us to another vampire. "No, don't know anything about that."

"It happened in the basement of Ferguson Towers," Vega said in the monotone of someone just going through the motions. "The two victims had their throats slashed."

Sonny's narrow nose let out a snivel. "Sounds like you've got a killer on your hands."

"Really," Vega said flatly. "And you don't have any information for us?"

"Why would I?"

"We're following up on a lead," she said.

Sonny dropped his chair and leaned over his desk. "Then you've been misled."

"No shit," she muttered under her breath, cutting her eyes to me as though to say, *Had enough of this dirt bag?*

But before she could stand, I placed a hand on her forearm. Sonny wasn't as pale as the creature Rancho had described, but I couldn't ignore his long hair—or the fact he would have employed hundreds of women over the years, maybe even made blood slaves out of a few of them.

"I imagine the turnover in your line of work is pretty high," I said.

"No flies on you," Sonny replied with a tired smile, front teeth glinting gold. "Just when you get them pulling in real money, too. They forget who *made* them that money, you know?" He turned toward the closed door that led onto the club, a den of black lights, thumping music, and sinuous, sweating bodies. Detective Vega hadn't been thrilled about having to walk through the club to get to the office. Neither had I, to be honest.

"Did any of them leave here with an appetite for blood?" I asked, raising a brow.

Sonny's gaze snapped back to mine, his left eyelid jittering faster. "I don't know what you're talking about."

"I think you do."

Sonny waved a hand of sharpened nails. "Once they leave, the girls aren't my business anymore."

In my peripheral vision, I could see Vega's gaze moving between us, brow furrowed, no doubt wondering where in the hell the interview was going. I wasn't sure myself. But I was getting the impression that if I could rattle Sonny hard enough, something useful might fall out.

"You're familiar with the big investment bankers downtown, right?" I asked.

"What about them?"

"They like a certain degree of invisibility, don't they? I mean, in terms of who they are?"

Sonny wet his lips with a pale tongue.

"It just strikes me that if they thought you were being, I don't know, *careless* with your women, they might decide to come uptown and have a word with you."

"Look, man," Sonny said, a note of fear entering his voice. I could feel cold power radiating from him, but it didn't compare to Arnaud's. A fact Sonny must have known too. "I hear what you're saying, but I don't do that to my girls. I don't turn them into anything."

At that moment, music burst through the opening door. A ginger-haired woman in glittering red shoes and a matching thong stepped into the office, her curves bared to the world.

"Sorry," she said between smacks of gum. "Didn't know you had visitors."

"No, I'm glad you came," Sonny said. He scooted back and patted his thighs. "Come over here, sugar. Have a seat."

She did as he said and plopped onto his lap, her mascara-lined eyes regarding us with utter disinterest.

"How long have you been with me, Casey?"

"I dunno." She shrugged. "Fifteen years?"

"Nineteen, sugar." He stroked her cheek with a long nail, sending chills through me. Everything about the vampire repulsed me. He cut his eyes to mine. "Nineteen years, and look at her. A hundred percent flesh and blood."

He was right. She exhibited none of the waxiness of a blood slave. And though her eyes verged on lifeless, I suspected that had more to do with a combination of drug use and regular blood draws. I studied Casey's neck and arms for marks. Sonny apparently caught on to what I was doing.

"You think I'd damage the merchandise?" he asked with a laugh. "Casey, show the man your ticklish spot."

"Now?" she said.

"Go on."

With a sigh, Casey set a high heel on the desktop and undid the thick strap across the top of her foot. She peeled back the strap to reveal angry-red punctures in the scarred skin—Sonny's watering hole.

"You see," he said. "I only take enough to keep me going, nothing more."

He brushed a thumb over the years' worth of punctures as though they were a work of art. Casey wriggled and let out a giggle. Sonny's eyes suddenly narrowed, and he shoved her off him.

"Hey!" She stumbled and braced herself against the wall, balancing on one high heel to refasten the loose strap on the other.

"Get back out there," Sonny barked. "You're not making any money in here."

"And you are?" she shot back.

In a flash, Sonny was on his feet. I didn't know what his intentions were—maybe just to yell some more—but seeing Casey flinch away was enough. I slammed Sonny into the wall and tackled him to the floor. A dry erase board with the dancers' schedules clattered on top of us. Sonny was stronger and faster than me, but I had caught him off guard. Before he could wrestle free, I yanked his head back by the hair and shoved Grandpa's ring against his throat.

"You might not know what this is," I said between gritted teeth. "But I know you can feel its power."

Sonny's shades were hanging from one ear, and his naked eyes seethed red with rage. "I can destroy you, human," he hissed, a second set of spiny teeth growing through his gums.

"The ring will destroy you first."

"Get up," Vega said, pulling the dry erase board away. "Both of you."

Sonny's eyes shifted to where she was standing over him, her pistol aimed down at his head. Her standard-issue bullets wouldn't kill him, but they would hurt like hell until he could reconstitute his form. Sonny must have decided it wasn't worth the hassle. He retracted his teeth and showed his palms.

"Jesus," he muttered. "You said this was gonna be an informal interview."

I got up and moved back, keeping my ring trained on him. He fixed his sunglasses as he stood, then gave his hair a light toss. When he noticed Casey still in his office, he flicked his hand.

"Go on, sugar," he said gently. "Back to work, huh?"

Thrusting her chest out defiantly, Casey turned and marched from the office, as though leaving of her own initiative. "Asshole," she said before the door closed behind her.

"Bitch," Sonny grumbled as he returned to his desk and sat down hard. "Always had a mouth on her. Probably getting too old for this gig, anyway."

Vega holstered her weapon and dropped a card in front of him. "If you decide you know anything about those murders, you give us a call."

I stepped up beside Vega and aimed a finger at him. "And if we find our killer and she has little puncture scars across the top of her foot, we'll be making some calls to the Financial District."

"I'm telling you, I don't turn them into anything."

"We'll see," I said.

"I don't!" he called at our backs as we left his office.

16

" A vampire," Vega mused as we drove south.

"Yeah, they're rare outside the Financial District," I said. "The banking class doesn't like having attention drawn to their kind—I wasn't lying to Sonny about that. Rogue vampires who get too homicidal get taken out pretty quick. Sonny knows this, which tells me he probably *has* been playing by their rules all these years. Snacking from his dancers' feet could well be the extent of his vampiric activities." I grimaced at the thought.

"So why did Arnaud send us to him?"

I was still trying to wrap my head around that one. I understood how a creature like Sonny would make the false lead appear more compelling, but a niggling feeling in the back of my brain told me Arnaud was trying to accomplish something more.

"I don't know," I admitted. "But I think it's worth getting a list of all the women who have worked for Sonny. Track them down."

"Three decades' worth?" Vega hit me with a hard stare. "Do you know how long that would take?"

"I know, but—"

"We've got two nights, Croft. Not two years."

"Maybe we'll get lucky," I suggested.

Vega's phone rang before she could voice the irritation on her face. "Yeah," she said, then listened. "Be right there." The engine hit another octave as she depressed the accelerator.

"What's up?" I asked.

"Hoffman's got the plans for the Towers at the office. He says he found a way the perp might have gotten in and out. Would you mind coming? If we have something we can act on, we're going to need to start planning. I don't know anything about taking down a blood slave."

What I really wanted to do was get back uptown to Seventieth Street and put eyes on the fae townhouse. But with Vega desperate for results in the face of a looming gang war, I knew leaving her was putting her son at risk. And if she tried to take on the creature alone...

I nodded. "Yeah, I'll go."

"Storm drains," Hoffman said, pointing them out on the blueprint he'd unrolled across Vega's desk. "A system runs directly underneath the towers. And right here's an access point, in the boiler room."

I remembered the rusty grate. "The pipe looked too small for a person."

"For you or me, maybe," Hoffman said, "but it's a foot and a half in diameter. Someone slender could've shimmied up it. And look." He unrolled another blueprint, angling it toward Vega. "After getting the plans from the Housing Authority, I went down to Environmental Protection, got a map of the storm lines in a sixteen-block radius."

I craned my neck to look over the gray paper and network of blue lines.

"Someone wanting to access the drain would've had a few choices," he said, tapping some entry points.

Vega's gaze rose from the map to my face. "What are we going to need?"

"Are you sure this is something you should be rushing into?" I asked.

"Who's this guy think he is?" Hoffman growled.

Vega moved her fists to her hips. I pretended to study the map, racking my brain for anything that would steer the investigation away from Ferguson Towers.

"Croft," she said.

"Have you ever been down a storm drain?" I asked, working out my argument as I spoke. "I did once when I was a kid, on a dare. They're confined, confusing. They take sounds and amplify them, bouncing them every which way. And a lot of stretches involve wading through water, some of it up to here." I placed a hand at thigh level. "My magic doesn't play so well with water. And with a blood slave's speed and strength, we'd be sitting ducks. As your consultant, I'm advising against it."

"You're still talking about blood slaves?" Hoffman asked, incredulous.

"We're going down." Vega's eyes remained hard as tacks. "Now tell us what we need."

She wasn't going to back off, and I couldn't warn her about the threat against her son. Arnaud's rules. I sighed and dragged a hand through my hair. "Silver bullets, for starters."

"And where can we get those?" she asked.

"I know someone, but I don't know what he has in stock. It might take a day or two."

"We both use standard nine-millimeter rounds," Vega said. "We can change weapons to accommodate the ammo, if needed. Find out what he can supply us *now*—not in one or two days. You can use my phone."

"Um, I'm not sure he has a number."

"What in the hell is this, Croft?" Vega demanded.

"What?"

"Every time something comes up that might advance the investigation, you start squirming."

"What are you talking about?"

"You know exactly what I'm talking about."

Anger sprung from my smoldering bed of guilt. "Look, whether you like it or not, part of my role as your consultant is keeping you safe from the horrors out there. I'm doing the job you're paying me for."

Hoffman snorted. "I'll tell you what's going on," he said to Vega. "Gandalf here knows we're about to find out there ain't no blood slave, or whatever he calls them, so he's milking us for as many hours as he can bill us for. Told you the man was a freaking hustler."

Vega's eyes didn't move from mine. "Do I need to drop you from the case?"

I held her gaze, the corner of my mouth trembling with emotion. In my mind, I was saying, *Fine, screw it. Go off and do whatever you want. Get yourselves killed. I don't need this.* But that was the stress talking. I took a deep breath and dropped my gaze back to the map.

"Fine," I said, holding up a hand. "I'll see what I can find out about those bullets."

An hour later, I exited Mr. Han's apothecary with two boxes of nine-millimeter silver bullets in my coat pockets, along with a third box packed with silver bullets and cold iron ones for my own use. I could have lied to Vega, of course, told her my source had been out, but she was getting better at seeing through my lies. The best I could do right now was stall her.

All right, I thought as I paced north. *Vega gave me three hours to track down the bullets, which means I have enough time to go home and try to prepare a spell or two to get into that fae townhouse and look for Caroline.*

"Well, lookie here," someone said.

It didn't occur to me I had crossed Canal Street and entered Little Italy until I recognized the voice at my back.

"We don't have to go to his place after all."

I wheeled to find Floyd striding up behind me, a pistol aiming from the waist of his cinched coat. To the left, Whitey was steering a Studebaker along the one-way street beside us, his pale eyes tracking me.

"C'mon, man," I said. "I told you I have an alibi."

"Yeah, and guess what," Floyd said. "It didn't check out."

"What? Who did you talk to?"

"Detective named Hoffman. Real helpful."

"Hoffman? He was the one who picked me up from the gala," I said, then stopped as cold understanding took hold. That was one way to get rid of someone you believed to be a con man.

"Not according to him, you weren't," Floyd said.

"Did you talk to Detective Vega? She'll vouch for me."

Floyd let out a barking laugh. "I bet she will. How much did that cost you?"

"Cost?" Great, so not only had Hoffman denied seeing me the night of Caroline's disappearance, but to discredit whatever Vega might say, he claimed I'd paid her off. That tire-shaped son of a bitch. "There were other officers at the scene," I said, backing away.

"Yeah, and you probably gave them a little something too. Now why don't you climb on into the car." He signaled with the gun.

God, I don't have time for this.

I nodded but angled my cane so it was pointing at his stomach. *"Vigore!"* I yelled, anticipating the force that would burst from my cane and hit Floyd hard enough to lift him from his feet. But the meager force barely rattled my cane. Some trash near Floyd's feet puffed up.

I refocused. *"Vigore!"*

"Yeah, that's real cute," Floyd said. "Now c'mon, you're testing our patience here."

He grabbed me by the shoulder of my coat and jabbed the

pistol barrel against my low back. A sharp pain opened in my left kidney, but I was still fixated on my cane.

"Respingere!" I cried, trying for a shield to shove Floyd off me.

"Let's go, let's go."

As Floyd walked me off the curb, I remembered the warping sensation of the fae threshold when I'd tried to force my way in. That bit of contact must have scrambled my abilities, knocked them offline. I hadn't noticed any changes at the time, but fae magic was often subtle.

Fantastic timing.

By the time we arrived at the car, Whitey had gotten out and opened a backdoor. Without my power, I had no choice but to duck inside. Floyd scooted in after me. He didn't need to warn me not to try anything funny. He was saying it all with the pressure of his barrel. The plastic-covered seat spoke volumes as well.

"Keep your hands where I can see them," Floyd said.

"Where are we going?" I asked.

"To talk to someone."

"Not the fish, I hope."

Floyd chuckled. "Well, that's gonna be up to you." He pulled a phone from his coat and made a call. "We picked him up in Little Italy," he said. "Yeah. Yeah. All right. We'll meet you down there."

He put his phone away and tapped Whitey's shoulder. "Pier sixteen."

Recent experience told me I was being taken to the mob boss—who had taken a keen interest in Caroline's whereabouts, for some reason. I examined my hands, my right pinky still a little off where Bashi had had it snapped a few months earlier. I just hoped Mr.

Moretti would prove less volatile, though mob bosses and piers rarely worked out for people like me.

Whitey drove us onto an abandoned shipping dock, where huge metal containers stood in rusting stacks. At a chain-link fence, he got out, unfastened a lock, and rolled the gate open. Seagulls scattered from what looked like a rotting dog carcass as we drove through. Whitey parked close to the water's edge, almost in the shadow of the Brooklyn Bridge.

I tested my cane with a whispered Word, but still nothing. When I tried to inch away from Floyd's pistol, he dug it even deeper into my ribs. "I'm telling you," I sighed. "Caroline didn't leave the party with me. She left with a guy named Angelus."

Floyd laughed. "Couldn't even come up with a regular-sounding name."

"Which should tell you I'm not lying."

"Shut it," Floyd said. "He's here."

I craned my neck around to see a black Escalade with tinted windows easing through the gate and onto the cement pier. It pulled up next to my side of the car and sat, engine idling.

"Let's go," Floyd said, shoving the pistol against me. "Slowly, though."

My door lock popped open and I stepped out, Floyd scooting across the seat after me. I considered making a run for it, but Whitey had chosen the spot for a reason. It was open, exposed, the closest shipping container a good fifty yards away. If I could summon a shield, piece of cake. But since my powers had taken a fae-induced crap, I had no choice but to follow orders.

Floyd seized me by the upper arm and opened the back door of the Escalade. "Get in," he said.

The back seat was empty, but I could make out the silhouettes of the driver and a large man in the passenger seat. Mr. Moretti, I presumed. Floyd prodded me, and I scooted across the seat—one not covered in plastic, I noted with some relief. After climbing in after me, Floyd closed the door. I shifted in a sudden darkness that smelled of oily hair tonic.

"Where is she?" the man in the passenger seat asked.

"I'm assuming you mean Caroline?"

He remained staring straight ahead, his silence thickening the air.

"Well, as I told Floyd here, I consult for the NYPD. I was called to a case last night and left Caroline in the company of a guy named Angelus. By the time I returned, she had already left."

"With someone who looked just like you," the man said.

"Apparently."

"You see, the problem I'm having here is twofold." The man's voice was low and husky, as though each word were passing over a grater. *Was* he Mr. Moretti? "One, we have several witnesses who saw you and her leave together. And two, no one in the NYPD can corroborate your story."

"Well, I can explain the second," I said, my voice thin and unconvincing. "Detective Hoffman doesn't like that I'm consulting for the Department. He did in fact pick me up from the gala last night, at about—"

"Enough bullshitting," the man cut in. "Where is she?" I could make out his hair now: iron-colored, combed back in severe lines. He shifted a pair of broad shoulders that were almost level with his ears.

"Believe it or not, I'm trying to find that out, too. I did manage to get an address for this Angelus. It's on the Upper East Side, Seventieth Street. A butler stonewalled me, but I'm—"

"Where is she?" he repeated.

"That's what I'm trying to tell you," I cried in exasperation. "I don't know where she is, but I've tracked down the address of the last person I saw her with. Someone who..." I stopped, uncertain how to complete the sentence. *...can change his appearance? ... has wild-crazy powers?*

"I'm going to ask you one more time," the man said. He turned until an aging face waxed into view. "Where's Caroline?" Familiar blue eyes stared hard into mine. "Where's my daughter?"

17

"**M**r. *Reid?*" I said.

I'd met him once, a year before, his hand crushing mine when we shook. I had known that if my trial relationship with his daughter progressed, there was a good chance I'd be seeing him more often—something I was inwardly dreading—but, Jesus, not like this, not on a pier in the back of an SUV with a wise guy jamming a pistol against my ribs.

"I spoke with your department chair," Mr. Reid said.

"Who? Snodgrass?"

"He said he's caught you watching Caroline through her classroom window while she teaches."

Heat broke out over my face. "Once or twice, maybe."

"And that you frequently ask her out to lunch."

"Well, yeah. But to which she frequently says yes."

"He described it as an unhealthy infatuation."

"I don't know about the unhealthy part."

"He also says you're unstable. That you were the main suspect in a homicide investigation a couple of years ago, a crime you were arrested for but made some sort of a plea deal to get out of."

"Well, Snodgrass doesn't like me much, either."

"Sounds like your unpopularity crops up whenever it's most convenient." Though Floyd snorted beside me, Mr. Reid didn't crack a smile. "Be that as it may," he continued, "Snodgrass was telling the truth. The records were buried, but everything he told me was in them."

"If you're implying I hurt your daughter, Mr. Reid..." I licked my lips. "God, nothing could be further from the truth. I've been trying to reach her on her phone since late last night—you can check the phone records. And right after Floyd and Whitey visited me this morning and I understood she was missing, I started looking for the man I'd last seen her with. I got a street, I found the townhouse, I interrogated the butler. I mean, we're wasting our time sitting here."

"The townhouse on East Seventieth Street?" he asked.

"Yeah."

"So what were you doing in lower Manhattan?"

"I was, um, helping the NYPD with something."

He sighed and turned away. "The NYPD again."

"I know how that sounds. I know how this all sounds." I had never felt more impotent in my life. Not only were my powers offline, but every word I spoke sounded like utter horse manure. And this in front of a man whose daughter I was in love with.

Though I did have to wonder how Mr. Reid had gotten mixed up with Moretti's men, especially since Caroline insisted he would never deal with gangsters. Either there was a side to her father she didn't know about, or, desperate for his daughter's safe return, he had decided to compromise his ethics. Filing a missing person report with the NYPD was no guarantee of action after all. If you wanted results, you had to pay for them. Hiring Moretti's men, who could probably use all the work they could get these days, fell into that category.

"There's only one way you're getting out of this," Mr. Reid said. "And that's by giving me something I can use."

I racked my brain. "I, ah..." I remembered something and leaned forward. "When Angelus first asked to speak with your daughter at the gala, she blew him off. But when he said it had something to do with her father, with *you*, she agreed."

Mr. Reid stared through the windshield in the direction of a garbage boat chugging up the East River.

"Do you know why that might have been?" I pressed.

He turned just enough to make eye contact with Floyd.

The pistol jabbed into my side. "Let's go," Floyd said.

"Wait. Mr. Reid," I pled, "I'm telling you the truth."

"The first time I met you, you struck me as a bullshit artist," Mr. Reid said. "I even told Caroline that. Wish she would've listened."

My door opened, and Whitey was there to yank me out by the arm. I stumbled into the harsh gray light, Floyd emerging against my other side. As the two wrestled me back toward their car, I heard the Escalade wheeling around behind me and leaving the pier.

"Where are you taking me now?" I asked. "The zoo?"

"No," Floyd replied. "But by the time we're through with you, you're gonna be singing like one of them macaws."

I planted my feet and resisted. I didn't have a plan, but I wasn't getting back into their car.

"You want us to work you over out here?" Floyd asked. "That it?"

"What can I say?" I grunted, resisting their efforts to drag me forward. "I'm an exhibitionist."

"Hear that, Whitey? Man wants to be beaten bloody for the world to see." He jerked the cane from my hand and sent it clattering across the pier. When he turned back to face me, I drove a fist into his nose.

"That's for this morning," I said.

Floyd staggered back, a hand to his spurting nose. "Y-you broke it!"

"Believe me, it's an enhancement."

"Oh, you screwed up." I turned toward Whitey's raspy voice and met a pair of pale eyes as devoid of empathy as the black bore staring at my forehead. "You screwed up big time."

"Waste him," I heard Floyd call from behind me, his voice clogged with blood. "Screw the job, just waste him."

I'd been gambling that Mr. Reid wouldn't want a professional hit on his hands. Plus, what good was I to him dead? What I had underestimated was Moretti's men taking matters into their own hands.

Whitey smiled thinly as he cocked the revolver.

I threw my forearms over my face and crouched away. But the shot never came. When I peeked out, Whitey was on his back, arms and legs spread like a man after a night of extreme bar-hopping. Floyd lay nearby on his side, blood pooling beside his head.

I turned around to find Blondie straightening the sleeves of his jacket. Two more blood slaves stood at his back.

"I hate to look a gift horse in the mouth," I said, peering back at Moretti's men, "but twice in one day?"

"Arnaud has another lead for you to give to the detective," Blondie said.

I accepted the piece of paper he held out and looked it over. Arnaud's spidery handwriting read:

Claudette Poole, Headmistress
Hangar Hall School for Girls
Hauppauge, New York

From a strip joint to a girl's boarding school?

"We still have eyes on the boy," Blondie reminded me.

I read the contact info a second time, wondering how in the hell I was going to convince Vega to pursue another Arnaud lead, especially one so far away.

"Fine," I sighed, pocketing the paper. "But do you mind telling me what the trip to Sonny's was all about?"

Intelligence seemed to infuse Blondie's empty gaze. "Well, it is like the old line goes," he replied in a familiar, taunting voice. "Do as you're told and no one gets hurt."

"Is he involved with the killer?"

"Sonny has been involved with many people," Arnaud-as-Blondie said. "And for some, that's a problem."

"Who?" I pressed.

"Who, indeed?" Arnaud smiled impishly as though to say the Q&A was over.

"Can you at least explain the new lead? Give me something I can use to convince Detective Vega?"

"For someone as resourceful as yourself, Mr. Croft, I trust you'll come up with a compelling reason all on your own."

He gave a small wave and disappeared from Blondie's eyes. I looked back at Floyd and Whitey, who had begun to stir. Time to make tracks. I would need to stop off at my apartment to grab a few things and explain the situation to Tabitha, but with Mr. Reid and Moretti's men after me, I wouldn't be able to stay there. I had to come up with another staging area, somewhere they wouldn't think to look for me.

After a moment's deliberation, I had one.

I grabbed my cane and left the pier at a run.

18

I poked my revolver into the East Village apartment. "Hello?"
No answer, no sounds of movement. I stepped inside and made a quick tour of the rooms. The unit appeared to have seen at least one more squatter since Clifford Rhodes, the stringy-haired vagrant who had summoned a shrieker six months earlier, but it was presently vacant. I set down two duffle bags loaded with items I'd gathered at my apartment and bought en route. Fortunately, Moretti's men hadn't recovered in time to head me off.

From one of the bags I pulled out a padlock, screwdriver, and two door-hasp kits. I spent several minutes screwing the thick metal hasps to both sides of the door and adjacent frame, then clicked the padlock home through the inside hasp. The security system was nowhere close to what I had at my own apartment, but

I hoped it would keep just anyone—and hopefully any*thing*—from wandering in.

And it looked like this dump was going to be home for a while.

I sighed as I made another tour of the apartment. No electricity, a trickle of cold running water, and from the bathroom, a sewer-like smell that could fell an ogre. On the plus side, the steel bed frame and roll-up mattress remained, as well as the table, Bunsen burner, and propane tank from Clifford's time here. With dusk dimming the unit, I set several candles around the old lab and lit them. I then pulled an iron pot and several spell items from my bags.

One of the spells I had been planning was a nullifying spell—to try to neutralize the fae magic protecting the townhouse. But with my powers scrambled, that spell was out. Instead, I would have to cook a potion to neutralize the effect the fae magic was having on me.

I opened the valve on the propane tank and fired up the Bunsen burner. I set the iron pot on a mesh platform above the burner and poured in some green absinthe. To the absinthe, I added salt, iron dust, and shavings of rowan wood, stirring the ingredients with my engraved spoon. With none of my own power to channel, I directed my intentions through what energy remained in my coin pendant, which I held over the potion.

I was just tapping the spoon against the rim of the pot and setting it on the table when the pager went off.

That'll be Vega, wanting her bullets.

I twisted the Bunsen burner to a low blue flame, checked the pager, and then left the unit, moving the padlock to the outside hasp and snapping it closed behind me.

Dusk had settled over the city by the time I stepped out onto the street. It took several blocks of wandering through the bombed-out neighborhood—the last place Moretti's men would think to look for me—before I found a working payphone.

"Did you get them?" Vega asked without preamble.

"Two boxes' worth," I replied. "What's up?"

"We're going down tonight."

"Into the storm lines?"

"No, Funky Town," she said in exasperation. "Yes, the storm lines."

"Well, look. Arnaud gave us another lead."

"Who?"

"I don't know, some administrator at a boarding school."

"Did he say why?"

"No, just that it's someone we would be interested in talking to."

"Where is this school?"

"Out on Long Island." I cringed before adding, "Hauppauge."

"Forget it," she said.

The finality in her voice was what I'd feared. "Why?"

"He's playing us."

"I don't know... That visit to Sonny's could well lead to something. I mean, the man did turn out to be a vampire."

"The only thing it's leading us down is a false trail."

"I just think—"

"Forget it," Vega repeated. "Where can I pick up the bullets?"

I thought desperately. Arnaud wasn't dumb. The second his blood slaves observed us descending into a drain, even a drain blocks from Ferguson Towers, he would guess what we were up to. Which would mean I hadn't kept up my end of the deal. Vega's child would be snatched—or worse.

"I'll bring them to you," I said finally.

"When?"

"Give me an hour?"

"Fine, but no more."

I hung up. I had bought some time, anyway. I turned from the phone and made my way around months-old trash piles back toward the apartment. A few blocks to the north, I could make out the silhouettes of ghouls in a roving pack. Before they could pick up my scent, I broke into a run.

I was going to love my new neighborhood.

"About time," Vega said with a huff.

"Yeah, sorry." I set the boxes of ammo on her desk. "Had a hard time catching a cab."

She wasted no time opening the top box, inspecting the ammo, and loading the silver bullets into her service pistol. I patted my waistband and pockets. Damn. Still not used to carrying a gun, I'd left my own at the East Village apartment. I eyed Vega's black body armor. A helmet with a headlamp sat on one end of her desk.

"So you're really serious about this," I said.

"Why wouldn't I be?"

"I just think we should give it another day. Check out the other lead first."

"You're doing it again," she said without looking up.

"Doing what?"

"Squirming." She checked her loaded weapon and holstered it.

"I've already told you, I can't help you down there."

"Who said anything about you going down?"

I stared at her. "Come again?"

"Do you think I'd put a civilian consultant in that kind of danger?" She gave a sharp laugh. "My new unit is under enough scrutiny as it is."

"You're planning on going down alone?"

"Not alone."

At that moment, Hoffman came waddling into the office in his own set of body armor. His eyes widened briefly when they met mine.

"Surprised to see me?" I asked.

"Disgusted is more like it." He fidgeted with his Kevlar vest.

"Thanks for the alibi, by the way."

"What are you talking about?" Vega asked.

"Do you want to tell her?" I asked Hoffman.

"You're making a big deal out of nothing," he said. "Couple of Moretti's men wanted to know what time I picked up Dumbledore here last night. Told 'em I couldn't remember."

"You told them a hell of a lot more than that," I said. "Including that Vega couldn't be trusted."

"Moretti's men?" Vega's eyebrows crushed down. This was going to be good. "You're talking to Moretti's men?"

"Naw," Hoffman said. "I mean, it's not a regular thing or nothing. Like I said, they—"

"Listen here." Vega drew herself up in front of him. "If I hear you're talking with Moretti's men—or *any* of the bosses' meat heads—I will personally walk you to internal affairs and see that your ass never wears the NYPD shield again. They might have worked their slimy tentacles into other units, but I'll be goddamned if they're going to infiltrate mine. Are we clear?"

"Sure," Hoffman said, scratching his nose. "Geez."

When he glanced over at me, I showed him my smuggest smile. There was a lot more I could have told Vega, but watching him being upbraided was worth it for now.

"So are we going or what?" Hoffman grumbled.

Vega glowered at him another moment before turning to collect her helmet.

"Guys," I said. "There's, ah, one other thing I need to do before you set out."

"What?" Vega demanded.

"It's a ritual of protection. Sort of a magical layer of armor against whatever you might encounter down there."

"I don't frigging believe this," Hoffman groaned.

I was already sprinkling a circle of copper filings over the floor.

"Is a ritual really necessary?" Vega asked, eyeing the symbol skeptically.

I nodded. *Yeah, but not for the reason I'm telling you.* I stepped into the circle and, ensuring I had a view of the security monitors in the main room, gestured for Vega and Hoffman to join me.

"If this is some kind of trap..." Vega said.

"I swear on everything I hold dear, it's not. Besides, I would be stuck inside it too."

Vega looked at me another moment, eyes narrowing, before stepping into the circle. She turned to her partner. "Hoffman," she ordered.

Still smarting from his dressing down, he muttered and joined us.

"In close," I said. "Arms around each others' waists."

Hoffman leaned away. "You serious?"

"Do it," Vega said, slipping her arm behind me.

"Can't you see he's playing us?" Hoffman said.

On the matter of holding waists, I was, actually. That part was completely unnecessary for the spell to work. I pulled Hoffman up against me and gave the fat roll on his far side a little pinch.

"All right," I said. "You might get swimmy-headed, but that'll pass."

I spoke a Word to close the circle, then centered myself. The potion I'd drunk an hour before to break up the fae magic was still working on me, still smoothing out the final wrinkles in my magical lines.

"Imitare," I said.

"What?" Hoffman barked.

Vega shushed him.

"Imitare," I repeated. Energy flowed through me like electricity, spilling into the circle at our feet, gaining strength. *"Imitare."*

I repeated the incantation, eyeing the security feed from the vehicle checkpoint at the front of the building. For several minutes, I watched the cars pulling up to the mechanical gate.

"What is this?" Hoffman grumbled, looking at the growing light around his feet.

A moment later, I had my car: a black sedan with tinted windows. With each spoken Word, I had been fashioning a three-dimensional likeness of us in my mental prism. Now, with an uttered *"Liberare,"* I released the projection onto street level. And there we were on the monitor, as if we'd just walked out of the building. I squinted at our likenesses, impressed by the detail. It was as though the remaining fae magic that trickled through me was acting as a booster now instead of a foil. I manipulated the projections, walking us toward the idling sedan.

"Aprire," I said.

The sedan's rear door opened. I manipulated our projections to make it look as though we were ducking into the back seat. A moment later, an actual passenger got out of the front seat, looked around in confusion, then slammed the rear door before climbing back in.

The access gate opened, and the sedan slid into the flow of city traffic.

Three shadows darted up the sidewalk, paralleling the car. It had worked. The blood slaves had taken the bait. Exhaling, I broke the circle. The remaining energy puffed out into the room.

"It's done," I said.

"About time," Hoffman muttered, jerking his arm from around my waist.

While he and Vega donned their helmets, I glanced over the schematic of the storm lines, noting the marks in red—their planned route to Ferguson Towers. The entry point was a drainage culvert on the East River, near Montgomery Street. I knew how to get there.

"Good luck," I told them. "If you run into the creature, be sure to aim for the heart."

19

A cold wind blew off the East River, batting my cinched coat and chaffing my cheeks. I could see the EPA man who had probably opened and closed the chain-link gate for Vega and Hoffman sitting in a parked van beyond, the orange ember of a cigarette drawing his face from the darkness.

I raised my gaze to where thick razor wire coiled along the top of the fence. Going over was out. I followed the fence until I could no longer see the van, and inserted the end of my cane into one of the lower links.

"Protezione," I whispered.

The small orb of a light shield took shape, stretching the steel wire. I willed the orb out until the link gave. The fence began to rattle as I pushed more energy into the spell, links contorting and popping around an ever-expanding hole. At last, it was large enough for me to withdraw the cane and duck through.

Deepening the shadows around me with another Word, I slipped past the EPA van and down a short drive until I was standing beside Vega's parked car, which faced the large drainage culvert.

The fence that guarded the cement cylinder stood wide, an open padlock hanging from one of the links. The security was as much to keep people out as to keep the ghouls in. Another reason I wasn't going to let Vega tackle this alone. I just had to pray the projection spell had thrown Arnaud and the blood slaves off long enough to keep Vega's son safe.

Straddling a trickle of slimy water, I entered the culvert's open mouth. The space smelled like a public restroom. I called light to my cane and held it out. A round graffiti-tagged corridor swelled into view. I started forward at a fast walk, trying to ignore the fact I was going underground.

At a four-way intersection beneath what I guessed to be Madison Street, I began to turn left, but quickly killed my light and drew back. Vega and Hoffman were down there, about fifty yards away, headlamps shining into another corridor along the north side of the tunnel. They spoke in rapid whispers, but the acoustics were making an echoing confusion of their words.

I tiptoed toward them, using my cane to deepen the darkness around me.

"...sleeping bag over here," I heard Vega say. She disappeared into what I realized wasn't another tunnel, but a service room in the wall, a couple of feet off the floor. "And that looks like dried blood."

"You think it's the killer's?" Hoffman asked.

"If the blood matches the saliva, we'll have our answer."

I was fairly certain what that answer would be. We were only a couple of blocks from Ferguson Towers, which made this a prime spot for a rogue blood slave to lair and rise whenever its hunger struck.

I pressed my body to the wall as Hoffman shone his light up and down the tunnel. He didn't spot me, but he had missed something far more important up the tunnel—eye shine.

I yanked my cane into sword and staff.

"Illuminare!" White light shot from my orb and down the tunnel, past where Hoffman stood, hitting the creature bearing down on him. Only it was no blood slave. Long hair draped glowing red eyes and a jutting jaw of bunched teeth. And the creature was too tall for a blood slave. She had to stoop as she ran toward Hoffman, long, naked arms knuckling the floor.

Hoffman raised a hand to block my light, oblivious to the danger behind him. "That Croft? What the hell are you doing here?"

"Get down!" I shouted, following it with, *"Vigore!"*

A blast chased the light and roared down the tunnel. Thanks to remnants of the fae magic, the force quickly grew beyond my control. The force pummeled Hoffman, sending him tumbling toward the creature, who had steeled herself in a crouch, head bowed.

Oh, shit.

"Croft!" Hoffman shouted in rage.

I ran forward, pushing more light through my staff, hoping to blind the creature from seeing the meal I had just shoved in front of her. Hoffman rolled to a flopping rest on his back, his silver-bullet-loaded pistol glistening in the shallow creek a good twenty feet behind him. He lifted his head, his breath choking off as the creature's nightmare face rose into his view.

"Vega!" Hoffman wheezed.

Striated cords popped from the creature's shoulders as she reared to pounce.

"*Protezione!*" I shouted.

The creature slammed into the shield of light I threw in front of Hoffman. But before I could shape it into a protective dome, the creature darted a clawed hand around the barrier and seized Hoffman's leg.

"Leggo!" Hoffman cried, kicking at her with his free foot.

I sprinted forward, the movement jostling my ability to hold the shield together, but I needed to get close enough to attack the creature without inflicting collateral damage on Hoffman. Explosions went off behind me and rang down the tunnel. Blood burst from the creature's shoulder.

Vega!

The creature threw her head back in a furious cry and released Hoffman. I wasted no time grabbing his pant cuff with a Word and dragging him from the creature. Water slewed up around him as I shoved him behind us.

"Her heart!" I called to Vega. "Aim for her heart!"

By the time I looked back, the creature had lowered herself to all fours and was bounding toward us in a rapid zigzag. Smoke rose from the spot where she'd been struck. Vega's pistol banged out another series of shots, bullets caroming off walls. But the creature wasn't slowing.

I stepped forward and raised my glowing staff. *"Protezione!"* I shouted.

A plate of light spread over the tunnel. I staggered as the creature rammed into it head first, breaking through in a bright shower of sparks. But I had slowed her, enabling me to close her in a second light shield. Snapping her protuberant jaw, she rammed against the barrier again and again.

"What in the hell is that thing?" Vega asked, coming up beside me.

"Don't know," I said, between strained grunts. "Some sort of vampire, but she's damned powerful. I can't crush her, and I'm not sure how long I can hold her like this. Going to give you a shot at her heart."

"Okay, but I need to reload."

Dipping into my power reserves, I flattened the shield until the creature's arms and legs were pinned. I then lifted her into a standing position. She snarled and snapped, muscles leaping from her bone-white skin. I'd been telling Vega the truth. I had no idea what the creature was, how she had come to be. I opened a hole in the shield over the creature's sternum.

"Don't know how you're doing this, Merlin," Hoffman said, circling the creature in a limp to retrieve his pistol. "But I'll be happy to do the honors."

"Fine," I grunted, "but hurry."

The creamy white light that heralded a Thelonious visit had begun to wisp around my vision. I was only vaguely aware that Grandpa's ring was squeezing my finger in urgent, pulsating beats.

Something solid struck my head. I splashed into the slimy drainage, but managed to keep my staff aloft. Dark suits flashed past. Gunshots banged around me as I strained to hold the invocation, to keep the creature entrapped. A leather shoe flashed into view and kicked my staff away.

The light shield around the creature wobbled and then broke apart.

20

Hands seized the lapels of my coat and slammed me against a wall.

"Did you really think you could deceive me," Blondie hissed, though I heard Arnaud's voice.

Sounds of struggle echoed up and down the tunnel. I turned my head to find another blood slave pinning Vega's arms behind her. Her headlamp jostled as she swore and kicked at his shins. Down the tunnel to my left, Hoffman was on his back, a third blood slave stepping on his throat.

Blondie shook me. "I gave you two simple directives. One, stay away from the Towers. Two, follow my leads."

"Wh-what happened to the creature?" I gasped, peering around. She should have ripped us all apart. She still could.

"Your only concern right now should be for the consequences of your insolence. But first things first."

Blondie seized Grandpa's pulsating ring and twisted. I shouted out in pain as bone crunched, and the ring, abrading the length of my finger in an attempt to hold on, finally popped free. He tossed the enchanted ring to a blood slave, who splashed off, no doubt rushing it to Arnaud.

I gritted my teeth. "Goddamn you."

"That's for violating our earlier agreement that you remain outside of the Financial District. As for our present agreement, you now have a choice to make." He clamped the top of my head with his fingers and twisted until I was looking at Hoffman, still down. "The detective?" He swiveled my head the other way, where Vega continued to kick and swear. "Or the detective?"

"What are you asking?"

"One lives, one dies," Blondie said. "The decision is yours."

"And if I don't play your stupid game?" My throbbing finger was making me nauseas.

"Then you are condemning them both."

The easy choice was Hoffman, but I wasn't going to be an accomplice to murder.

"Fine, kill me," I said. "Spare them."

"Oh, no." Blondie laughed. "That would be letting you off too easy." His lips straightened. "Now choose."

With Vega struggling and Hoffman down for the count, neither could hear our exchange, neither knew that their lives rested in the hands of a wizard in entirely over his head.

"First tell me what the creature is to you," I said.

"You're stalling for time, Mr. Croft."

"Why are you protecting her?"

"That's the shame of it," he said. "Had you listened to me, who knows what you might have discovered?"

"Why can't you just tell me?"

"We've wasted enough time," Blondie said. "My men are getting restless. If you do not choose within the next ten seconds, your friends will both suffer broken necks."

"Sure you want the attention a couple of dead detectives are going to bring?" I asked.

"Oh, the attention won't be on me, Mr. Croft. By the time the bodies are found, my associates will be long gone, and it will be *your* evidence investigators will discover around the victims."

"Bullshit."

"Five seconds, Mr. Croft."

I took a quick peek at Vega and Hoffman. I stopped and looked at Vega a second time. Behind her, several figures were easing up the tunnel. More blood slaves?

"Three," Blondie said. "Two..."

One of the figures aimed what looked like a shotgun.

"All right, all right," I said. "You want my choice?"

"One."

I thrust my arms out, driving both palms into Blondie's chest. Caught by surprise, he teetered back on his heels, arms flailing for balance. I crouched and turned as the shotgun went off, shots nailing my whipping trench coat, one grazing my hip in a bright flare. The blast blew Blondie halfway around, tearing skin from his face, as though by a sandblaster.

I dove for my sword, grasped the handle, and rose to face Vega's blood slave. But he had released Vega and was sagging, a long, slender blade skewering his chest from behind. The sword's owner gave the blade a hard twist and then drew it free. When the slave splashed to the tunnel floor, I did a double take at the female figure now beside Vega. Remembering Hoffman, I wheeled toward him. His blood slave was down too, gargling and pawing at a dagger in his throat.

A slender figure arrived above him, leather glistening in the detectives' headlamps, and drove another dagger into the slave's heart. He twisted the blade each way and pulled it out.

"Goodnight, sweet prince," he said, drawing a forearm across his brow.

The shotgun went off a second time, and Blondie landed on his back beside me, his chest blown open.

I looked from the downed blood slaves to the new arrivals. As Vega went to help Hoffman up, I retrieved my staff, calling light to it. The three figures that glowed into view were instantly familiar: a towering tattoo-faced man holding a pump-action shotgun, a rail-thin woman with spiked pink hair, and a lithe man in leathers, his hair dyed neon green.

"...the hell?" I whispered.

Tattoo Face squinted at me before his face lit up like a bulb. "I don't believe it! Mr. Wednesday Night!" He hustled over and wrapped a huge arm around me, pulling me into a crushing side hug.

"You know each other?" Vega asked.

"He came to one of our house parties back in October," Tattoo Face said. "The guy's a freaking animal."

Blade's pink lips smirked. "You should see him when he disrobes."

My cheeks blazed as Vega looked from the punks to me in

puzzlement. I hurried to explain. "They lived below someone involved in that case we worked together in the fall. I sort of … bumped into them." I left out the part about Thelonious paying our world a visit, downing a bottle of cheap liquor, crashing their party, and then depositing me on a mattress, half-naked, with Blade.

Vega nodded slowly as though I'd explained absolutely nothing.

I looked from the shotgun Tattoo Face held, to the leather-wrapped sword handle showing above Blade's left shoulder, to the pair of ninja swords Green Hair had sheathed across his chest in an X. I was still trying to figure out how and why they had ended up in the storm line.

Vega showed her badge and introduced herself and Hoffman. "And your names are…?"

Acting as spokeswoman, Blade stepped forward. "This is Bullet," she said, slapping the back of a hand against Tattoo Face's chest. "I'm Blade. And our sometimes guitarist over there is Dr. Z."

Green Hair bowed slightly.

Hoffman limped forward. "How 'bout giving us some real names," he said, his throat still hoarse from being stepped on.

"How about we don't," Blade said. "And I never heard a 'thanks' from you."

"You have permits for those weapons?" he demanded.

Vega shook her head for him to back down. "We appreciate you helping us out," she said to Blade. "But we do have to know what you're doing here. You've walked into the middle of a murder investigation."

I caught Bullet and Dr. Z glancing over at one another.

Vega must have caught it too. "Something you guys want to tell me?"

"Have you found anything?" Blade asked.

"That's not something we can discuss with the public," Vega said.

"Why?" I asked Blade. "Are you looking for someone?"

It had taken me a few moments, but I had connected their presence to the weapons they carried to the skill they had just shown in destroying the blood slaves. They might have been punk rockers for kicks, but they were vampire hunters by trade. They were trying to track down the killer.

Blade's dark eyes met mine. "That's not a matter we can discuss with the public."

Vega opened her mouth to say something when her phone rang. She drew it from a back pocket. "Vega," she barked, pulling off her helmet. *"What?"* The latte skin of her face went pale in the light of my staff. "All right, stay in the apartment. I'll be right there."

"What's going on?" I asked.

Vega jammed her phone away and began running back toward the main line.

"Hey, what happened?" I asked, splashing to keep up. I heard Hoffman laboring into a limping run behind us.

"Some men grabbed Tony," Vega said.

"Tony?" I struggled to place the name.

"My son."

A boulder dropped into my stomach.

Oh, shit.

21

When we arrived at Vega's apartment, the door was hanging from one hinge, and a middle-aged woman, who I guessed to be Tony's babysitter, was pacing and sobbing hysterically.

"Tell me exactly what happened," Vega said, her voice as tight as a suspension cable on the George Washington Bridge.

When the woman wheeled toward us, her face was a disaster of mascara and bloated eyelids. "Oh, Ricki," she said. "Oh, Jesus. They come and—and they take him."

"Who came, Camilla?" Vega demanded.

"I didn't see," she said. "I go to bathroom. Tony asleep over there." I followed her trembling finger to where a multi-colored heap of Legos were scattered across a couch. "And when I come out, the door broken, and—and—and—"

Her voice seemed to stick as she wrung a ball of stained tissues in her hands.

"And what, Camilla?" Vega seized her shoulders.

Camilla managed to swallow, which opened the pipes to more sobbing. "And they gone, Ricki. I run out, but men already at staircase. Door close behind them. By time I get there, I can no see them."

"What did the men look like?" Vega asked.

"Too far away. Too dark. Light by staircase still broken."

"Did you go to a window? Did you see what kind of vehicle they left in?"

Camilla shook her head in anguish. "Oh, God. I so sorry, Ricki. Oh, Jesus."

I watched the whole exchange numbly, knowing full well who had taken her son and why. I hadn't been able to steer Vega from the Towers. I hadn't kept her chasing Arnaud's so-called leads. Worse, three of his blood slaves had been killed. I examined my skinned and swollen middle finger, which I'd managed to put some healing magic to on the ride here. Knowing Arnaud, he would feel perfectly justified having Tony slaughtered as retribution for his losses. The vampire had committed acts more heinous in his time.

"All right," Vega said, sitting Camilla on the couch. "I'm going to call it in as a kidnapping. Hoffman, I want you to canvass the neighborhood, see if anyone might've witnessed Tony being carried down the street or put into a vehicle. I'll start a search by car."

With practiced eyes, Vega scanned her walls of framed photos, no doubt looking for the most recent image of her son. "Take this," she said, removing a close-up of Tony's smiling face and handing it to Hoffman. He stared down at it gravely, nodded, and left the apartment.

Vega was pulling her phone out when I heard myself speak.

"Detective, wait." I cleared my throat. "I know who took him."

Vega stopped scrolling and looked up at me. "What?"

"I know who took your son."

Without moving her gaze from mine, she said, "Camilla, why don't you go lie down? Use my bedroom. Close the door behind you."

"Yes, Ricki," she said, sniffling and sponging her nose.

When the bedroom door closed, Vega stepped toward me, eyebrows knifing down. "Start talking, Croft."

"Earlier today, when I met with Arnaud, he gave me the job of keeping you away from Ferguson Towers. He didn't say why. If I failed or told you what was up, he threatened to take your son."

"Is that what those leads were about?" Vega's voice sounded distant, dangerous.

"Yeah."

"And it never crossed your mind to clue me in."

"Of course it did, but he said if you changed your son's routines or put any kind of extra protection around him, he would know."

"So you've been working against me this whole time."

"I wouldn't put it in quite those terms. And it wasn't like I had a choice."

"What else did he offer you?"

I swallowed. "What?"

"If you had told me yesterday, I could've figured something out. I could have worked the Towers case from a distance and kept my son safe." Her voice faltered for the first time.

Even though I felt like the world's biggest asshat, my throat tightened defensively. "Look, when I met with Arnaud, he exuded this mind-fogging toxin. He practically fumigated his office with it. I couldn't think straight. I agreed to his terms because I couldn't see another way out."

"And he didn't promise anything else?"

Such as what became of your dear mother.

"No."

She searched my eyes, then turned toward the bedroom. "Camilla," she called, "stay here. I'm going out."

"Yes, Ricki," came Camilla's muffled voice.

"Where are you going?" I asked.

At the door, she checked her service pistol. "To make Arnaud tell me where my son is."

"Wait, wait, wait." I hustled after her into the hallway. "Do you think he's just going to let you into the Financial District? Let you up to his office? There's a reason he's built a fortress around himself."

"I could give two fucks."

I caught up to her at the door to the stairwell and seized her arm. She stiffened. "You don't release me in the next second," she said, "and I'm breaking the rest of your fingers."

"Just stop and think about this. You're scared, you're angry—I get it. But what you're talking about is only going to get you killed. Or turned into something awful. Then where will your son be?"

"Let me go, Croft."

"I'll use magic if I have to."

"Do that and I really will arrest your ass this time."

"I have an idea," I said, working it out as I spoke. "Something far more likely to get results. Something much safer for you and your son." I released Vega carefully, unsure whether she was going to resume her determined march or drive a fist into my face. I could see both impulses in her eyes.

"Talk fast," she said.

"We meet with Arnaud through one of his blood slaves. See what he wants."

"And where in the hell are we going to find one of them? Three are dead and at least another two took off with Tony."

"Arnaud still has an interest in Ferguson Towers, which tells me he's still keeping eyes on you."

She took a second to absorb the info. "We'll see."

We descended the stairwell to the lobby and pushed open the steel door to the street. Bits of the lock littered the stoop where the blood slaves must have forced their way in. I peeked over at Vega, who was peering up and down the deserted sidewalk, eyes dark and mercenary. Since receiving the call in the storm line, she had maintained a rock-hard composure, the dials of her maternal instinct to protect all locked on ten.

Guilt burned through me as I considered my recklessness. I had gambled with Vega's son and lost, goddamn me.

"Where are they?" she demanded.

I cupped a hand to the side of my mouth. "Arnaud!" I called into the night. "We're here to do as you say!"

My words had barely echoed away when, down the block, a slender shadow separated from the side of a building and began strolling toward us. The figure was dressed in a long black coat, formal shoes glinting beneath the streetlights. Vega and I turned our bodies to face him. When he had come to within a few feet of us, I recognized the monk's bangs.

"Well," Zarko said, "things have taken an interesting turn tonight, hmm?"

Vega drew her pistol and aimed it at his forehead—just what I was afraid she'd do. "Where's my son?"

"Hey, c'mon," I whispered. "We're not going to get anywhere that way."

"Your magic-wielding consultant is correct," Zarko said, his lips forking into a grin. "Especially when I presently hold the cards."

"Keep smiling, you piece of shit," Vega said. "This thing's packed with silver; not something your kind handles very well. Your buddies made a real mess of themselves in that tunnel under Madison Street."

"Oh yes, a pity." Zarko's hand gestures and turns of phrase suggested Arnaud was present in every way but form. "I *will* miss them. Fortunately, there is no shortage of ambitious young men in this city."

"Is he safe?" I asked.

"The detective's son?" Zarko smiled. "For now."

"Okay, you hold the cards," I said with a hard breath. "Just tell us what we need to do to get him back."

"My, that is a tricky one." Zarko clasped his hands behind his back and began to pace, unconcerned by Vega's pointed pistol. "I don't take broken promises lightly, Mr. Croft. And can I assume you have disclosed our little agreement to the detective? So there they are: two broken promises." He made a *tsk*ing sound. "And with a beautiful little boy at stake."

"You lay a finger on him..." Vega warned, eyes narrowed.

Zarko stopped pacing and spun toward her. "Though I have every reason, Detective, I am going to show some *humanity*, as your kind calls it. I am going to exercise restraint."

"What do we need to do?" I repeated.

"Well, it seems the first order of business is setting things to rights."

I didn't care for his chipper tone. "And how would we do that?"

"First, you're going to drop this business with Ferguson Towers." He showed a palm as I opened my mouth. "No more questions on the matter, Mr. Croft. I have told you all you need to know. Second, I have given you another lead, the name of a headmistress. I suggest you pick up there."

"Now?" I said.

"The sooner the better." His eyes cut to Vega. "For *all* concerned."

"I need proof that he's all right," she said.

"Very well." Zarko reached into his inside coat pocket and pulled out a smartphone. He spoke as he tapped. "This is a live feed, though the location will have to remain undisclosed, I'm afraid."

Not wanting to interfere with the technology, I stood back as Zarko held the phone out for Vega. The screen showed Tony curled on a couch in an affluent-looking room, sound asleep. A colorful afghan over him rose and fell with his breaths, his lips sputtering slightly. The boy seemed safe—were it not for the shadows of blood slaves drifting shark-like around him.

Vega nodded once, and Zarko returned the phone to his pocket.

"So, I stay away from Ferguson Towers," she said, still training the gun on him, "and I go interview this person, and you'll return my son unharmed?"

"It will certainly go a long way toward straightening the mess your consultant here made of things," Zarko replied. "After that, we'll see where the situation stands, how adept you've proven yourselves."

"Selves?" Vega said. "Unh-uh, he's not coming with me."

"I'm sorry," Zarko said, "but you and the professor complement each other far too well. I insist you work together. Consider it another condition for your son's release."

"I need a guarantee you'll keep your word," Vega said.

"Oh, Detective. You of all people should know there are no such things as guarantees. Odds. Chances. Those are life's precious currencies. You will improve both considerably if you get started now."

I nodded, knowing it was the best deal we were going to get out of him. Vega sighed as though arriving at the same conclusion and lowered her pistol from the blood slave. But Zarko was no longer there.

22

"Look, I'm really sorry," I said.

Vega's gaze didn't shift from I-495 East, down which we were barreling at over ninety miles an hour, lights flashing.

"You're absolutely right," I went on. "I should have told you about my deal with Arnaud."

"Stop talking," she said coldly.

"Like I said, I wasn't thinking clearly."

"Did I stutter?"

"I just don't want you to think—"

"I don't give a shit about your feelings," Vega cut in. "My only goal right now is getting my son back. Whether or not you meant to put him in jeopardy, you did. That's the bottom line."

I tapped my cane slowly between my shoes, eyes fixed on the dull opal.

"And when I do get him back," she continued after several beats of awful silence, "you and I are done. No more consulting, no more calls. I don't even want you stopping in to wish me a Merry Christmas."

I struggled with something to say, but she was right about me, about everything.

"Are we clear?" she asked, glaring over at me for the first time. A painful knot filled my throat. "Yeah."

Twenty minutes later, we pulled into a semi-circular drive that delivered us to the front of the mansion-like school. Small floodlights illuminated white columns, dark-red brick, and sheets of English ivy.

As Vega and I stepped from the car, the paunchy security guard who had let us onto the grounds arrived in a golf cart. He hustled up the steps, a ring of keys jingling in his right hand. "Her room is going to be at the end of the main hall," he said, opening the front door for us. "Last door on the left. Just be careful not to wake the students."

Vega charged ahead without thanking him. I caught up to her at a door with a brass plate that read, "Mrs. Poole, Headmistress."

Ignoring the security guard's directive, Vega knocked five times hard, the blows resounding up and down the hallway. A moment later, the door opened onto a tall woman in a white robe, graying hair pinned back from a worried face. She wasn't another vampire, in any case.

"You must be the detectives," she said.

"Dete*ctive*," Vega corrected her, leaving me to explain myself.

"Consultant," I muttered.

"Well, come in," Mrs. Poole said, standing to one side and closing the door behind us.

We stepped into a carpeted administrative office. "Please, have a seat." Mrs. Poole gestured to a pair of chairs in front of a desk. She closed the door to a back room—her living quarters, I surmised by the tabby cat that had begun to poke its head into the office. Mrs. Poole joined us on the other side of her desk.

"Thanks for seeing me on short notice." Vega scooted her chair forward.

"Anything I can do to help," Mrs. Poole said. "But what is this about, exactly?"

Good question, I thought. *Arnaud sent us to you with absolutely no explanation as to why. And yet he seemed determined that we come out here—and not just to keep us away from Ferguson Towers. Vega already agreed to that.*

I snuck a peek at Vega, wondering how she planned to proceed.

"There was a double murder in lower Manhattan a couple of nights ago," she began. "Two residents of a low-income housing project had their necks bitten into. They died from loss of blood."

"Oh my," Mrs. Poole said, touching her own throat. "I'm very sorry to hear that, but I'm not sure what that has to do with me or my school."

Vega had given the bare facts to see if they would prompt the headmistress to volunteer something. She hadn't. I scooted my own chair forward, trying to anticipate Vega's next move.

"Are you aware of any cases like that in the area?" Vega asked.

"People having their throats bitten?" The lines of Mrs. Poole's face deepened. "Why, no, Detective."

"And your students are all okay?" Vega asked. "No attacks on campus?"

"No, nothing like that." Her eyes moved between us, as though beginning to sense we had come on a blind cast.

Something Arnaud had said through Zarko was sticking in my head: *After that, we'll see where the situation stands, how adept you've proven yourselves.* It was that last part: *how adept you've proven yourselves.* He wanted us to find something. He had already sent us to Sonny, the vampire strip club owner, and now here. There had to be a connection.

"Well, if anything comes to you," Vega was telling the headmistress, "here's my card."

"Sorry I couldn't be of more assistance." Mrs. Poole rose as Vega did.

"Um, if you don't mind," I said. "I just have a couple of questions."

"No you don't," Vega said.

"I do, actually."

"I'm sorry," Vega said to Mrs. Poole. "My consultant suffered some head trauma earlier. He thinks he's an investigator now. That was all. We'll be leaving now."

"Have any of your girls left school since the start of the semester?" I asked quickly.

"Well, ah ... two, actually," Mrs. Poole said.

"Did they give reasons?" I hooked my feet around the chair legs and leaned away from Vega, who had seized my arm and was trying to haul me up.

"Sheila's family moved to the west coast, and Alexandra left for unspecified reasons."

I gripped the chair's armrests. "Did Alexandra's parents sign her out?"

"She didn't have parents. She was a ward of the state. A private donor sponsored her attendance here." Mrs. Poole's eyes shifted between us in growing anxiety as we continued to struggle. "But Alexandra turned eighteen this summer. She was a legal adult and didn't need permission to leave the school. She'd been having some problems. Perhaps that's why she left."

Vega's grip eased from my arm and she turned toward the headmistress. "What kind of problems?"

"Oh, well, acting out, unexplained absences. A search of her room didn't turn up anything suspicious, but her behavior was enough to put her on probation and into mandatory counseling."

"Do you have her sponsor's contact information?" Vega asked. "Also, a photo of Alexandra would be helpful."

"That would be in our admissions office," Mrs. Poole said. "I can make a copy of her file."

"Please do." Vega sat back down as Mrs. Poole left the room. When I started to speak, she said, "Not a word."

I crossed my arms and quietly considered how Arnaud's two so-called leads might overlap. If there was a similarity between Sonny and the boarding school, it was young women. What if this Alexandra had gotten fed up with school and moved to the city? With few work prospects, she might have had no recourse but the Forty-second Street clubs. I pictured her standing outside of *Seductions*, gazing up at the lurid flashing marquee, then making the stomach-curdling decision to cross the threshold, to reduce herself to eye candy. What then? Had Sonny bitten her? Turned her? My fists clenched at the idea of that sleazeball feeding on her foot. Had she become the creature we'd faced in the storm lines? Sonny swore he didn't turn his girls into anything, but there was a first time for everything.

Out of the blue, Vega said, "Why would Arnaud protect the killer while leading us to who she is? It doesn't make any goddamned sense."

"No, it doesn't. But vampires often follow their own logic."

"I wasn't talking to you."

I grimaced, but I had to admire her. Even with her son missing, she was still thinking about how to apprehend the creature and spare the residents of Ferguson Towers an all-out war.

"Sorry," Mrs. Poole said, returning to the office a few moments later. "It took a minute for the copier to warm up. Here's Alexandra's student file. I found an extra photo."

Vega accepted the stapled-together packet and looked it over. I scooted nearer and checked out the photo paper-clipped to the first page. The face above the girl's collared school uniform was sullen but pretty. Dark auburn hair fell in layers down the front of her shoulders. I tried to line the face up with the creature we'd battled in the storm line, but there was no resemblance. The girl's full name was Alexandra Mills.

"This is a P.O. Box," Vega said tapping the sponsor's information—a *Mr. John Smith*. "Do you have a physical address for him?"

"No, I'm sorry," the headmistress said. "That would be the only information."

"At least there's a phone number," I said.

Vega squinted as though my voice were an irritant.

"Are there any other questions I can answer?" Mrs. Poole asked.

I was about to shake my head when Vega surprised me by asking, "Did Alexandra have a roommate?"

"She did. Dominique Easly."

"I'd like to have a word with her."

Mrs. Poole looked at her wristwatch. "Right now? The girls are all asleep."

"It's important," Vega said.

23

"Is Alexandra in some kind of trouble?" The colored beads at the end of Dominique's cornrows clicked as she looked from Vega to me and back.

"We don't think so," Vega replied. "We just have a few questions."

Vega was sitting on the other end of Alexandra's old bed from me. She hadn't used *we* to be inclusive, but to put Dominique at ease. The young woman sitting cross-legged on the bed opposite us was tense, fingers picking at the tassels of a throw pillow.

I glanced around a room that I could have sworn carried traces of spent magic, but nothing suggested that Dominique dabbled. Her room was a hodgepodge of school books, stuffed animals, and posters of inspirational messages, favorite singers, and shirtless hunks. Standard dormitory décor.

"What do you want to ask?" she said.

"How long have you known Alexandra?" Vega asked.

"Since freshman year, but we didn't really become friends until last year."

"Is that when you decided to become roommates?" Vega asked.

"Yeah."

"Your headmistress said she started acting out," Vega said. "Missing classes. Do you know why?"

Dominique shrugged and dropped her eyes.

"Did *you* notice any changes?" Vega pressed. "Did she seem like a different person?"

"She just lost interest in some things," Dominique said, her gaze still lowered.

"When did she start using drugs?" I cut in, a shot in the dark. In my peripheral vision, fury radiated from Vega's eyes. But when Dominique's own eyes jumped up, they were large and rimmed with worry.

"What are you talking about?" she asked.

She was too young to be a convincing liar. Vega must have seen it, too.

"You're not going to get anyone in trouble," Vega said. "Whatever you say stays between us. Not even Mrs. Poole will know. We just want to help Alexandra."

Dominique glanced at her closed door, as though the headmistress might be standing inside it, then back at us. She sighed and leaned her arms against her thighs. "It was stupid," she said quietly.

"What was stupid?" Vega asked.

"I was visiting my aunt and uncle in the city this summer. They live in Brooklyn, sort of a junky neighborhood. Wasn't always that way, but after the Crash..." Vega and I both nodded for her to continue. "Anyway, I ducked over to the corner bodega for some coffee one morning, and I saw this tiny white envelope right outside the door, like someone had accidentally dropped it."

"Heroin," Vega said.

Dominique nodded. "I put it in my pocket and brought it back to the school. It was stupid. I could have been expelled, but I'd never done anything like that. I just wanted to understand what it was, how it could destroy lives, whole neighborhoods. But I was afraid to do it alone."

"So you talked Alexandra into trying some, too," I said.

"I swear it was only a little bit." Tears stood in Dominique's eyes. "Like this much." She pinched her first finger and thumb together. "And we didn't shoot it, we sniffed it, and then flushed the rest away."

Vega frowned. "Then what happened?"

"Well, you know, the drug started working. And yeah, it was strong. Real strong. I felt like I was riding these huge waves. But Alexandra, she turned into some kind of a monster."

I sat up straight. "Monster?"

"You know, storming around the room, knocking down furniture, throwing things. She cracked the window with her fist. Then she left. It was nighttime, eleven o'clock, and she didn't come back till the next day."

"Did she say where she'd gone?" Vega asked.

"She couldn't remember, but she didn't want to talk about it."

I snuck a look at Vega, whose eyebrows were bent in thought.

"But, yeah, she was different," Dominique said quietly. "She slept all the time, for one. That's why she was missing so much class. And when she was awake, she just wasn't there. She had the best laugh. Infectious, you know? But after that night, I never heard it again."

"Was she going out at night?" Vega asked.

Dominique nodded. "A few times I woke up, and she wasn't in her bed. I never asked her about it, though. A couple of times I saw blood on her clothes. She was starting to scare me." Dominique's lips moved silently before she was able to frame her next question. "Can heroin ... can it cause, you know ... mental illness?"

"No," Vega said. "It's been known to exacerbate existing conditions, though."

"Oh God." Tears leaked from Dominique's eyes, and she wrung the pillow on her lap. "I did it to her." Her next words came out as sobs. "I made her s-s-sick."

"*If* that's what happened," Vega said, "you couldn't have known. It was stupid, but you couldn't have known."

Dominique nodded reluctantly and wiped her eyes with the collar of her cotton nightshirt.

"Have you heard from Alexandra since she left?" I asked.

"No. She didn't even say goodbye. When I left for class one morning, she was still in bed. When I came back after lunch, she was history, half her closet cleaned out."

"Do you know where she might have gone?" Vega asked.

Dominique shook her head.

"The city, maybe?" Vega prompted.

"Maybe. I have no idea."

I thought about what Mrs. Poole had said regarding someone paying her tuition. "Did you ever meet the person sponsoring her to attend Hangar Hall?" I asked. "A Mr. Smith?"

"Sponsor?" Dominique said. "I didn't even know she had one."

"Alexandra never mentioned him?" Vega asked.

"Nun-uh."

"Where would Alexandra go on holidays and summer breaks?" I asked.

"She was a foster kid—no relatives—so friends would invite her to stay with their families. She came down to D.C. with me last year. My brother and his wife live there. We had a blast."

"I'm sure she enjoyed that," Vega said, standing. "I'm going to leave you my card. If you think of anything else about Alexandra or if you hear from her, I want you to give me a call."

"I really hope I didn't get her into trouble," Dominique said.

As Vega reassured her that she hadn't, I leaned back until I could touch the floor on the far side of Alexandra's old bed. I ran my fingers along the gritty junction between floor and wall until I encountered a strand of hair. Pinching it, I sat up again. I cleaned the dust off the dark-auburn strand and placed it into an inner coat pocket.

Might come in handy.

24

"Great," Vega said into her phone in a way that suggested whatever she had just learned was anything but, and hung up.

"What's up?" I ventured.

Vega returned the phone to her jacket pocket and narrowed her eyes at the highway ahead.

"Look," I said. "We're both after the same thing—piecing together whatever it is Arnaud wants us to find so we can get your son back. Wouldn't it be better if we worked together? I mean, there's a whole supernatural dimension to this that I know a helluva lot more about than you."

Vega passed two cars and a semi and veered back into the right lane.

"I screwed up," I said. "I admit it. You never have to talk to me again, just—"

"John Smith relinquished the P.O. Box last month," Vega said suddenly. "No forwarding address. The number on file is to a burner phone, untraceable, no longer in use. And there are a couple thousand John Smiths in the five boroughs—if that's even Alexandra's sponsor's real name."

"What about the payments to the school?" I said. "Checks or wire transfers would lead somewhere, right?"

"He mailed cash."

"So, whoever was financing Alexandra's education wanted to remain anonymous," I said, more to myself than Vega. *Why, on both counts?*

"Is she the killer?" Vega asked bluntly.

"May I?" I said, reaching for Alexandra's student file on the dashboard. When Vega didn't answer, I lifted the packet and examined the photo more closely.

Could that one dose of heroin have triggered a change in the young woman? A transformation into a blood-thirsty creature? I thought of the bone-white monster in the storm line, the protruding jaw, the red eyes and long, muscle-roped limbs. If so, I wasn't aware of any similar cases. I needed my research books, but Moretti's men would have eyes on my apartment, dammit.

"Hard to say," I hedged.

"Thanks for your contribution."

"I did manage to pick up a hair in her dorm room, though." I patted the breast of my coat. "When we're back in the city, I can cast a hunting spell. If it pulls us back into the tunnels, we'll have our answer."

Vega knifed her eyes toward me. "You mean the tunnels below Ferguson Towers? Are you *trying* to kill my kid?"

"Okay, okay," I said, my face hot with frustration. "We'll put that on hold for now. If Arnaud expects us to make a connection, and all he's given us so far is Sonny and the boarding school, then we should pay Sonny another visit, see if he knows anything about Alexandra."

"I didn't need you to tell me that."

"Great," I said, replacing the copy of Alexandra's file on the dashboard and sitting back. "The vamp's place it is, then."

"Sonny!" Vega hollered. "Open up!"

She waited five seconds, then hammered the paint-chipped door with the side of her fist again. I peeked down the narrow stairwell we'd just climbed, the red lights of *Seductions* flashing over the sidewalk outside.

"Who's there?" Sonny demanded from the other side of the door.

"Detective Vega."

"I already talked to you."

"We need to talk again."

"We? Is that screwball wizard with you?"

Vega looked over at me. "It will only take a minute."

"Unless I'm under arrest," came Sonny's receding voice, "take a hike."

"Sonny!" Vega shouted.

When he didn't respond, she shook the knob and looked up and down the lock-riddled door.

"Stand back." I unsheathed my sword and aimed it at the door. *"Vigore!"*

My goal was to bust the locks, but the force that shoved me into the rear wall ripped the door from the frame and sent the whole thing somersaulting into the apartment. The door upended a couch and crashed into an entertainment center, a television screen exploding in white sparks. Piles of DVDs spilled to the floor.

The door had just missed Sonny, who was sitting at a card table over a plate of food, a towel bib tied around his neck.

"What the fuck?" he cried, hair whipping as he looked from his displaced door to the two of us approaching through the haze of dust.

"Maybe you'll answer next time," Vega said.

"Who's gonna pay for all this?"

We were close enough now that I could see what was on Sonny's plate: pig parts in a soup of blood.

"I don't know," Vega replied. "Maybe you can file a complaint with the NYPD. I'm sure they'll fall all over themselves to help an upstanding citizen like you."

As Sonny's left eyelid jittered faster, his lips pouched out. I imagined his set of retractable teeth emerging through his gums.

"Oh, no you don't." The tip of my sword met the center of his bloody bib before he could lunge from the chair.

In the time it took Sonny to shift his red-glinting eyes from Vega to me and back, Vega had drawn her service pistol. He sat back with a sigh. "Come in here and ruin my dinner," he muttered, yanking his bib from around his neck and spiking it beside his plate. "What do you want?"

Without lowering her pistol, Vega held out the photo of Alexandra. "Do you know her?"

I watched Sonny's face. For an instant the resistance etched around his mouth smoothed. But only for an instant.

"A lot of girls come through my establishment," he said, raising his eyes.

"Look again," Vega said. "This would have been in the last month or so."

"What'd you say her name was?"

"I didn't. Alexandra."

"Don't know any Alexandras," Sonny said. "And I haven't seen anyone that looks like her in the last month."

"Sure she didn't come looking for work?" Vega pressed.

"If someone had come to me looking like that, I would've hired her on the spot. My clients love the innocent schoolgirl type. Never goes out of style." His narrow nose leaked a snivel.

Frowning severely, Vega pulled the picture away from him. "Do you keep records of your hires?" She must have seen the same flash of recognition on his face that I had a moment before.

"What if I do?"

"I want to see all of your hires since August."

"Fine. Get a warrant."

"The NYPD doesn't exactly follow the letter of the law anymore," Vega said, retraining her pistol on his forehead, this time with both hands. "In case you haven't heard."

"What? You gonna shoot me?"

"I'd be doing this city a favor," Vega assured him.

"Oh, some pretty important people would beg to differ." Though he said it with a grin, his left eyelid was beating furiously. "You'd be surprised at the names my girls entertain."

I stepped forward. "Well, what if we circumvented your VIP list and called the Financial District?"

"Be my guest."

I caught the faltering defiance in his voice and leaned closer. "Remember our visit earlier today? Guess who sent us?"

"Think I care?" Sonny picked up a pig's leg by its pale hoof and sunk his teeth into the meatiest section. Pink blood dribbled down his chin as he sucked and slurped, the pig's tangy odor making me queasy.

"Arnaud Thorne," I said.

Sonny's narrow eyes flicked up at me.

The Arnaud part was true, of course. What I was preparing to say, not so much.

"He thinks you're mixed up in those messy murders at Ferguson Towers. And he's—how should I put it?—*deeply* concerned. So if I were you, I'd be doing everything I could to prove I had nothing to do with Ferguson Towers. Starting by showing us your hires since August."

"I already told you I don't turn my girls," Sonny said.

"Your hires," I repeated.

"Christ," he muttered, the shriveled pig leg splashing onto his plate as he stood and scrubbed his mouth with the bib.

Ten minutes later, Vega and I stood behind Sonny in his club office as he hunkered in front of a vertical filing cabinet.

"September," he announced, holding up a file behind him. "Aaand October." Another file appeared, and Vega took that one, as well.

As Vega appropriated Sonny's desk to examine the files, I wandered the motley collection of filing cabinets against the back wall. Yellowing placards on the drawers listed months and years. Vampires were known to be meticulous, but holy hell—his records went all the way back to the 1980s.

"Impressive," I remarked.

"Hey, the city might be falling apart," Sonny said, "but I still get audited, if you can believe that shit."

"Cost of doing business, I guess."

"No kidding." He peeked over at Vega before sidling up to me and lowering his voice. He must have figured me for the good cop. "Hey, were you serious about Arnaud sending you and the detective down here?"

"Serious as anemia."

"And he thinks I'm mixed up in those slashings?"

I shrugged, which seemed more threatening than a nod. Plus, it was more honest. I didn't know what Arnaud thought. All I knew—or rather, suspected—was that Arnaud wanted us to discover something that, for whatever-odd reason, he couldn't spell out himself.

"Christ," Sonny muttered, dragging his hands through his hair.

"Do all the women apply under their real names?" Vega asked from the desk.

"I make them show ID," Sonny said, turning and ambling toward her. "And I can always spot the fakes. I know you think I'm the scum of the earth, but no way am I gonna hire an underage girl."

Sure, I thought, *only because you know you'd get shut down.*

Vega looked over the files again, then closed them with a sigh.

"See?" Sonny said. "Told you I didn't know nothing about your school girl."

"But you recognized her," I said. "When you first saw the photo."

"What are you talking about?"

"Don't screw with us," I warned. "Because when you screw with us, you screw with Arnaud."

Sonny held up his pale palms. "Look, I just thought she looked like someone who used to dance here."

"Who?" Vega asked.

"You know how many girls have come through these doors in the last thirty years?" Sonny said with a snort. "A thousand, probably. I can't remember all their names. I just thought your girl might've been one of them, until you told me it would've been in the last couple of months. The girl I was thinking of was here much longer ago. Fifteen, twenty years, at least. I can see her face, but that's it."

The admission sounded incidental, but my wizard's intuition was tapping away again, telling me we'd just found a shallow toehold.

Before I could press the vampire, Vega's phone went off.

"Rancho," she said, "what's going on?"

It took me a moment to place the name. Stiles's henchman, the bulky Mexican we'd met at the diner.

"When?" she asked coldly. "Okay. Thanks for telling me." She hung up and studied the phone's screen for a long moment, her face seeming to turn the color and texture of slate.

"What's the matter?" I asked.

Vega squeezed her eyes closed, then opened them. "Another murder at Ferguson Towers. Same M.O. as the last two. Stiles is convinced it's Kahn, even though Rancho told him the drain in the boiler room was busted open. Stiles is mobilizing, but so is Kahn. The war's going down tonight."

25

I studied Vega's set face as she sped south on Broadway. "You heard the terms," I cautioned her. " 'Stay away from Ferguson Towers.' I don't remember hearing a clause."

"Arnaud meant in relation to the murder investigation." Vega squealed around Union Square and onto Fourth Avenue. "I'm not going there to investigate. I'm going to stop a war."

"It's still a risk," I said. "Why don't you call for backup?"

"Even if they responded, that's just asking for a bigger blood bath."

"Vega, your son..."

Her eyes burst into black flames. "I know the fucking stakes, Croft!"

I stared ahead at the line of street lights, my cold hands wringing my cane. I shouldn't have pressed. Vega had made her decision. If sparing the lives of hundreds of children meant placing her own child in deeper danger, she had no choice. The vow to serve and protect was emblazoned on her soul. Like my magic, it was a part of her makeup.

A light rain began to streak the windshield as we approached Ferguson Towers. The sedan scraped over the curb and onto the sidewalk before barreling through the project's main gate. The water on the windshield spangled the lights of the east towers. Beneath the lights, hundreds of figures had amassed. On the far side of the plaza another army was gathering in front of the west towers.

"Shit," Vega spat.

She accelerated toward the east towers and slammed on her brakes. The front line of men pulled back as the sedan skidded around on the slick concrete and came to a sliding stop in front of them. I peered past Vega. The men wielded weapons, several of them aimed at the sedan. I was no expert on arms, but I recognized the green grenades jutting from shoulder rocket launchers.

"Hey," I said to her, "maybe we should reconsider—"

Vega threw her door open and got out. "Stiles!" she shouted.

Oh, Christ. I got out on my side and hustled around the car until I was beside her, the rain flicking against my face. The armed men pressed forward until Vega and I were enclosed in a semicircle.

"Where's Stiles?" she demanded.

Murmurs went up about cops on their turf. As I looked from face to hostile face, I understood why Vega hadn't wanted to get a larger police force involved. The NYPD was just as much the enemy as Kahn.

"Stiles!" she shouted again.

The crowd shifted, and Stiles emerged in a boot-length leather coat, his shades and bald head glistening with water. "Ricki," he said calmly.

Vega stomped forward until she was standing in front of him. "What the hell do you think you're doing?"

"I could ask you the same."

"We had an agreement," she shouted.

"Yes, *had*," he said. "The situation changed."

"Bullshit!" Rainwater flew from Vega's mouth. "You were planning this stupid war before the latest victim turned up."

"I've told you in the past, you live by your rules, we live by ours. Rule number one is to never give ground to your enemy."

Vega stepped closer. "And I told you, *goddammit*, Kahn's not behind the killings."

"You've been gone too long, kid," Stiles said. "You're out of your depth. Shove off, and take Pasty here with you."

"She's right," I said, struggling to keep my voice from shaking in the sudden cold. "We're closing in on the perp. We almost had her apprehended earlier tonight."

"Where I come from," Stiles said, "*almost* doesn't mean much." Laughter erupted around him, and I could see how he had maintained control over his towers. In addition to whatever violence he wielded, he had the coolness factor down pat. But the line of his jaw suddenly hardened. Vega was pointing her pistol at him.

"Call it off," she said, "or I'm bringing you in."

Stiles shook his head. "Don't be stupid, Ricki."

Metal flashed, and two dozen barrels stared at Vega and me. I concentrated into my casting prism, ready to conjure a shield. *C'mon,* I thought to Vega. *I know you've got history here, but is this worth it?*

"Call it off," Vega repeated.

Grumblings went up, but Stiles silenced them with a raised hand. "Everyone chill. This is between me and Ricki."

"So what's it gonna be?" Vega asked, the rain water that beaded over her pulled-back hair beginning to trickle down her face. Her pistol didn't waver.

Stiles shook his head. "Still the same spitfire you were twenty years ago, never knowing when to back down."

"Yeah, well this isn't twenty years ago, and we're not arguing over whether you're two-timing me—which I knew you were. You've got enough artillery to reduce the west towers to a sandlot. And I'm guessing they've got enough to do the same over here. Look around, goddammit. Look at all the lives you're putting in danger."

I peeked up the east towers. The same silhouettes I'd seen last night stared from the windows. It was the smaller ones, low to the sills, that bothered me the most, the ones belonging to children.

Though Kahn's army waited across the plaza, the aim of Stiles's sunglasses didn't shift from Vega's face.

"She's right, boss." I looked over to see someone large pushing his way to the fore. It was Rancho, his own rain-streaked face tense and fearful. "I-I've got a family up there. A lot of us do."

Several of Stiles's men shifted, necks craning back toward the towers. The movement created a shudder through the ranks, through Stiles's generalship.

"Is that right?" he asked calmly, drawing a black pistol from his waistband. "You're worried about your families?"

Still looking at Rancho, Stiles pivoted his arm and shot Vega pointblank in the stomach.

My heart stopped as Vega collapsed to the concrete. Stiles's men backed away.

"If you know how to drive, I suggest you collect your partner and get off my plaza." It took me a moment to realize Stiles was talking to me.

I dropped to my knees beside Vega. She was still alive, thank God, her breaths coming in choked gasps. The bullet had pierced the body armor in a small burst of mesh. There was no way to tell how deep the bullet had penetrated, but blood was seeping from the hole. A lot of blood.

Anger burned in my gut. "She was only doing her job."

"Did you say something to me?" Stiles asked, his voice even, menacing.

I rose and rotated toward him. "She was only trying to protect your residents."

"She knows better."

I had no more words for the cold-blooded creature. A man who would hurt a former friend, a mother, the most dedicated public safety officer I had ever met. I glanced around at the crowd through the tapering rain.

"Anyone with a family to protect," I said. "I suggest you go to them now."

"You don't talk to my men," Stiles said. "*I* talk to my men." He raised his pistol until it was staring at my face. "I'm not going to say it again. Take your partner and get the fuck off my plaza."

I stooped toward Detective Vega. Her cheek was pressed to the concrete, face clenched in agony. Rain water mingled with the blood from her wound and pooled pink around her knees. My intention had been to pick her up and load her into the car, to get her to a hospital. Instead, fury threw me into a pivot. Sweeping my cane in a wide arc, I shouted, *"Forza dura!"*

The force blew from me with the roaring power of a jet engine. It slammed into Stiles and his men, sending them airborne in a wave. A chorus of cries rose. Shoes and weapons spilled to the plaza. I glimpsed Stiles's flapping leather coat before he disappeared into the wave of bodies crashing against the nearest towers. I drew my cane apart.

"Protezione!" I called, forming a light shield around Vega and me.

Bullets sparked off the glowing dome, but not from Stiles's men. The commotion had spurred Kahn's army into action. They were charging from the west towers, gun muzzles flashing.

I glanced around. Many of Stiles's men remained down. Others staggered into the east towers. A few had reclaimed weapons and were firing back at Kahn's men.

I looked down at Vega. I needed to get her out of here, but I couldn't let the situation degenerate into the war she'd been trying to prevent.

Flares burst across the plaza and two, three rockets blasted toward us.

"Respingere!" I shouted.

The pulse from my shield pummeled the rockets, knocking them off their trajectory. They wriggled skyward and detonated like brute pyrotechnics, the Manhattan Bridge to the north flashing in and out of view. Shrapnel rained down over my shield. *Christ.* My abilities had been developed to cast nether creatures back to their realms, not to carry out urban warfare. And with the fae magic still bolstering my powers, I possessed punch but not precision.

I opened a rear door of the sedan and scooped Vega up. She felt too limp as she sagged against me.

"Hang in there," I said. "I'm going to get you to a doctor."

I fed her through the door and lay her across the back seat.

I was pulling away when her left hand reached out and seized the lapel of my coat. Words hissed from her grimacing lips. "Don't you ... *dare* ... put me in a hospital."

She released me, her hand falling back to her wound. I read between the lines. A hospital would mean being sidelined, unable to work on reclaiming her son. We'd have that fight later.

I slammed the door closed and grew the shield to enclose the sedan. Kahn's army had reached the plaza's center, and heavy fire was coming from both sides. Stiles's retreating men had taken up positions inside the apartments, gunfire flashing between window bars.

That's nice, you idiots, I thought, *drawing fire toward your families.*

A rocket launcher spewed gas from an upper-story window, and a missile dove toward the plaza. My force invocation was too slow. The missile detonated in front of Kahn's men, blasting back the advance.

How in the hell am I going to end this conflict?

The short answer was I couldn't. The best I could do was give the two sides a common enemy.

Me.

26

I dropped into the driver seat and slammed the door. Vega had left the sedan running. It was a different vehicle from the one I'd driven in October, but the same make and model. I took a moment to refamiliarize myself with the controls before pulling the gearshift into drive.

I glanced back to check on Vega. "Hold onto something," I told her and waited for her to wrap a hand around one of the safety belts.

I stepped on the gas and peeled around until I was bearing down on Kahn's army. Bullets flashed off the shield that glimmered around the sedan. I felt the impact of bullets from the rear, meaning I was taking fire from Stiles's men as well.

Perfect.

Kahn's soldiers began to back away, then scramble from my oncoming vehicle. When I was almost to the front lines, I shouted, "*Respingere!*"

With the fae magic acting as a catalyst, the pulse from the shield detonated like a daisy bomb, blowing men as far back as the fence ringing the project. I steered through the fallen men and ruined weapons, careful not to run over anyone, then wheeled around and accelerated back toward the east towers. More shots rattled and popped, impacts flashing beyond the windshield.

With another shouted Word, my shield expanded rapidly, knocking back Stiles's men in the plaza. I cut the sedan hard right and steered toward the main gate. In the rearview mirror, I caught combatants from both sides giving chase, no longer shooting at one another.

How long the temporary truce would hold, I had no idea. But I'd done all I could.

The sedan's passenger side scraped through the gate in a sharp keening. I braked too late, launching off the curb and into the rusted husk of a car that had been left curbside. I cursed and reversed, then took off west, away from the chattering gunfire still directed at me.

I jagged left at the next intersection, then right, then left again pulling up to a four-way stop. I was far enough from the Towers that I dispersed my shield to allow my powers to recharge. I twisted and peered into the back seat. "You all right, Vega?" I still had to figure out where to take her.

I didn't notice the dark van slide up beside us, lights off, until my driver side door cannoned open. A fist crushed my jaw and wobbled my casting prism. A pair of hands seized the front of my coat, jerked me from the vehicle, and pinned me against the car's side. I stared at an unfamiliar face.

Wait ... I do know you.

Stiles's sunglasses had no doubt come off when I'd blasted him. Now, small, nervous eyes stared into mine.

"You couldn't leave the Towers to us," he said, a bloody cement rash glistening over his right brow. "You had to come and interfere."

When he reared back to punch me again, I jabbed a thumb into his right eye. He grunted and released my coat. I dove for the open car door, for my sword, but he grabbed the back of my coat and swung me out. I slammed into the side of the van, head ringing.

I turned, fists raised, and threw a lunging punch. Stiles leaned away, a switchblade popping from his own fist.

We circled. I blinked sweat and rainwater from my eyes, tried to focus, but my head was too foggy to cast. The van's front doors opened and closed, and two of Stiles's armed henchmen took positions to box us in.

Stiles stepped forward and drove the blade at my gut. I skipped backwards, got my feet tangled, and fell to the street.

The ganglord stood over me. "I don't know what the hell you are," he said, holding up the blade. "But something tells me you still bleed."

A shot rang out. Stiles staggered to the side. One of his hands drifted to his throat. When it came away, he stared at his palm for a long moment. A gout of blood spurted from his neck. He dropped straight down, collapsing onto the seat of his coat, then fell against the side of the van.

I turned. Vega's pistol was pointing from the front door of the sedan. Stiles's henchman moved toward her, rifles aimed.

"Stand down!" Someone hustled up from a side street, a shotgun raised. It was Rancho. "I'm next in command, and I don't want any dead cops. Put Stiles in the van. We need to get him back to the Towers."

The henchmen hesitated before lowering their rifles. They pulled open the side door of the van and lifted Stiles's limp body. While they loaded him into the van, Rancho grasped my arm and hauled me to my feet. He helped me into the sedan, squinting into the backseat.

"You gonna be all right, Ricki?" he asked.

She nodded and lay back, the hand holding her pistol pressing against her stomach.

"Don't worry about the Towers," he said. "With Stiles out of commission, I'll get them back under control." His gaze shifted to me, and he lowered his voice. "Don't let her die, motherfucker."

I nodded, and he closed the door.

"I'm taking you to a hospital," I said as I turned down Canal Street.

"You do, and I'll kill you," Vega whispered.

"Duly noted, but I've never treated a bullet wound before. And even if I knew what I was doing, my powers are all out of whack. I wouldn't be able to put any healing magic to it."

"There's a medical kit in the trunk," Vega murmured. "I'll tell you what to do."

I started to shake my head, but then I had an image of pulling up to an emergency room only to have Vega brace herself inside the car like a cat. I sighed. "All right. I'm staying at a place not far from here. But if I can't help you, I will take you to a hospital. No more arguments."

"Fine," she said. "Just shut up and drive."

I kicked the apartment door closed behind me and set Vega on the bed in the back room. The medical kit I'd pinned beneath my arm fell to the floor. I stooped over Vega and freed the Velcro straps of her vest. She inhaled sharply through her teeth as I peeled the vest away. She was wearing an army-green wife beater underneath, its stomach plastered with blood.

I steeled myself before lifting the hem of her shirt to her sternum and tucking it beneath her sports bra. Her stomach was awash in blood. An angry hole stared up at me from beneath her right ribs. It opened and closed like a small mouth with each pained breath.

Vega lifted her head to see. "Oh, crap," she muttered, and let her head fall back.

Okay, that's not very reassuring. "Listen, you're going to be all right," I said. "But you have to tell me what to do."

"Bullet broke through the vest," Vega whispered. "But I don't think it made it through the muscle. Go ahead and open the kit."

I opened the medical kit and dumped the contents onto the floor.

"Put on the blue gloves and grab the peroxide and some gauze."

I sifted through the contents until I found the gloves in a plastic bag. I tore open the bag with my teeth and pulled the gloves on. I then ripped open a package of stacked gauze and twisted the cap from a brown bottle of peroxide. "All right," I said. "I've got everything."

"Pour the peroxide over the site." She wrapped her fingers around the edges of the metal frame. "Need to disinfect it."

"Do you want a countdown?"

She shook her head, eyes squeezed closed.

I tipped the bottle over her stomach, soaking it with peroxide. Her muscles clenched into a small six-pack as the peroxide foamed white in the wound. I wiped around the hole with a handful of gauze, sponging up the pink runoff. After several seconds, Vega let out her held breath in a grunt.

"Good, Croft," she whispered. "Now find the extra long tweezers."

"Got 'em," I said, tearing away the sterile wrapping.

"Have to get the bullet out."

"I was afraid you'd say that." I looked back down at the medical supplies. "Isn't there something I can give you for pain?"

She shook her head. "When morphine started disappearing from the kits ... NYPD stopped including it."

"Wonderful." I swallowed and held the tweezers over the wound. "Just tell me if you need me to back off, all right?"

She nodded.

I winced as I lowered the tweezers into the opening. I tried not to touch the walls of flesh, as though involved in a macabre version of Operation.

I had only gone in a few millimeters when I encountered something foreign beneath the pool of blood. Vega's stomach tensed as I tried to grip the object with the tweezers.

"Sorry," I said.

"Just grab it, dammit. Grab it and pull it out."

I pressed the tweezers in more deeply, got a solid grip, and drew the flattened chunk of metal free.

"It's out!" I said, like someone who had just landed a fish.

"We're not done," Vega panted. "Look for a package labeled Celox."

I dropped the bullet and tweezers in the wadded-up gauze and looked through the contents of the medical kit. "Celox... Celox... Okay, found it." I picked up the metallic pouch.

"It's a coagulant," Vega said. "Pour it over the wound."

I opened the pouch too aggressively. The corn-meal-like granules spilled across her stomach, clumping where it met blood. Using a finger, I shoveled the Celox into the wound until it was full, then patted it down. I looked at Vega's face. She was sweating heavily, a forearm to her brow.

"Hey, hey, are you all right?"

She waved weakly toward the medical supplies with her other hand. "Just dress it."

I covered the wound with a small stack of gauze and then affixed the gauze with a compression dressing. I reinforced everything with medical tape. It didn't look half bad, but the mess around her was another story. I appraised her soaked vest, the pile of dirty gauze. She had lost a lot of blood.

"Just need a little rest," Vega said. "Then we'll talk to a blood slave."

She wasn't going to be in any condition. "Why don't you let me?"

"Forget it."

"Why?"

"Because it's not your son."

I covered her with a clean sheet I had grabbed from my apartment and looked at her pallid face. A fresh wave of guilt at endangering her son, endangering *her*, seared through me. She needed to be in a hospital. She needed blood.

I pulled my cane from my coat belt and looked at the opal. What was the bigger risk, attempting or not attempting to heal her through magic?

"Try it," Vega mumbled, an eyelid cracking open. "I'm going back out there regardless."

I had no doubt she would.

Setting my legs apart, I touched the end of the cane to the mound of dressing beneath the sheet. I leaned back against the power flooding toward my prism as I incanted, allowing only the smallest trickle through. The orb glowed softly, enveloping Vega in a thin, cottony haze of light. She murmured as her eyelids trembled closed. I pulled energy back from the spell and broke it. The room dimmed again. I had given her as much magic as I was willing to risk. Hopefully it would be enough to jump-start the healing.

From one floor down, the room shook with the march of footsteps and doors opening and closing. The vampire hunters were home. I wanted to remain with Vega, to monitor her condition, but a quick trip downstairs could help fill in some holes in the Ferguson Towers murders. Such as why Bullet, Blade, and Dr. Z had been tracking the creature.

Vega had curled onto her side and seemed to have drifted off, her vulnerable body rising and falling in an even rhythm.

"I'm going to step out, but I'll be right back," I whispered. And then I did something I never would have attempted while Detective Vega was awake. I leaned down and kissed her cheek.

27

"Mr. Wednesday Night," Bullet said upon answering the door, but without his usual enthusiasm.

"Mind if I come in?" I asked.

The giant of a man frowned his tattoo-patterned face and looked behind him, as though seeking approval from someone beyond my view. "Yeah, sure," he said, opening the door wider.

Blade and the green-haired Dr. Z were sitting on a couch, holding half-eaten slices of pizza. They had changed out of their battle gear. Blade now sported a camouflage tank top and Dr. Z a hooded shirt. Bullet joined them on the end, setting his shotgun beside the couch. Blade jutted her chin toward a greasy pizza box standing open on the coffee table. "Help yourself," she told me.

"Thanks, but I'm watching my complexion."

"How about a beer, then?" Dr. Z offered.

"Yeah, guess I could use one of those." I pulled a gold can from the six-pack on the table and settled into an old rattan chair facing the couch, the exhaustion of the day weighing on my bones. I cracked the tab and took a long drink. The beer went down warm and thick.

"Let me guess," Blade said, watching me lower the can. "You're a Jehovah's Witness and you want us to take a look at some pamphlets."

"I'm a consultant for the NYPD, and I want to know what you were doing down in the storm lines. Armed with silver weapons," I added.

"I thought you were a professor," Bullet said, biting into his pizza, the cheese stretching into strings as he drew it from his chomping jaws.

"I'm that, too."

"All the shit going on in this city," Dr. Z cut in, "and you're worried about *us*?"

"Look, you guys aren't in any trouble. In fact, I think we're after the same thing." The three of them fell silent, suddenly more interested in their dinner. "All right, why don't you start by telling me what happened after the detectives and I left? We all thank you for bailing us out, by the way."

"We followed a blood trail," Blade said.

"Detective Vega hit the creature with a silver bullet," I said, nodding for her to continue.

"Well, by the amount of blood, I'd say she hit it pretty good. But the trail led to a mainline where water was really gushing, probably from an opened hydrant. That's where we lost the trail.

And in that maze, forget it. We must have been down there for two hours before deciding to pack it in."

"The creature killed again," I said.

The three of them looked up. "Where?" Blade asked.

"The Ferguson Towers Project. We think she's climbing up through the storm drain." I wondered now if the creature's injury had driven her to feed. "How did you learn about her?"

"Someone hired us," Blade said.

That much I had guessed. "Who?"

"Sorry," Blade said. "We guarantee our clients complete confidentiality. It's one of our selling points."

When I could see she wasn't going to budge, I relented and took another swallow of beer. "Fine. Why don't you just tell me what you know about the creature?"

"She's a hybrid," Blade said.

"A hybrid? Of what?"

"Vampire and werewolf."

"More of the first than the second, though," Dr. Z put in.

I had never even heard of that, but I supposed it was possible. "Hybrid by birth?"

"Could be," Dr. Z said. "But there's always the lightning strikes twice scenario. You know, some unlucky bastard getting the lycanthrope infection, then later being turned into a vampire."

"And someone hired you to put this one down?"

"We don't chase after these things for our health," Blade said.

"No, I guess not. Care to tell me your next move?"

"And tip off our competition?" Blade smirked. "In case you haven't noticed, we're a little cash starved." She glanced around a living room of second-hand furniture, sagging punk posters, and stacked amps.

"I think I can convince the NYPD to let you have this one." Especially since that would free us up to focus on Arnaud's leads. I just prayed he hadn't already taken punitive action against Vega's son.

"Well, thanks to your blundering into the tunnels," Blade said, "who knows where the creature ended up. It won't be lairing in that little service room again, though, I can tell you that much. It's too smart."

"And damn near invincible," Dr. Z said. "Those silver bullets you were packing wouldn't have done the job."

"No?" I set my beer can down with a shaking hand. Some consultant I'd turned out to be. "How do you kill a hybrid, then?"

Dr. Z drew a finger across his neck. "Decapitation, baby."

"We'll probably have to wait for it to strike again," Blade said. "That'll give us an idea where it's holed up."

I remembered the hair in my coat pocket, the one I had collected in Alexandra's dorm room. If she *was* the creature, a hunting spell could lead us to her. But the creature wasn't my immediate priority. That honor went to Detective Vega's son. Which meant taking up Arnaud's game again, connecting the dots he was setting out for us until a picture emerged.

"How did you know to look underground?" I asked.

Blade chewed slowly on her next bite of pizza, as though considering what to divulge. "We were told the same thing as you," she said at last. "That the creature was using the storm drains."

Only we weren't told that, I thought. *Vega and Hoffman figured it out. Which suggests that whoever hired you three either has access to the case file or to someone working the case.*

"Can I assume your employer is someone powerful then?" I asked.

Blade and Dr. Z gave me poker faces, but I caught Bullet, the weak link, glance quickly down.

Blade tossed her crust into the box and closed the lid. "Time's up, Everson. Dr. Z and I need to rehearse. Big show next week. If you can promise to keep your pants on, you're welcome to come."

"One last question," I said, ignoring the dig. "With this job, have you been meeting any resistance from the vampires?"

Dr. Z snorted. "Only about every time we turn around. Too bad no one's paying us to knock off blood slaves."

"Any idea why?" I asked as I handed them cards with Vega's contact info.

Blade shrugged. "Someone hired us to kill the hybrid. Maybe someone hired a vamp to keep it alive."

28

I rushed to where Vega stood at the side of the bed, adjusting her service belt around her waist. Her wife beater was dark but no longer bloody. She had already rinsed it in the sink and wrung it out.

"What are you doing up?"

"I didn't want to sleep too long," she said. "Whatever you did helped."

When she raised her face, strands of damp hair clung to her brow. Though her color remained pale, it had improved from only a half hour ago.

"I still say you need your rest. You lost a lot of blood."

She ignored the comment, wincing as she straightened. "Where did you run off to, anyway?"

"That trio that helped us out with the blood slaves? They're squatting in the same building." At that moment, the muted sounds of electric guitars came up through the floor. "They've been hired to hunt the creature. That's why they were down in the storm lines."

"Hired by who?"

"They wouldn't tell me, but I say let them hunt it."

Vega nodded as she stepped past me. "I agree for once. Now let's go find Arnaud's spokesperson, see where things stand."

"That won't be necessary." I held up a piece of paper. "It was stuck in the door when I got back here."

Vega snatched it from me, her eyes already moving over the spidery script. I came around behind her and reread the message:

Your return to Ferguson Towers violated the letter of our agreement, but perhaps not the spirit. I am giving you the benefit of the doubt and will consider the detective's injury penalty enough. Rest assured, the boy remains safe in our care. As for the leads, I applaud your thoroughness thus far. It seems you are making progress. Keep it up, and the conditions for the boy's return will soon be fulfilled. I have another person you will no doubt find interesting. I advise you to see her forthwith.

Lady Bastet
59 Carmine Street

"The name ring a bell?" Vega asked.

"Not from personal experience, but yeah. Lady Bastet lives in the West Village. She also happens to be a mystic."

"An old woman with a crystal ball?"

"Old in years, maybe, but not looks. And I don't know about the crystal ball, but it wouldn't surprise me. That address is for a rug store she owns, but her real business is divination and spells."

"Good mystic or bad?"

I thought as I retrieved my revolver. "Neutral."

"Think she'll be open this late?"

"Probably, but you're going to need something warmer." I dug into one of my duffel bags and pulled out a gray sweatshirt I had planned to sleep in. "Here." I tried to help Vega into it, but she pulled it out of my hands and put the sweatshirt on herself, rolling up the sleeves to her wrists.

"Let's go," she said.

A plain sign over the sidewalk pointed down a staircase to Lady Bastet's basement-level business. Despite Vega's assurances that she was all right, I had her keep a hand on my shoulder as we descended. I had already seen her stumble once.

At the bottom of the steps, an old paint-chipped door creaked open before I could knock. A striking eye with a white kohl peered out.

"Yes?" a woman's voice asked.

"Lady Bastet?" Vega said, shouldering me aside. "I'm Detective Vega with the NYPD. Do you mind if I ask you a few questions?"

"And who is your handsome associate?" She spoke in an

accent that was hard to place.

"That's Everson Croft. A consultant."

Lady Bastet opened the door until we were looking at a dark-skinned woman in a white peasant blouse. A gold band with an ankh symbol in its center held a pile of dark hair from a face whose age lines enhanced her appearance. Lady Bastet smiled at me with lush lips, then seemed to tease me with her cat-green eyes to follow. It was a compelling look.

Vega shot me a consternated glance as Lady Bastet led us through a display room of Middle Eastern rugs to a back room. The space smelled of harsh incense and magic. While cats squinted at us from various perches, Lady Bastet gestured for us to sit at a stone table in the room's center. After covering what looked like a scrying globe with a cloth, she joined us on the table's opposite side.

"You are missing someone close to you," she told Vega.

Vega set her jaw. "We're investigating a series of murders, and we'd like to ask you some questions."

"As a consultant?" Lady Bastet asked.

"As a person of interest," Vega replied.

I half expected Lady Bastet's eyes to widen in alarm. Instead they pinched at the corners, as though she were smiling inwardly. Perhaps our visit had livened up an otherwise dull night.

"Please," she said, opening a hand of long nails. "Proceed."

"I'm going to give you some names," Vega said, "and I want you to tell me whether they mean anything to you." She took Alexandra's photo from the file and pushed it across the table. "This is Alexandra Mills."

Lady Bastet lifted the photo. "She is beautiful."

"Do you know her?"

"Beautiful and tortured," Lady Bastet went on. "It is there in her eyes, as though something is fighting to claim her very soul. She is winning, though. At least at the time of the photo."

"You haven't answered my question," Vega said.

Lady Bastet placed the photo on the table and slid it back. "I am sorry. Sometimes the impressions just come." When her eyes touched on mine, she might as well have winked. "No, I do not know her."

Vega's shoulders slouched as she returned the photo to the file. "How about a Sonny Shoat? He runs an establishment on West Forty-second Street called *Seductions*."

Lady Bastet repeated his name. "Do you have something of his I might touch?"

"I'm not asking for a reading," Vega said, her voice thinning with frustration. "I'm just asking if you know him."

"I do not deal with those types."

"What types?" Vega asked.

"I think you know."

She meant vampires, which put us in a quandary. If she didn't know Alexandra or Sonny, why *had* Arnaud sent us to her? I peeked over at Vega. With her mundane line of questioning all but exhausted, I decided it was time to take a supernatural tact.

"What sorts of services do you offer?" I asked.

"Readings, divinations, communication with the deceased. Spell work, occasionally."

"What kind of spell work?"

"That depends on what my client wants," Lady Bastet replied. "And what they are willing to give."

I noticed she didn't say *pay*.

My eyes roamed the room in thought. The space was crowded but neat. Cats large and small crouched on shelves stocked with items like crocodile teeth, falcon feathers, and the colorful shells of scarab beetles.

I nodded toward a clutch of dried purple flowers. "I see you have wolf's bane," I said. "Do you ever treat clients infected with the lycanthropic virus?"

"From time to time, yes."

"Ever encountered a werewolf-vampire hybrid?"

"Once."

"An infant, right?" I said. "About eighteen years ago?"

Now Lady Bastet's eyes did widen slightly. "May I ask how you know this?"

I glanced over at Vega, who had one hand turned up as though to say, *Were you ever going to tell me you'd figured something out?* But the pieces had snapped together in the last moment. Sonny the vampire. The creature we had encountered in the storm line. The remnants of a spell I had sensed in Alexandra's old dormitory. Lady Bastet's reaction to the photo.

Alexandra hadn't worked for Sonny. Her mother had.

"Someone brought an infant to you," I said. "A young woman, I'm guessing. She was worried about her little girl's ... makeup. She asked you to cast a spell to fix her, to make her human."

"But I could not," Lady Bastet said, picking up the story. "She had not been infected by a werewolf, nor had she been turned into a vampire. Those elements belonged to her by birth. As such, I could only suppress her vampire and werewolf natures, keep them from maturing."

"Through a powerful binding spell," I said.

"May I see the photo again? Yes," Lady Bastet said after Vega had handed it to her. "I remember the eyes. So intelligent." She sighed sadly. "Am I to presume the spell has been broken?"

"About two months ago," I said. "Alexandra took a powerful street drug. Detective Vega and I happened to visit the room in which she ingested it, and I detected the remnants of the binding spell."

"It probably occurred on or near the full moon," Lady Bastet said. "This Alexandra would have gone into the wilds at night, fed on the blood of animals, and then slept in the daytime to avoid the most intense light." I nodded, remembering what her roommate had told us. "Eventually, she would have developed a craving for human blood. It would have been irresistible to her. Are you trying to find her?"

"Yes," Vega said.

"No," I said over her. "Well, not right now. We're trying to find the mother." Something still told me that was what Arnaud was after. "Do you remember her name? Anything about her?"

"She did not give me a name. She was young and frightened, though she hid both well. I noticed she had no wedding band. She looked a lot like this young woman." Lady Bastet tapped the photo with a fingernail.

I turned to Vega. "Do you remember Sonny's reaction to the photo? How he said it reminded him of an employee from decades earlier."

"He knew the mother," Vega said.

"Intimately," I added. "Because he's Alexandra's father."

Vega's head tilted. "That son of a bitch," she whispered.

I turned back to Lady Bastet. "Did you treat the mother, too?"

"She did not ask me to. Perhaps because she was not a full-blooded werewolf."

"What did you charge the mother to help her infant?" I asked.

"Her hair."

"Her hair?" Vega said.

"She had very powerful hair, the color of wild honey, all the way to her waist. Her wolf nature gave it added potency. Some of my most powerful enchantment spells came from that hair."

"Do you have any left?" With even a single strand, I could cast a hunting spell.

"I am afraid not. Word spread quickly. The supply could not keep up with the demand."

Crap.

"Can you, I don't know, *divine* anything about her whereabouts?" Vega asked.

"Do you have something that might connect me to her?" Lady Bastet asked.

"We have no idea who she even is," Vega said.

"Then I'm sorry."

"Wait." I reached into the inner pocket of my coat and withdrew the long strand of Alexandra's hair. "This belonged to her daughter."

Lady Bastet accepted the hair and drew it between her finger and thumb. "A cellular as well as an emotional connection." Lady Bastet's lips turned up at the corners. "Most powerful."

"Will it work?" Vega asked.

"That depends on what you are prepared to give."

"What do you charge?" Vega asked, already pulling out her wallet.

Lady Bastet's attention shifted to me. My skin tingled uncomfortably as her kohl-lined eyes roamed my body. At last, her gaze settled on mine, and she smiled again. "His blood."

"What?" Vega said.

"Not all of it." Lady Bastet stood and retrieved a clay tube from a shelf. "This much."

I sized up the tube. She was clever, asking just enough to weaken my powers without it being a deal breaker. But I was more concerned with how she planned to employ my blood. Wizard's blood could be used in powerful spells. And if those spells took a dark bent, the wizard was on the hook with the Order—especially if said wizard had given his blood willingly.

I glanced over at Vega, who was watching me for my answer, one hand to her bandaged stomach. "It's a deal," I said. Before I could reconsider, I pushed up my right coat sleeve and placed my arm on the table.

"Very good."

I shuddered as Lady Bastet's fingernails caressed the network of veins on my upturned forearm. She uttered an incantation, and the veins bulged in a painful spasm. Drawing what looked like a wooden needle from her hair, she said, "You'll feel a small prick."

She placed the needle against an especially thick vein. A second later, the needle bit into me. A greedy suckling commenced, and I watched blood fill the clay receptacle she held below the needle's other end.

When the tube was full of dark blood, Lady Bastet pulled the needle free and capped the container. With another incantation, the puncture closed and my veins relaxed. Giving the tube a light shake, she whispered, "Perfect."

She shooed away a cat perched on a small wooden box and placed the tube inside among some others. Back at the table, she removed the cloth from the scrying globe. The pad of her first finger caressed the length of Alexandra's hair as she whispered in old Egyptian.

The marble-like pattern of the globe began to shift and glow.

"The mother is in the city," Lady Bastet said after a moment. "She is involved with disreputable people, but she cannot disentangle herself from them, like she did Sonny. The years have made her more wily, though. She uses them."

I glanced over at Vega, who mouthed, "John Smith." I nodded. Alexandra's sponsor. He was connected to the mother somehow. And if he had been paying Alexandra's tuition in cash all those years, he was someone of means. Lady Bastet stared into the globe until I couldn't help myself.

"Is there a man in her life?" I asked.

"Because the hair is not hers, I see only glimpses of those around her. There are two men of significance, though. One strong, the other weak. Power binds her to both. Not love." Light seeped from the globe as it stopped shifting.

Lady Bastet raised her eyes. "I have told you all I can see."

"No name?" Vega asked.

The mystic's gold hoop earrings rattled when she shook her head.

"There's Sonny's files," I said to Vega as Lady Bastet covered the globe. "Alexandra's date of birth gives us the year she was conceived, probably when her mother worked for Sonny. Going name by name through the file for that year, Sonny should be able to make the match to the woman he remembered, the one who looked like Alexandra."

Vega nodded and stood. "Thanks for your help," she told Lady Bastet.

"Are you sure there is nothing else?"

"Not right now," I said.

Vega hesitated. "Actually... a friend of Everson's is missing."

I looked at her in surprise. Vega tilted her head toward Lady Bastet. I pulled out my wallet, digging through the leather sleeves until I found Caroline's business card from the College. I slid it halfway toward the mystic, then stopped. "What are you asking for this time?"

"We will discuss payment afterwards." Lady Bastet's lids fell slightly as she stroked the card. The globe returned to life and glowed against her face.

But after only seconds, the globe dimmed again.

"I am sorry," Lady Bastet said. "Your friend is no longer in this world."

My heart stopped for a beat before lurching into a sick rhythm. "Wh-what do you mean?"

The black cloth the mystic replaced over the globe looked like a funeral shroud.

"That is all I can tell you. And for that, I ask nothing."

29

"You going to be all right?" Vega asked.

I looked from the dark storefronts skipping past on Seventh Avenue to Detective Vega, who had insisted on driving despite her bullet wound. They were the first words either of us had spoken since leaving Lady Bastet's.

"Still processing," I replied numbly. "But her pronouncement could mean a couple of things besides, you know..." I swallowed.

My best hope now was that Angelus had taken Caroline to the faerie realm.

"If there's something you need to do, I can probably take it from here."

I shook my head. "No. I'm the reason we're in this mess. The priority is getting your son back safely. I'll look for Caroline afterwards. Anyway, Arnaud insisted we work together."

"All right. Let's just take a few minutes to make sure we're on the same page." Vega coughed weakly into her fist, wincing at the pain in her stomach. "This mother, who has werewolf blood in her, has a child with Sonny, and they give birth to a—what did you call it?"

"A werewolf-vampire hybrid," I said.

"The mother takes the hybrid to Lady Bastet, who casts some sort of spell to keep her as human as possible. Then the mother puts her child, Alexandra, in the care of the state. Years pass. The mother's left Sonny, but she gets involved with some disreputable people."

"People with the money to pay the tuition at the boarding school."

"Yeah," Vega said. "Which tells me 'John Smith' is probably the mother."

I paused to consider the P.O. Box and burner phone. "You're probably right. Great catch."

"Alexandra seems to be doing all right at school, but her roommate brings home a street drug. Heroin laced with God knows what. Alexandra takes it and ... it breaks up the spell somehow?"

"With the kinds of forces that spell was holding back," I said, "it might not have taken much. Sort of like a tire that gets nicked on the highway. First little bits of rubber start flicking off, then huge chunks, until you're down to rim."

"And she became a werewolf-vampire?"

"Right."

"But what brought her to the city?"

"Help? Answers? A larger food supply?" I shrugged. "There's no telling. Not with the information we have."

"So why is Arnaud protecting her?"

I thought about what the vampire hunters had said right before they kicked me out of their apartment. "Maybe he isn't protecting her out of self-interest," I said. "Maybe someone hired him to protect Alexandra."

"The mother?"

"Seems the most likely candidate. But it still begs the question: Why is Arnaud having us chase leads to find out who the mother is if he already knows? I mean, look at what he's given us so far: the creature's identity, the father's identity, the fact the mother brought the creature to Lady Bastet. He doesn't *need* us to connect the dots."

"Then there's the question of who hired the vampire hunters to kill the creature."

"Ah," I said. "I actually have a lead there. Who did you inform about your trip into the storm lines?"

"So far? No one."

"Did you write it down anywhere, like in a report?"

Vega shook her head. "There wasn't time. I was planning to write the report after."

"So you didn't tell anyone?"

"No, Croft. Just you and Hoffman."

"Hoffman," I groaned.

"Why?"

"When I asked the vampire hunters how they ended up in the storm line, Blade said, 'We were told the same thing as you. That the creature was using the storm drains.' Which can only mean someone got that information from Hoffman and then passed it along."

Vega's eyes narrowed as she shook her head. "He knows he's not supposed to share info on an investigation without my authorization."

"Yeah, well, he's not exactly up for a Meritorious Police Duty medal."

"All right, I'll call him after we deal with Sonny." She pulled up curbside near the staircase leading to Sonny's apartment.

I got out and came around the car to find Vega leaning against her car door, holding her stomach.

"Let me take a look," I said.

"I'm fine." She pushed my hand away.

"If you're bleeding again…"

"I'm not." She strode toward the staircase.

I followed, watching her closely. I could sense the dose of healing magic I'd applied earlier still moving around inside her. She really needed to be resting for it to work, though.

At the top of the steps, I could see where Sonny had leaned his blown-out door against the frame. The spaces around the door's edges were dark.

Vega knocked. "Sonny? It's the NYPD."

When no one answered, I lifted the door and walked it a few feet into the living room, setting it against a wall of risqué *Seductions* calendars. Vega slipped past me, her sidearm gripped in both hands. She cleared the living room and turned toward the hallway.

"Sonny?" she called again.

As I drew my cane apart, my gaze dipped to Vega's stomach. A small point of blood had struck through the sweatshirt. She'd lied, dammit. She was bleeding through the dressing. Before I could say anything, she disappeared down the hallway. I poked my head behind the kitchen counter. In the sink, I glimpsed Sonny's dinner plate, the pig parts sucked dry.

A light flicked on in a back room. "Croft," Vega called.

I followed her voice to a bedroom of purple walls and thick black drapes. She nodded at the king-sized bed. Sonny lay spread-eagle in its center, a blade-shaped hole puncturing his crusty chest. With the death blow, centuries of aging had collapsed back into his body, claiming him in an instant. He looked like a mummy.

"Any idea who would want him dead?" Vega asked.

I circled the bed, remembering what Arnaud had told me on the pier: *Sonny has been involved with many people. And for some, that's a problem.* "The question is why someone would want him dead *now*."

"Maybe someone observed our earlier visits," Vega said.

"Yeah, that's what I'm thinking."

I leaned over Sonny's body. Several small perforations pocked his face. I reached into my coat, pulled out my notepad, and drew the pencil from the spiral binding. With the pencil's sharpened tip, I probed a perforation on his cheek until I encountered something hard.

"What the hell are you doing?" Vega asked.

I pried a small shot free and placed it in my palm for Vega to see. "Silver ammo," I said. "I'll bet you anything it's the same ammo that did damage to Blondie earlier tonight."

"The vampire hunters?"

I nodded, thinking of Bullet's pump-action shotgun. "Did Hoffman know we interviewed Sonny?"

"He knew about our first interview, yeah. I told him before he went off in search of the plans for Ferguson Towers." Vega's eyebrows crushed down as she made the connection. "That means he turned around and informed the person who hired the vampire hunters."

"The client must have thrown in a bonus for Sonny."

"Kill the hybrid, kill its origin story," Vega said.

"Tells me someone wants to bury the matter in the worst way." A disturbing thought came to me. "Did Hoffman know about our trip to the boarding school or to Lady Bastet?"

"I didn't tell anyone about those."

"Good. Let's keep it that way." The world wasn't going to miss Sonny, but I didn't want innocents becoming targets. "Let's head down to Sonny's office. I want to check out those files."

"Why? All he has down there are names and tax IDs. They won't mean anything to us. The whole point of coming here was to get *him* to identify her." She shot Sonny's corpse an exasperated look that seemed to blame him for his own death.

"Well, we won't know unless we look."

"What do you know?" I said, stooped in front of the file cabinet drawer labeled *2001*.

"What?" Vega came up behind me.

"The entire second half of the year is missing."

"Probably when Alexandra's mother started here," Vega said. "The mysterious client had the vampire hunters grab six months' worth of hires to bury the name he or she was trying to hide."

I lifted out the files for the first half of the year.

"What are you doing?" Vega asked.

"Here." I handed half of the files to her. "Look for any unusual last names. Dancers who would be easy to track down. If they were hired before Alexandra's mother, they might still have been here when she came on board. They might be able to give us a name. We can show them the photo of Alexandra. Seems she inherited her mother's good looks. She sure doesn't resemble Sonny."

"A blessing for her," Vega muttered.

We carried the files to Sonny's desk and set up on either side.

I was halfway through the March hires when a name jumped out at me.

"Hey," I said. "That dancer who came into the office earlier today. What did Sonny call her?"

Vega grimaced. "You mean besides 'sugar'? Casey."

"There's a Casey right here. And didn't Sonny say she'd been with him for almost twenty years?"

At that moment, the door to the office opened, and the six-and-a-half-foot bouncer who had admitted us poked his head in. "You two gonna be in here much longer?"

"As long as it takes," Vega told him.

"It's just..." The bouncer scratched his curly hair and glanced behind him. "I know you're police and all, but the boss don't like people nosing around his stuff. He might smile and play nice when you're here, but he takes it out on the rest of us when you're not. He's got a temper like a pit bull."

"I don't think that's going to be a problem anymore," I said.

"Where can we find Casey?" Vega asked.

"Casey? She worked a double today. She's in the dressing room on a smoke break."

"Can you ask her to come in here?" Vega said.

"I can ask."

The bouncer disappeared. A minute later, Casey stood in the doorway in a pink silk robe, her red hair pinned up in a messy pile. She placed a hand on a cocked hip, a stench of cigarette smoke and perfume radiating off her.

"What?" she demanded.

Vega gestured to the chair next to mine. "Have a seat."

"Why?"

"Relax," Vega said. "We just want to ask you a couple questions."

Casey shot me a sour smile as she landed in the chair.

"Is your full name Casey Lusk?" Vega asked.

"What if it is?"

"Do you remember when you were hired?"

"No."

"Does March 2001 ring a bell?"

"Not really." She crossed her long legs.

"A young woman was hired shortly after you," Vega said, pulling out Alexandra's photo and placing it on the desk in front of Casey. "She would have looked like this, but with hair to her waist."

Casey scowled at the photo.

"You knew her?" I took out my notepad.

"She played little Miss Innocent, but she didn't fool me. Manipulative piece of trash. Had Sonny wrapped around her pinky finger. She even got him to propose to her." She let out a sharp laugh. "Can you imagine that? Sonny? Married?"

"Can you give us a name?" I asked.

"Chastity Summers," Casey said with exaggerated sweetness.

I jotted the name down and looked up to find Vega's dark eyes staring back at me. I nodded. We might just have connected the final dot. But man, the detective was not looking good. Way too pale.

"Whatever became of Chastity?" Vega asked.

Casey shrugged. "Hell if I know. She was here for about six months and then took off. Sonny moped for the next year. Serves him right, the dumb bastard. Tried to warn him she would rip his heart out."

"And she never showed up here again?" I asked.

"Nope."

"Do you know anyone who might've kept up with her?"

"Kept up with her? We all hated her." Casey glanced around before leaning forward and lowering her voice to a husky whisper. "But I know for a fact Sonny hired some sort of private investigator to look for her. Didn't find shit." She gave a self-satisfied snort as she sat back.

"Thanks for talking with us," Vega said. "You've been very helpful."

"That's it?" Having attained a degree of authority, Casey was reluctant to relinquish her chair. I felt a prick of pity for the aging dancer as she stood slowly, tugging her robe by its fraying hem.

"If anything else comes up, we'll be in touch," I assured her.

After Casey left, I looked at Vega. "Think we have enough?"

"I'd like more info on this Chastity," she said, "but if a P.I. couldn't track her down almost two decades ago, I doubt we'd do any better."

"Lady Bastet said she's in the city."

"Still a needle in a haystack, especially since Chastity wouldn't be Chastity anymore."

"Think she changed her name?" I asked.

"I'm sure of it." Vega spun her chair from the desk and stood. "Let's go out and see if we played Arnaud's game to his satisfaction." She took two steps toward the door and collapsed.

I caught her before she hit the floor and lowered her the rest of the way, one hand under her head. The stomach of her sweatshirt featured a fist-sized spot of blood. I didn't have to look underneath to know the bandage was a sopping mess.

"Detective," I whispered, patting her cheek.

Her eyelids fluttered open, and I watched her pupils sharpen. "Did I trip?"

"You passed out. You're running on empty."

"I'm fine." She sat up and blinked as though to straighten her vision. "Just stood too fast." She extended a hand for me to pull her to her feet. I complied, wrapping an arm around her waist to steady her.

"Would you stop?" she said, elbowing me away.

"Would you let me help you?" I cried. "You can't do this alone."

She wheeled on me, staggering slightly before regaining her footing. Though her body was about to wilt, her dark eyes burned with emotion. "We'll worry about me after this is over. But I am *not* going out there to face the creatures holding my son with you propping me up. Got it?"

I relented with a sigh. "Am I allowed to catch you, at least?"

Vega turned and opened the office door onto the beating lights of the club. I followed, hoping to hell we had met Arnaud's terms. Vega wasn't going to be able to hold out much longer.

30

We emerged from the club and looked up and down the block of flashing marquees and pay-by-the hour hotels. If blood slaves were lurking among the skeletal street walkers, I couldn't spot them.

"Arnaud!" Vega called, her voice hoarse.

When no one appeared after several moments, I hooked a thumb toward the sedan. "He might want to meet someplace less public. Why don't we drive a few blocks and park?"

Vega shivered as she nodded.

"I'm going to have to ask for your keys, though," I said.

"So you can finish the demolition job you started at the Towers?"

I *had* banged up her car pretty badly. But Vega relented,

slapping the key chain into my palm. She shivered again as she dropped into the passenger seat, eyes closed, the cuffs of the sweatshirt I'd loaned her balled inside her fists.

I cranked the engine and turned up the heat. I was about to pull the gearshift into drive when I caught the silhouette of someone's head and shoulders in the backseat. I wheeled with my revolver.

"At ease," Zarko said, almond eyes glinting red in the darkness.

My heart slammed through my breaths. "You could've given us a little warning."

"I just thought the detective would want to meet out of the cold," Arnaud said through his blood slave. "She is not looking at all well, is she?"

I peeked over at Vega, whose eyes remained closed.

"Chastity Summers," she said. "That's the name of the mother."

"*Was* the name of the mother," Zarko corrected her. "But I think you know that."

Rage burned through me. "Can't you see the condition she's in?"

He gave a mysterious smile. "But you are so very close."

"To what?" I shouted.

"The truth."

"Look." I paused to control my voice. "Just release her son, let her get some medical care. We'll continue the search. We'll find out who this Chastity Summers is. You have our word."

"Amend the original agreement?" Zarko chuckled. "I wouldn't think of it. Besides, it would seem we are in a race against someone intent on keeping that information in the dark, no?"

"Look at her, for God's sake. The situation's changed."

"No, Mr. Croft. The situation has only become more interesting. I have placed associates of my own at stake. I have even lost a few. It would only seem fair that you have skin in the game as well."

"Is that what this is to you? A goddamned *game?*"

"A figure of speech, Mr. Croft, I assure you." The smile on his lips thinned. "The revealed truth would have profound consequences. Why, it could change the very landscape of this city. Why do you think someone is going to such great lengths to suppress it?"

"But you already *know* the truth," I said.

"A truth I can do nothing with at the moment."

"Why not?" I demanded.

"Perhaps I have already hedged my bets, and there is no gain in it for me. I am an investor after all. And the best investors cover all sides of a trade. *Or...*" The word lingered, teasing, on his tongue. "Or perhaps it is that you are not the only ones bound by an agreement."

Vega stirred in the passenger seat. "Does this have something to do with you being hired to protect her daughter?"

"Very astute, Detective. There is hope for your son yet."

I expected the not-so-veiled threat to light a fire in Vega, but she remained slumped against the seat back, eyes closed. With her blood loss, everything probably seemed dull and hazy. "He's still safe?" she asked.

"Sleeping like an angel."

"And once we find out who Chastity Summers is," I said, "you'll release him?"

"Yes, but you should be quick. While the boy sleeps, a little blue vessel on the side of his neck pulsates away. My associates have taken an interest in that conduit of precious fluid. I have control over them, of course. But as that interest turns to real hunger, why, a brief lapse on my part..."

"If he's hurt," Vega mumbled, "I will hunt you down myself, and I will kill you."

"What energy!" Zarko said, laughing. "Yes, take that spirit and rally yourself. I would hate to see you fail at this late stage and with so much at stake. The truth is not as distant as it might seem—especially for you, Detective. Find out who wants the creature dead, and the answer will reveal itself like a magician's coin."

In a burst of cold wind, the rear door opened and closed, and the backseat was empty.

I sighed and looked over at Vega, who was fumbling for her smartphone.

"Who are you calling?"

"Hoffman," she said. "Need to find out who he's been supplying info to."

"Wait," I said, holding out a hand just enough to freeze her display. "Let's think about this for a minute. If Hoffman knows he's doing something below board, he'll deny it. Not only that, he'll tip off whoever he's informing. Instead of confronting Hoffman, what if we laid a trap?"

"What kind of trap?"

"We debrief him on the investigation, leaving out the parts about the boarding school and Lady Bastet, of course. Tell him we're close to knowing the mother's identity. We'll put together a file of fake names and contact info—leads you'll instruct Hoffman to follow up on. Whoever Hoffman's talking to is going to want that file. We'll see what Hoffman does with it."

"Tail him?"

"Even better, I can infuse the file with a hunting spell."

She nodded weakly. "Fine, but you were right, dammit. I'm not going to make it without some blood."

"There's a medical center a few blocks away."

Vega shook her head and scrolled through the contacts on her smartphone. "No hospitals. I have an EMT friend who owes me a favor." She tapped a number and activated the speaker. "Larry," she said when a man's voice answered. "It's Detective Vega. You on duty?"

"Yeah, what's up?" he said.

"I'm gonna need an ambulance for an emergency blood transfusion. B positive. One unit should do it. Is there somewhere I can meet you?"

The voice hesitated. "You're bringing the victim to us?"

"I am the victim."

"Oh, geez. Yeah, yeah. Where are you now?"

"Near Forty-second and Broadway."

"Okay, how about in the valet garage across from Grand Central?"

"How soon can you be there?"

"I'm headed there now." The sound of a siren rose through the speaker.

Vega hung up. "You heard the man."

The ambulance was already waiting, its rear doors open, when we pulled into the garage. I parked and ran around to Vega's side before she attempted to stand. A portly man in blue coveralls and with graying hair appeared from the ambulance and jogged up to her other side.

"Christ, kiddo, what in the hell happened to you?"

"Stopped a bullet with my stomach," Vega said as she staggered between us toward the ambulance. "Thanks to my vest, it wasn't deep. But I lost some blood. Everson removed the projectile."

"All right," Larry said. "While the drip's going, I'll stitch up the wound."

We helped her up into the ambulance, where she collapsed onto a waiting gurney, the interior lights bleaching her remaining color. While Larry busied himself with the IV bags, Vega clutched my coat sleeve.

"This is gonna take about an hour," she said. "If you need to do something for your friend, go ahead."

My gaze dropped to the spreading stain in her sweatshirt.

"That's an order," she added.

I pulled up a mental map of Manhattan. The fae townhouse was a straight shot north, about thirty blocks. I could be there in under ten.

"You sure?" I asked.

She shoved my arm toward the door. "Go."

"All right, but..." I patted my coat pockets until I felt the pager in its iron case. "Call if you need me back before then."

She nodded, then looked down at where Larry was inserting a line into the crook of her left elbow.

I checked my watch: 2:40 a.m. I hopped from the ambulance and jogged to the sedan. As I wheeled the car around, I caught the first droplets of blood filling the tube to Vega's arm.

"Fifty-nine minutes to find Caroline and make it back," I whispered.

I sped from the lot.

31

I pulled up a half block from the townhouse and parked. When I squinted, the narrow domicile across the street wobbled into focus for a few seconds before the veil pushed my gaze to the neighboring address. I squinted again. Light glowed from the four ascending windows, which was no surprise. The nighttime enhanced fae magic, and so the fae were more active at night.

Active enough to show their faces outside the townhouse, I hoped.

Without time to cook up a spell, I lacked the ability to break through the threshold. That left a stakeout. As I replaced the silver bullets in my revolver with iron ones, I replayed the sequence of events surrounding Caroline's disappearance, starting with the gala.

Angelus pursues Caroline and asks to speak with her. She wants nothing to do with him until he mentions her father. While they're talking, I catch something about "a fair exchange." I head out with Hoffman to the crime scene, and Caroline and Angelus apparently leave the gala together, Angelus casting a glamour to look like me. The next morning, Moretti's men come to my apartment, looking for her. That they were hired by Caroline's father tells me she really is missing. I get the address to the fae townhouse from the night hag, only to be stonewalled by the butler. But he knows where Angelus is, and probably Caroline. Fast forward to the meeting with Lady Bastet and "She's no longer in this world."

That Caroline might be in the faerie world was nothing to feel optimistic about, but it sure as hell beat the alternative. Judging by the secrecy of the townhouse, and the sudden burst of voices I'd heard while talking to the butler, I was willing to bet there was a portal to that world beyond the threshold.

I clicked the cylinder of my revolver home and scanned the street in front of the townhouse. I just needed someone to show up who could give me some damned answers.

"Well, what do we have here?" I whispered.

A Clydesdale clopped into view from down the street, pulling a dark carriage. In front of the townhouse, the horse slowed to a stop. A man in a black top hat and cape climbed down from the driver's bench and opened the carriage door. Laughter bubbled out as a well-heeled man and woman appeared on the carriage's far side. Their formal dress and the woman's blatant show of jewelry, coupled with their being out so late, screamed "fae."

I climbed over the sedan's console and exited on the passenger side. Using the cars parked curbside as cover, I slinked along the sidewalk until I was across the street from the carriage.

The man handed something to the driver, who bowed, climbed back onto the carriage, and snapped the reins. The horse and carriage moved away, leaving the frosted-haired couple giggling on the sidewalk. The woman took the man's arm in an exaggerated stumble, and the two broke into louder laughter.

Drunk fae. Even better.

I waited for the sound of the horse to diminish before jogging across the street. I pulled up behind the couple and drew my revolver.

"Stop right there," I said.

The couple looked at one another, then wheeled clumsily.

"This thing's loaded with cold iron," I said, "so I want you to listen."

"And who are you?" the man asked in a vaguely English accent.

"I'm looking for someone. I'll release you as soon as you can tell me where she is."

Their drunkenness seemed to have subdued their magic as much as their reaction times. They continued to blink at one another and at my revolver, their faces a blend of surprise and amusement.

"Well, are you going to tell us who you're looking for?" the man asked.

"Caroline Reid."

The woman's face brightened. "Caroline Reid?"

"You know her?" I asked.

"Oh, yes. A lovely, *lovely* young woman." She turned to the man. "You remember her, honey? She came over to interview you about your time in Mayor Alito's administration."

"What?" I said.

"For a book she was writing," the woman said, wavering on her feet. "We have a signed copy on our..." She hiccupped and circled a hand as she tried to come up with the word. "...our *mantel.*"

I looked from the woman to the man. *Were* they fae?

"Who are you?" I asked.

At that moment, the door to the townhouse opened, and a pale rectangle of light spilled into the street. I squinted at the slight figure bisecting the doorway. "Mr. and Mrs. Darby? Is everything all right?"

I couldn't make out his face, but I recognized his voice. The butler.

"Oh, fine, Jasper," the woman slurred. "We were just chatting with our new friend here."

"Hey!" I called, swinging my revolver toward the butler. "Stay right there!"

"I suggest you come inside," the butler said to the couple. "It *is* late after all."

The well-dressed man staggered as he turned to me and bowed. "Very nice to meet you."

"Yes," the woman called over a shoulder. "And please tell Caroline hello for us. Such a dear."

I tried to climb after them, but I couldn't seem to lift my feet, which had suddenly taken on weight. The same leaden weight forced my revolver arm down until the weapon clicked against a stone step. I watched the couple disappear through the light and into the fae townhouse. The oppressive weight dropped me to both hands and knees, and I tried to crawl. Soon, I couldn't even do that.

"Good evening, Mr. Croft," the butler said with stern finality.

"Wait..." My lungs could barely fill the word. I strained to breathe against the growing pressure.

The butler receded into the townhouse, the light narrowing until the door clicked closed. Whatever enchantment he had cast released me, and I could inhale a full breath again.

I stood from the steps and whispered an incantation to test my magic. The barest force rippled through me. My powers were in remission again. Fan-flipping-tastic.

"Thought we might find you here," a stuffy voice said.

I wheeled to see Floyd and Whitey stalking up the sidewalk, Floyd with a triangular cast over his busted nose. Both were wielding their vintage Colts. I backed away, wondering how in the hell they had known to come here, when I remembered my conversation with Mr. Reid in the Escalade. I'd given him the street.

"That was some stunt you pulled on the pier," Floyd said. "And getting your buddies to jump in?"

I glanced around as Moretti's men strode nearer, but something told me Arnaud's blood slaves wouldn't be bailing me out this time. Once Vega received her transfusion, she would be able to connect the final dot, find out who the mother was. Arnaud didn't need me anymore.

"This is the house," I said, pointing up the steps. "This is where that guy took Caroline."

"You're wasting your breath." Floyd raised his gun.

"Why the hell else would I be standing out here at three in the morning?"

"The hell should I know? To make yourself look innocent? Anyway, I don't know what house you're even talking about."

I glanced over. *Damn. The veiling spell.*

"Drop the gun," Whitey said in his raspy voice.

"Sorry, guys. I'm not leaving here until I find Caroline."

"Drop the gun," Whitey repeated, cocking his hammer.

"Yeah, I heard you the first time. But I'm pretty sure Mr. Reid doesn't want a dead body attached to his name."

"Yeah, but Mr. Moretti does," Floyd said. "You just popped up on our list."

"Mr. Moretti?"

"Shut it," Whitey said to his partner. I read the narrow look he shot Floyd. They were planning to collect twice on me. First from Mr. Reid for extracting the information on his daughter's whereabouts, and then from Mr. Moretti for delivering a hit on me. I adjusted my slick grip on my revolver.

"You want to know where Caroline is?" I nodded past them. "Ask him."

Still wary from their surprise beat-down at the pier, Floyd and Whitey chanced peeks behind them. But I wasn't bluffing. Someone was walking up, and that someone was Angelus.

He was wearing the style of suit I'd seen him in at the gala, formal and dark, the shirt underneath his jacket open at the collar. He approached from the direction of Central Park, as though returning from a nighttime stroll—completely insane for anyone but a powerful supernatural. I squinted past him in the faint hope of seeing Caroline, but he was alone.

A half block from us, Angelus slowed, but he didn't stop. I trained my revolver on him. Moretti's men glanced between us, their guns still on me, but their faces now squinting with uncertainty.

Angelus drew up to within a few feet of us and stopped. "Is that Everson?"

"You know damn well who I am," I said. "You assumed my appearance when you left the gala last night. What did you do with Caroline?"

"Caroline is fine," he replied neutrally.

"I didn't ask how she was. I asked what you did with her."

"I coerced Caroline into nothing."

Despite my cold fury, I noted the precision with which Angelus was answering my questions. The fae were master deceivers, but they couldn't lie. "Where is she?" I asked, stepping closer, revolver pointed at his chest.

Floyd and Whitey stood off to either side, eyeing our exchange.

Angelus's face, a handsome bronze when he had arrived, now greened a shade. He was reacting to the iron bullets in the revolver. I watched for the least sign he was preparing to cast magic.

"Where is she?" I repeated.

"Caroline is home," Angelus said.

"Bullshit, buddy," Floyd cut in. "Whitey and I were just over there."

"Where's home?" A sickness crawled around my belly as the first line of an obituary scrolled through my head: *Caroline Reid was taken home to be with her Lord on the night of...*

Angelus looked at the three guns aimed at him and raised his gaze to the townhouse. "It's late, gentlemen." His slate-blue eyes fell back to mine. "And I'm sure we all have places to be."

"You don't get it." I stepped over to cut him off. "You're not going anywhere until you tell me where Caroline is and how I can reach her. Try to force your way past me, and I will shoot you. I know for a fact cold iron kills your kind, especially when it's blown through your heart."

"Yeah," Floyd put in.

"You will not kill me, Everson Croft," Angelus said calmly.

"Oh, no?" I applied pressure to the trigger.

"Your magic is weak, but I can read it like the stars. You have never used it to perform ill. And as goes the magic, so goes the man. Now if you will excuse me." He raised a hand as though to step past me.

I fired twice. First into Whitey's chest and then Floyd's. They dropped like sacks to the pavement. I trained the gun back on Angelus.

"This ain't magic."

Angelus studied the two dead gangsters. "I do not wish to harm you, Everson."

"That's pretty funny, considering which end of the gun you're standing on. I'm through screwing around. I catch even a whiff of enchantment coming off you, and you'll be joining them." My heart slammed harder at what I was about to ask. "Is Caroline still alive?"

"Goodnight, Everson."

Angelus stepped past me, and I squeezed the trigger. Nothing happened. When I squeezed again, my revolver moved. I looked down and hollered. In the place of the revolver, a hermit crab-like creature with a black shell clung to my hand, its hairy legs pricking my skin.

I swore and tried to shake the creature off me. Angelus's magic was so subtle I hadn't felt the transformation. The creature hit the pavement and scuttled away into the shadows.

I wheeled and lunged for Angelus. If he reached the door, I'd lose my only lead to Caroline. My fingers touched the back of his jacket, but before I could grasp it, the material turned as slippery as a buttered pan. My fingers scrabbled against it, and I fell forward onto the sidewalk.

Angelus jogged up the steps.

Something in my pocket dug against my hip as I rolled and pushed myself to my feet.

Wait. The pager.

I reached into the pocket and gripped the casing. Cold iron. I yanked out the pager and winged it at Angelus. The pager struck him in the low back. He grunted and seized the spot with both hands as though he'd blown a lumbar disk. The pager clattered to the bottom of the steps. I picked it up mid-stride, palmed it in my right fist, and took the steps three at a time.

"You're not going anywhere," I said.

When Angelus twisted around, I shot the iron-loaded fist into his mouth. Something broke beneath my knuckle. He clutched my jacket. I reared back and threw another punch. The looping blow caught him behind the ear. We went over together, tumbling down the steps. When we hit the sidewalk, I straddled him and mashed the pager against his cheek.

"I want answers, goddammit," I panted.

Angelus squinted up at me from a scraped and bleeding face that had taken on a blue hue. Though the iron was dissolving his glamour, he still bore the sharp angles and self-possession of royalty.

"Where is Caroline? And I don't want to hear that she's *home*. I want a fucking location, an address."

"She's where she belongs."

"See? That doesn't help me, either."

I pressed the pager harder until Angelus hissed and smoke began to curl from his face. When his pupils shrank, I noticed a pale light had fallen over us. The door to the townhouse had opened.

"Everson," someone said, but it wasn't the butler.

A hand to my brow, I squinted up to find the light filtering around an angelic being.

My breath caught. "Caroline?"

32

She wore an airy gown, a white cape fluttering from her shoulders. Light from the townhouse shone through her golden, brushed-down hair, but it seemed longer than Caroline's. She stepped forward until she stood at the top of the steps.

"Caroline, is that you?"

I pushed myself off Angelus and climbed the steps cautiously. Fae power glimmered around the woman, something I had *definitely* never sensed around Caroline.

I came to within two steps of her and stopped. It was Caroline. And yet … it wasn't.

She regarded me with blue-green eyes, almost too intense to meet.

"Are you all right?" I asked.

"You shouldn't be here, Everson."

"What's happened? What have they done to you?"

"I'm fulfilling an agreement made on my behalf."

"Agreement? By who?"

"My mother."

She had never mentioned her mother before. And what connection would her mother have had with the faeries? Unless...

"She was a fae? Your mother?"

"*Is* a fae, Everson."

"So you're, what, half-fae?"

"Yes, but I relinquished that part of my heritage as a girl."

I grappled with the seismic revelation. "I ... I had no idea."

"Just as I had no idea the power you wield. But I can see it around you now, a living force."

"I meant to tell you."

"As I meant to tell you." Her voice carried a hint of sorrow, as though something had been lost.

I glanced back at Angelus, who remained down on the sidewalk.

"What was the agreement?" I asked Caroline.

"Not now, Everson. You should leave."

"Please. I've been worried sick about you."

She studied my eyes before dropping her gaze with a sigh. "My mother is royalty. She rules a kingdom parallel to New York. She met my father when the fae were active in human politics. They fell in love, they had me. But the fae can be whimsical. She left my father without his knowing what she was. As a part-fae, I had a choice—to embrace my fae nature or become fully human. I chose the second, severing all connections with that world. For years I had no contact with my mother."

"What changed?"

"My father's sick. He was diagnosed with cancer this summer. He'd been undergoing aggressive treatment, but the cancer wouldn't budge. Angelus told me my mother was willing to heal him, but on the condition that I honor the agreement she made before I chose mortality."

A cold shadow moved through me. "What agreement?"

Caroline's eyes shifted past me. Angelus joined her on the top step, his glamour restored. "That we be wed," Angelus said, slipping an arm around her waist, "as it was decided."

I moved my gaze between them. "Wait, you're *married?*"

Caroline tilted her head and touched my arm, which was answer enough. That was what Angelus must have meant at the gala by "a fair exchange."

"How?" My heart felt as though it had been punched numb. "When?"

"I made the decision after you left the party. To reclaim my fae nature and accede to the arrangement my mother had made. I wanted to tell you, but the window was closing. The ceremony had to be performed before the full moon, and there were days of preparation involved."

"Days? But the gala was last night."

"The wheels of time rotate differently in our worlds. A day here could be a week there. I thought I would be able to complete the ceremonies and return before anyone knew I'd been gone."

"Well, why the deception?" I demanded. "Why did pretty boy here assume my form? What in the hell was that about?" I wasn't sure whether I was more angry at Angelus now or Caroline.

"That was my idea," she said. "Angelus has advised the

opposition, and I didn't want word getting back to Mayor Lowder or my father that I'd been seen leaving with him. I hope that didn't create any problems for you."

"Problems? Oh, just a few."

"I'm sorry," she said.

"Can I talk to you alone for a minute?" I asked.

Caroline looked over at Angelus—her frigging *husband*—and nodded that it was all right. I bristled as he kissed the side of her head and then walked into the townhouse, closing the door behind him. Without the backlighting, Caroline seemed almost mortal again.

"Are you sure you know what you're doing?"

"It wasn't an easy decision, of course. But yes."

"I don't know a lot about the fae," I said, "but they have a reputation as manipulators. How do you know they didn't give your father his illness? I mean, maybe your mother's taken a fresh interest in New York politics. If so, I can't think of a more valuable asset than you."

"Believe me, Everson, I thought about all of that." She lowered herself to sit, her gown spilling down the steps like mist. "But it wouldn't have changed the fact that my father was dying."

I sat beside her and gazed out over the still street. We could have been back on the balcony overlooking Central Park the night before, all of this talk of the faerie realm and arranged marriages a distant dream—or nightmare.

"Do you love him?" I asked.

"I told you, it was arranged."

"Why Angelus?"

"His father has a small kingdom in a realm parallel to upper Manhattan."

"Two kingdoms on Manhattan Island?"

"Several kingdoms, in fact. The island is much larger in the faerie realm, more like a small continent. But the societies are feudal, arranged marriages between ruling families common. Angelus may seem cold and formal, but he's … he's decent."

"I bet he is," I grumbled. "So now what?"

"I'll have duties in the faerie realm as well as here." She turned up her palms. "This is all new to me, Everson. I guess I'll just take it a day at a time."

"And your job at the college?"

"I'll keep that for the time being."

I swallowed. "And us?"

When she looked over at me, her eyes glimmered with emotion. "I'm married now."

I nodded vaguely and dropped my gaze to my hands. *Figures. The only woman I really loved as an adult.*

The pager went off, Vega signaling she was ready.

"Well…" I slapped my thighs and rose. "I guess that's that." As incredible as it seemed, I had forgotten about Floyd and Whitey until their fallen bodies entered my peripheral vision. "Just do me a favor and let your father know you're all right. I think he was worried about you."

"I will."

I descended the step. "Goodnight," I said without looking back.

"Everson."

I didn't stop. She caught up to me on the sidewalk and grasped my arm.

"Look," I said, turning. "You don't have to—"

Her lips pressed against mine, silencing me. I tasted the subtle power of the fae, like spring water and honeydew. Her soft hands held my cheeks. I raised my own hands, clasping the backs of hers. Worlds spun around us.

When at last Caroline broke away, tears shone on her face.

"I am sorry," she whispered.

"Yeah. So am I."

She gave a final sad smile before climbing the steps and disappearing into the fae house.

33

When I swung the sedan into the parking garage across from Grand Central Station, Detective Vega was sitting on the rear step of the ambulance, a blue blanket over her shoulders, Larry the EMT beside her. I pulled up in front of them and got out to open the passenger side door.

"Feeling better?" I asked.

Vega shed the blanket and climbed into the car. "Good enough."

"She let me give her a unit of red and half a bag of saline," Larry said. "She could really use another of each, but she promised me she'll go to an ER whenever you two wrap up whatever you're doing."

"And we're off the books on this one?" Vega asked.

"What books?" Larry made a shooing gesture with his hands. "Go on, get out of here. Go save New York."

We pulled out of the garage and onto Lexington Avenue.

"I've already called Hoffman," Vega said. "He's going to meet us at the office downtown. How did everything go with—"

"She's fine," I interrupted.

"So she wasn't missing?"

"Yes. Well, no." I stared at the empty road ahead. "It's complicated."

"O-o-okay."

I changed the subject. "Did Hoffman sound suspicious when you talked to him?"

"No, but he seemed a little too interested when I told him I had info on the creature's mother. Probably can't wait to get his grubby hands on it so he can run it to whoever he's informing."

"I think it's Mr. Moretti."

"The washed-up gangster?"

"I ran into a couple of his men just now," I said. "One of them let slip that I'd popped up on Mr. Moretti's 'list,' which I can only assume meant his hit list. Think about it. Someone has Sonny killed but without knowing what the vampire might have told us. So he has to play it safe—"

"And eliminate us, too," Vega finished.

"But I think our plan buys us time. Mr. Moretti's going to want to know exactly how much we know. That info will be in the fake file that Hoffman will hopefully deliver to him."

Vega was silent for a moment. "Why Moretti, though?"

I'd done some thinking on the drive back from the townhouse. Lord knew I'd needed to occupy my mind with anything but the bombshell Caroline had dropped on my heart. "The hit was the first clue," I said. "I then went back over what Arnaud told us outside of Sonny's. He said, 'The truth is not as distant as it might seem, especially for you, Detective.' That last part didn't click for me at the time, but Little Italy is just a few blocks north of your office, right?"

"Moretti's fiefdom."

"And think about Arnaud's parting advice: 'Find out who wants the creature dead, and the answer will reveal itself like a magician's coin.' A coin has two sides, right? So if one side is Moretti, the other side is probably—"

"His wife," Vega said.

"I met her last night at the gala. She fit the bill. Long, auburn hair, orange-tinted irises. And she had this feral air about her, like she wasn't entirely human. That could be accounted for by werewolf blood."

"That also fits with what Lady Bastet said about her being mixed up with disreputable people. The Italian mafia isn't what it used to be, but it's still plenty criminal. And there's probably enough in the till for the wife to have helped her daughter without anyone in the organization noticing."

"I didn't sense a lot of love between Mr. and Mrs. Moretti last night, either," I said.

"But why is he so desperate to cover up his wife's past?"

I shrugged. "To protect their reputation? The man's been trying to wheedle his way back into the upper echelons of organized crime in the city—*honorable* organized crime, as he probably thinks of it. Maybe he considers having a homicidal creature for a daughter a handicap."

"Maybe," Vega said, but without sounding convinced.

"We'll find out for sure, in any case. What time did you tell Hoffman?"

"Four thirty."

I checked my watch. "All right. That gives us enough time to create the file and for me to put a spell..." My voice petered out as I remembered the fae's neutralizing effect on my magic. I powered down the window and aimed my cane at the approaching street light.

"What are you doing?" Vega asked above the roaring wind, a hand to her whipping hair.

"A test," I said. *"Vigore!"*

I watched for the street lights to rock on their wires. With even a small return of my powers, I could cast a weak hunting spell, something that might hold up provided it didn't start raining again.

The street lights erupted in an explosion of sparks. Wires snapped, and one of the traffic-light bodies plummeted onto the roof of the sedan before clunking away behind us. I drew my cane back into the car and powered up the window.

"Successful test?" Vega asked thinly.

"Yeah," I said, reflecting on Caroline's parting kiss.

I wasn't sure, but I think she had restored my powers.

"So what do we got?" Hoffman asked, waddling into Vega's office in one of his polyester suits.

"The list of women I mentioned." Vega tossed the file of fake names and addresses onto the desk. A light blue aura that only I could see hummed around the manila folder. "I want you to follow up. They're all in the city."

Hoffman squinted over at me with naked disdain as he grabbed the file and dropped into the chair next to mine. He flipped it open and frowned over the list. "And you're sure the mother's one of these?"

"Almost positive," Vega said.

"Where'd you get the info?"

"A nightclub owner named Sonny," Vega said. "The one we talked to earlier."

Hoffman nodded and tucked the folder under an arm. "I'm on it." Halfway to the door, he stopped and turned. "Oh hey, were you able to find your kid?"

"Yeah," Vega said.

"And he's all right?"

Vega's eyes dropped to the folder. "He will be."

"Good to hear, good to hear."

I waited until Hoffman left and I heard the elevator door close behind him before holding up my trembling cane. "It's locked onto the folder."

"And I was able to pair to his cell," Vega said, showing me her smartphone.

"All right, but keep that thing away from me. I don't want to mess it up."

Vega was preparing to say something when the phone rang. She raised a finger for silence and carried the phone to the far corner of the office before activating the speaker.

Someone picked up.

"Yeah?" a man's voice asked.

"I've got the file," Hoffman said through the crackling exchange.

"Good. You know where to drop it."

"I'll have it there in a few," Hoffman said.

Vega swore under her breath as she put the phone away.

I stood. "Sounds like the hunt is on."

Vega drove while I aimed my cane out the window, calling out the turns. The streets were practically deserted, one of the reasons for the hunting spell. Hoffman would have spotted us had we tried to tail him.

The spell directed us into Little Italy and down Broome Street, confirming my suspicions.

"There he is," Vega said, easing off the gas. Blocks ahead, a blue sedan was turning left, brake lights glimmering red off the still-wet asphalt.

"He's already made the drop," I said.

"How do you know?"

"Because my cane's pulling us to that corner."

In fact, my cane was jerking like it had hooked a marlin. I choked up my grip to keep the spell from yanking the cane from my hands.

Vega pulled up to the corner and idled.

"The mailbox," I said, cane aimed at the squat blue receptacle bolted into the concrete.

"All right, we'll put eyes on it." She drove through the

intersection and U-turned at the next one, parking in front of the rolled-down steel door of a butcher shop about a half block from the box.

She killed the lights and engine.

"The son of a bitch lied to my face," she said.

"Hoffman?"

"You were there. He looked me straight in the eyes and told me he had nothing to do with Moretti." She shook her head. "And I trusted him. When this is over, his ass is history."

"I know I don't consult on hirings and firings, but that sounds fine with me."

"Shh," Vega said, sliding down in her seat.

I did the same and peeked over the dashboard. Headlights were swimming into view from straight ahead. We slid even lower as the car behind the lights took shape—a classic sports car. At the corner with the mailbox, the car cut right and droned out of sight. I glanced over at Vega as I scooted back up.

"False alarm?"

"Stay down," she said. "The driver's probably circling to make sure he's not being tailed."

She was right. The same headlights reappeared a minute later. This time, the car pulled up to the corner. A man in a hat and coat got out of the passenger's seat, looked around, and hunkered on the far side of the mailbox. Seconds later, he stood and returned to the car, a familiar-looking folder in hand.

"Recognize him?" I asked.

"Yeah, it's one of Moretti's men. How's your spell holding up?"

"Should be good for another thirty." I watched the car turn left onto Bowery.

"Moretti's place isn't far from here, but they'll probably tool around the neighborhood for a little to make sure no one's following."

We gave them a few minutes' head start before Vega pulled from the curb.

My cane tugged us north onto Bowery. Following a couple of jags, we ended up on Second Avenue, skirting the worst of the East Village. Blocks away, ghouls rummaged through garbage piles. They were getting bolder, something that was going to become a problem for Mayor Lowder as eyewitness accounts increased and more New Yorkers went missing.

When the spires of Midtown rose around us, Vega asked, "Still north?"

I could hear the uncertainty in her voice. We were miles from Little Italy. "Until my spell says otherwise."

Her smartphone rang, and she pulled it from her pocket. "Vega," she said.

On the other end, I picked up what sounded like a woman's urgent voice.

Vega squinted as she listened, as though trying to hear better. "Where are you?" she asked. The woman's voice was interrupted by a shotgun blast before she resumed.

"*Shit,*" Vega spat, more to herself, it seemed. "All right. Hang on. We're on our way." She threw the phone onto the dash and performed a vicious U-turn, mashing me against the door. "That was your vampire-hunter friend Blade," she said when we'd straightened.

"Blade? What's going on?"

"They've got the creature pinned in a basement at Frederick Douglass Apartments, a project just north of Ferguson Towers."

I glanced back in the direction we had been heading. "But ... the file." I had very nearly said *your son.*

"The hunters can't stop the creature. She's out of control. And right now Blade and her friends are the only thing standing between her and the thousand-odd residents of Frederick Douglass. They need backup."

"How did they even know where to find her?"

"They picked up some chatter on their police scanner. Someone called in a murder in progress. Another junkie."

"That's what Alexandra came to the city for," I decided. "Heroin."

"What?"

"Well, blood and heroin. She's targeting junkies, not because they're low-hanging fruit, but because she's feeding an addiction. Remember the victims at Ferguson Towers? The way the blood had been lapped up? I'm betting it was because the blood had been freshly injected."

"Great," Vega said. "So we've got a werewolf-vampire hybrid who also happens to be a raging addict."

I dumped the iron ammo from my revolver onto my lap and began pushing silver bullets into the cylinders. As I worked, I noticed that Alexandra's photo had slipped from the file on the dashboard such that the young woman seemed to be looking at me. I considered what Dr. Z had said about killing a hybrid: *Decapitation, baby.*

God, I hoped it wouldn't come to that.

34

We pulled up in front of a single grim housing tower. Before Vega could get out, I seized her arm.

"What are you doing?" she said.

"I want you to go back to Lady Bastet's."

"What? Why?"

"To see if she can perform another binding spell."

"Croft, the creature's killed four people that we know of, and—"

"And inside that creature is a young woman who didn't ask to become what she is," I said. "That's why there's a mother out there doing everything she can to protect her. That's why Arnaud forbade us from hunting her. The mother was afraid we would kill her."

Vega looked from me to the tower and sighed.

"I'll keep her from the residents," I said. "Wizard's honor."

"All right, but I'll hold you to that."

I got out and slammed the door closed before Vega could change her mind. As she took off west, I ran toward the tower. The front door was unlocked, the blacked-out lobby empty. I called light to my cane and found a door that opened onto a plummeting staircase. I swore as my chest began to tighten.

Why do these big showdowns always have to happen underground?

Shouts and violent clangs rose as I descended. At the bottom I made out Blade and Bullet, their headlamps slicing through the darkness. Nearby, a thick pipe braced a metal door that shook with blows and screams.

"Don't shoot," I said as Bullet swung his shotgun toward me. "It's Everson."

Bullet nodded quickly, eyes huge, and returned his aim to the door.

When I was almost to them, my light glowed over Dr. Z. He was propped against a wall behind them, the chest of his leather outfit ripped open. In his right hand, he gripped the handle of a broken ninja sword.

"What in the hell happened?" I shouted above the noise.

"What's it look like?" Blade said, her mouth bloody, samurai sword gripped in both hands. "We got our asses handed to us."

I knelt beside Dr. Z, who stared straight ahead, his breaths shocked and gasping. I moved his hand from his chest and winced at the damage. The creature had clawed him to the bone.

Hovering my cane's orb over his chest, I spoke Words of healing. A soothing force moved through me, emerging as a cottony aura that enveloped Dr. Z. His eyelids fluttered closed, arms relaxing to his sides. Caroline had not only restored my power, it seemed, but my control. I hoped both would be enough to handle the creature until Lady Bastet arrived.

I stood from Dr. Z's side and turned to the clanging door. "Is that her?"

"Yeah," Bullet said, "and the door's not going to hold her much longer."

"No?" It still looked solid to me, especially with the pipe bracing it.

"Check out the hinges," Blade said.

The hinges were as thick as toilet-paper tubes, but old. With each blow, rust sifted from them. Beyond the door, nails screamed over metal, sending a sharp shudder through me.

"We had her cornered in there," Blade said. "Bullet tossed a frag grenade into the drain she'd come up through, collapsing her escape. The creature was injured, too. Then a band of frigging blood slaves jumped us, giving the creature time to recover. She tore into Dr. Z good. We were lucky to get her off him and get ourselves the hell out of there. The only reason we haven't ditched the job is because I don't like the idea of that thing above ground."

"Yeah, that makes a few of us," I said, drawing my revolver. "Look, I've got someone on the way. Someone who may be able to transform the creature back to the human she was."

"That thing's human?" Bullet said, squinting from me to the shaking door.

"An eighteen-year-old girl," I said. "If we can keep her in there for another twenty minutes or so, we might not have to fight her."

"No argument here," Blade said.

With the next collision against the door, something snapped in the lower set of hinges. The pipe bent at its middle and shifted. *Crap.* The door wasn't going to contain her for twenty more minutes. More like two.

"Back up," I said as the door shook with another blow.

Blade eased toward the rear wall, adjusting her grip on her sword. Bullet backed up beside her, shotgun aimed at the door from his stomach. Neither of them knew I was a magic user, but they weren't exactly strangers to the supernatural. I would explain later.

Aiming my cane at the door, I murmured, *"Vigore."*

A low-level force shook from the sword and met the door as the creature collided into it again. My casting prism buckled. The bracing pipe folded at its middle and clanged to the cement floor.

"Vigore," I repeated, leaning into the increasing force flowing from my cane.

The creature's next collision broke the lower hinge and cracked the upper one. I staggered but kept my footing. The door tilted in the cement frame, creating a narrow space along the top edge. Bloody talons jabbed through the space, the creature's scream cutting deep into my ears.

"Someone get Dr. Z out of here," I shouted.

Blade cocked her head of pink-spiked hair at Bullet. "You're almost out of ammo."

"Yeah, but you gonna be okay?" he asked.

"I've got a professor-cop-wizard in my corner," she said with a smirk. "Who knew?"

Bullet holstered his shotgun on his back and scooped up Dr. Z like he weighed nothing.

The talons disappeared from above the door.

At the foot of the steps, Bullet leaned toward me and said, "Blade can get a little bold for her own good. Keep an eye on her."

I nodded quickly and braced for the next impact. The creature hit the door like a truck, destroying the upper hinge and dropping me to my knees. The door threatened to collapse. With a shouted Word I slammed it back into its frame, muscles burning, body streaming sweat.

The door rattled and shook. I had expended too much power in too little time and could feel my hold failing, could feel Thelonious whispering around my thoughts. "She's coming through," I grunted.

"Let her," Blade said from her crouch.

"Huh?"

Blade licked her pierced lips. "Just partway. If you can pin that thing in the doorway, I can make her think twice about wanting to come out the rest of the way."

The door stopped rattling. Beyond, I heard talons scratching over cement, gaining speed.

I braced as the creature collided into the door, overwhelming my counterforce. The weathered rectangle of metal crashed to the floor, and the creature filled the doorway, larger than she had appeared in the storm drain. A fang-filled jaw jutted through shanks of dark hair, her muscled body bloodied from her assault on the door. Her red gaze cut from me to Blade, a deep growl growing in her chest.

The space rang with explosions as I aimed my revolver and squeezed off two shots. Black blood burst from the creature's chest, and she recoiled.

I took aim at her heart—to stun her, if nothing else—but Blade darted into my line of fire. Silver sword flashing, she slashed the creature back into the basement room. Aluminum cans and debris scattered around their feet. The creature screamed and threw her arms up to block the slicing blows. I followed, glowing cane held aloft. But as hard and fast as Blade struck, the creature's tissue was regenerating too quickly. And the creature was no longer backing up.

"Blade!" I called. "Get behind me!"

With an angry scream, the creature swiped a clawed hand at Blade's face. Her sword flashed into a parry, catching the creature's wrist. Though talons didn't rend flesh, the force knocked Blade to the floor. The creature pounced, her jaw of nail-sharp teeth diving for Blade's throat.

"Forza dura!" I cried, aiming my cane.

The explosive force blew the creature into a graffiti-smeared wall. Blade's sword went along for the ride, clattering beside her. The creature recovered and watched us from a snarling crouch.

"Alexandra, listen to me." I pushed power into my entrancing wizard's voice, remembering how I had been able to reach Father Vick when the demon possessed him last fall. "You're a bright young woman in her final year of high school, not the monster that's taken you over. If there's the smallest part of you that can hear me, stand your ground. Don't allow these impulses to drive you. They are not you, Alexandra. Do you hear me? They are *not—*"

The creature's muscles bunched up and she sprang at me, not a spark of humanity in those glowing red eyes.

I backed from her bounds and fired twice, missing high. My heel caught what felt like a stuffed sack. I lost my balance backwards. The cane tumbled out of my grasp as I slammed into the floor. When the creature was almost on me, she buckled off course, skidding over the trash-strewn floor.

She righted herself and rounded on Blade, who had rammed into her side. A pair of spear-head-sized blades flashed in the punk rocker's hands.

"Come and get some," Blade said.

She ducked and spun beneath the creature's leap, finger blades flashing up. The creature screamed as she passed overhead, blood spraying from her stomach. Staggering to a stop, the creature turned around. Blade, whose face was stippled red, grinned back at her.

She's dancing with death, I thought.

As I pawed behind me for my cane, I saw that I had tripped over a blood slave, their bodies littering the room in shapeless mounds. Against a far wall lay the creature's latest victim, his neck obliterated.

The hybrid charged again. Blade ducked low, but the creature didn't leap this time. At the same moment I grasped my cane, her lowered head cracked into Blade's, the concussive sound resounding throughout the cement space. Blade was out before she even flopped onto her back, the finger blades spilling from her grasp.

"*Protezione!*" I shouted, bringing the cane overhead and aiming between Blade and the creature. A light shield glimmered into being, the creature's jaw smashing into it in a spray of sparks.

"*Respingere!*" I cried.

A force pulsed from the shield, shoving Blade toward the doorway and the creature deeper into the basement room. But I had sacrificed too much energy. The shield faded out. I pushed myself to my feet and stumbled forward until I was standing between Blade and the creature.

Straining to see through wisps of Thelonious's creamy white light, I aimed the revolver at the creature's head.

35

Panting, blood and adrenaline souring my mouth, I stared at the creature across the room. The creature glared back, torn and blood spattered but healing. I wasn't going to be able to stop her. Not with three bullets. Not with my powers running near empty and no useful spell items to speak of. Maybe not even with my powers running at full.

The vampire and werewolf parts of Alexandra seemed to be having a boosting effect on one other. Strength, brutality, the uncanny ability to heal... *Damn near invincible is right*, I thought, remembering what Dr. Z had told me back at their apartment.

I holstered my revolver in the front of my pants and drew my cane into sword and staff. My best chance was to keep her off balance with low-level blasts while attempting to sever her head at the neck. The hybrid's death would also mean the death of the young woman inside her, but I probably wasn't going to be alive long enough to weigh the morality of that decision.

I cleared the aluminum cans from around my feet and widened my stance.

The creature crouched back on her hands and haunches, nostrils flaring. Distracted, she broke eye contact to sniff something near her hand—a cast-off drug envelope. When she raised her eyes again, I could feel the violent hunger radiating from them, could see it in her drooling mouth.

She needed her fix.

I chanced a glance around the room. My gaze hit on more drug envelopes, cans, empty snack bags. A flicker of hope took hold inside me. I didn't have my spell items, no, but perhaps I didn't need them. *A few small investments of energy, a few lucky breaks...*

I sheathed my sword and stooped slowly to retrieve one of the drug envelopes. I ran a finger around the inside of the brown package, my skin picking up a faint coating of dust. The creature sprang.

"Fuoco!" I shouted, blowing on my coated finger.

The spell that I used on dragon sand to create fire was an amplifier. Now, a burst of energy entered each tiny granule sailing off my finger, intensifying its chemistry a hundredfold. I held my breath and scrambled back from the pluming white cloud as the creature plunged into it.

She emerged on the other side in a stagger, eyelids sagging, jaw hanging to the side. She blinked around languidly, but the muscles of her face were already beginning to tighten. I didn't have much time.

I jabbed my cane around the room, calling everything conductive. Cans, metallic snack bags, scattered change. They tumbled and skittered inward. With another incantation, I arranged the items into a casting circle around the creature, pushing as much energy into it as I dared.

The creature stared at the garbage glowing into formation around her feet, an angry roar building in her chest. Her muscles bunched up to spring.

"*Serrare,*" I called.

The circle snapped closed. The creature rebounded from a manifested wall of energy. A wall the casting symbol was now sustaining. Exhausted, swimmy-headed, I tamped down my power and leaned back against a wall. I'd gone to the very brink. One more invocation and Thelonious would come sweeping in to pay the ladies of Frederick Douglass a visit.

The debris comprising the circle rattled as the creature took up her attack against the field. As with the door, the field wouldn't be able to contain her for long, but I was shooting for long enough.

With the creature's next strike, the aluminum cans shuddered and the field wavered.

"*Cease,*" a voice commanded, its power propagating through the room.

The creature halted her assault and stared past me. I turned to find Lady Bastet stepping through the ruined doorway, Vega close behind, her pistol drawn. I laughed in weary relief.

"All hail the cavalry," I said.

In one of Lady Bastet's hands, a clutch of what appeared to be dried wolf's bane plumed smoke. In her other, she carried a bejeweled flail, with which she beat the air in rhythmic strokes.

"I bound you once," she said in ancient Egyptian, striding forward. *"I tied your lupine and vampiric natures together. Fastened them with intricate knots. As each struggled to free itself, they only pulled the knots tighter, allowing the child to live a life unencumbered. But a foreign substance broke those knots, undid what had been done, and your lupine and vampiric natures fed. By the grace of Mut, I will bind them again. I will free the girl inside."*

A snarl curling her bloody lips, the creature watched Lady Bastet circle the field.

Vega came up beside me. "Are you all right?"

"Yeah, just weak." I pulsed energy into the symbol to help sustain the casting circle. I nodded toward Blade, who was struggling to sit up, a hand to her head. "Would you mind checking on her?"

Vega nodded and went over to Blade.

"Sleep, slumber, dream," Lady Bastet chanted.

I eyed the creature, who didn't appear on the verge of any of those. But the smoke from the wolf's bane had begun to change, the strokes of the flail shaping it into small hawk-like spirits. They sprang from the air and into the casting circle. The creature screamed and swiped at them, but they evaded her hands. One by one, they thinned and slipped into her nose and mouth. In weakening fits of coughing, the creature sagged to the floor.

"Release the circle," Lady Bastet said.

I looked from the slumbering creature to her and back. "Are you sure?"

"Release it," she insisted.

I did as she said, drawing energy until the field collapsed.

Lady Bastet caught the creature's head and, kneeling, cushioned it with her thighs. She brushed the dank hair from the creature's temples, then pressed her palms to them, incanting in whispers, her head bowed.

I walked over to where Vega had helped Blade to a wall, against which the vampire hunter now sat. An angry gash cut across Blade's brow, and her eyes looked bleary. "So who are you guys?" she asked. "Magic Inc?"

"Something like that," I said. "Here."

I applied enough healing energy to Blade to stabilize her. Then we all watched Lady Bastet work. A turquoise aura enveloped the creature, who lay supine, legs straight, arms across her chest, as though the energy were swaddling her. Muscles trembled and jumped and she bared her teeth, but her eyes remained closed. I sensed the battle raging inside her, the vampire and werewolf parts of her makeup resisting Lady Bastet's magic. But Lady Bastet worked meticulously, moving from one binding to the next. What bindings the creature pulled free, Lady Bastet refastened. And I recognized the pattern of the bindings as one large plaited knot. I had a flash of an Egyptian goddess on the banks of the Nile, weaving strips of palm leaves. Now, when the creature parts of Alexandra strained, the fibers pulled taut, securing the larger knot.

At last, Lady Bastet sat back with a sigh.

"It is done," she said.

The aura dimmed, and the creature it had once held was a young woman. Her dark auburn hair was distressed, her body bruised and bleeding, but she was the girl in the photo. Alexandra Mills. Shedding my coat, I stepped forward and placed it over her. I then lifted her limp body into my arms.

"Looks like she needs a hospital," I said.

"No, the binding is too fresh," Lady Bastet said. "Western medicines may undo it. I can care for her at my place."

We left the basement, Vega helping Blade up the stairs and out to the street. When we reached the sedan, I set Alexandra in the back seat, and Lady Bastet got in on the other side.

"This is where I split," Blade said.

"Can we drop you off somewhere?" I asked.

"No need." She nodded toward an old blue paint truck rumbling toward us. As the truck pulled up beside us, Bullet leaned across the passenger seat and opened the door. Blade sheathed her samurai sword into a scabbard on her back. "A pleasure working with you," she said as she climbed into the truck. "Even if it cost us thirty grand."

"*Now* will you tell us who hired you?" I asked.

"Nope." She waved from the window. "Don't be a stranger."

"I won't," I said. "Take care."

It certainly didn't hurt to know a few vampire hunters in the city.

When I dropped into the passenger seat, Vega was staring at her smartphone, the glow paling her tense face.

"What is it?" I asked.

She turned the image for me to see. I squinted a moment before I understood what I was looking at. Hands twisted my heart. It was a close-up shot of her son's neck. A small blue vein had been pricked, as though by a pin, and a thread of blood leaked from the vessel.

Beneath the picture, someone had typed, "Better hurry. The scent alone is *intoxicating*."

36

We dropped Lady Bastet and Alexandra off at the rug store. While Vega waited stiffly in the car, I carried Alexandra inside, setting her on a cot Lady Bastet had unfolded in the back room. "Tell no one she is here," Lady Bastet warned me as I left.

Back in the car, I focused on my cane, tapping into what remained of the hunting spell. My cane vibrated and then jerked in my hands. *Good. Still connected to the file.* But probably not for much longer. I powered down the window and aimed the cane outside. The spell tugged northwest.

"That way," I said.

Vega peeled from the curb. At my directions, we ended up on Second Avenue near where we had aborted our earlier pursuit of Moretti's men.

"Hold this course," I said.

"I need you to be damn sure about this."

"I am," I said, but I understood what she meant. With her son imperiled, every second mattered. And in the time it had taken for us to deal with Alexandra, Moretti's men should have circled back. The spell should have been pulling us south, toward Little Italy. Not north.

When we reached the East Seventies, Vega blew out her breath. "This isn't right. What in the hell would Moretti's men be doing way up here? We're getting into the Russians' territory. I'm going to ask you again. Are you sure you're—"

"Turn right!" I cried, clutching the bucking cane in both hands.

Vega slammed the brakes and cranked the wheel. The sedan skidded over the slick road, grazing a parked car, then leapt forward again, blowing through the next intersection. Three blocks later, with the night sky beginning to pale over the East River ahead, the cane steered us left onto an affluent street. A tree-filled park rose outside my window.

"Slow down," I said. The cane was rotating toward an opening in the tall security gate ahead. "There," I said, nodding at a driveway and what appeared to be a guard house beyond.

"I don't believe it." Vega slowed to a stop and cut her lights.

"What?"

"You don't know where we are?"

I looked around, trying to get my bearings. It was a corner of the city I rarely visited. The closest intersection was with East Eighty-seventh Street, which was telling me something.

"Wait a minute. Is this..."

Vega nodded, her eyes hard. "The mayor's mansion."

"Budge is involved in this?"

"Apparently."

"I don't get it. He's working for Moretti?"

Vega narrowed her eyes at the guard house. "More likely Moretti's men are working for him."

I clenched my brow, trying to make sense of the development. Now the shock of revelation opened everything wide. Alexandra was the stepdaughter of someone powerful, but not Mr. Moretti.

"Budge is the stepfather," I said numbly.

"Meaning his wife's the mother."

I thought of the soft-spoken woman at the gala. "Penny is Chastity Summers?"

"That's what Arnaud meant by the truth not being far from me," Vega said. "Little Italy is close, but City Hall is a hell of a lot closer. Practically across the street from police headquarters."

Vega pulled out her smartphone and began tapping the screen.

"Who are you calling?"

"I'm replying to Arnaud, telling him we know who the mother is."

Moments later, her phone blipped with a response. Vega sighed harshly through her nose.

"What?"

"He wrote back, 'Is that your final answer? Tick-tock, tick-tock.'"

Vega started the engine and veered into the driveway.

"Hey, what are you doing?"

"Making sure," she said.

"Shouldn't we, you know, strategize?"

"There's no time."

She pulled up to the guard house, stopping in front of the mechanical gate barring our way. The man inside the booth, though big and bulky, didn't look as mercenary as the guards for the Financial District. Then again, he was a public employee.

"Detective Vega with the NYPD," Vega said, holding up her ID. "I need to see Mayor Lowder immediately."

The guard consulted a console, the screen glowing green against his face. "Is he expecting you?"

"No, an emergency came up."

"Those usually come from the police commissioner. But I can ask him." He picked up a phone and punched a button. "Good morning, Mayor. There's a Detective Vega here to see you regarding an emergency."

"Tell him it concerns his family," Vega said.

"It has to do with your family." The guard scratched his chin. "All right, sir. Thank you."

When the guard stooped down, I called power to my prism, ready to cast. But instead of a weapon, he reappeared with a clipboard, which he asked Vega to sign. Vega passed the clipboard back. The gate blocking our way rose while a row of bollards beyond sank into the driveway.

"That seemed too easy," Vega muttered as she crawled the sedan forward.

I uttered an invocation, and a shield glimmered thinly around the car as the mayor's mansion rounded into view. The city used to give weekly tours of the mansion before the Crash, but I had never been back here. The yellow two-story house looked plantation style, with its wide front porch, second-story balcony, and line of stately columns. A handful of cars sat in spaces out front, including the sports car Moretti's men had been driving.

Vega parked beside it.

"What's our plan?" I asked.

"Let me do the talking." Vega drew her sidearm and got out. I climbed from the passenger side and strained to reshape the shield so that it protected the two of us. My powers had recharged on the drive up, but remained short of full strength. "Notice anything strange?" she asked.

"No guards?"

"Bingo."

Shots cracked from the sides of the house, sparking off the shield.

"*Vigore!*" I shouted, directing the force into a cluster of bushes to the left of the porch. In a burst of leaves, one of Moretti's men somersaulted skyward. Vega aimed and shot twice. Both bullets found their target, silencing the man before he crashed to the ground. The man on the right side of the house stood to run. Vega shot him once in the back. He face-planted on the lawn and went still.

I caught up to Vega on the front porch, where she seized the door handle. She stood back and nodded at my cane. With another "*Vigore!*" the door blew inward. Vega entered low, swinging her firearm from side to side. I moved in behind her, the final tugs of the hunting spell indicating we had the right address.

"Mayor Lowder," she called.

"In here," a man's voice answered from the next room.

We followed the voice to a large antique-furnished sitting room. To one side of a crackling fireplace, Budge reclined in a leather chair, a brown bathrobe fastened loosely around his belly, his slippered feet propped on an ottoman. He peered at us over a pair of reading glasses, a newspaper spread over his lap.

"Detective," he said, cordially. "And is that Everson Croft from the gala? Have a seat, have a seat."

While he gestured to the other chairs in the room, Vega swept the space with her pistol before taking a position where she could watch both doors and the staircase. "I'll stand, thank you," she said.

Mayor Budge folded up the newspaper and dropped it on an end table. He swapped his reading glasses for his round pair and finger-combed the cowlick from his brow as he put them on. "Now, what's this about a family emergency?"

Vega leveled her gun at him. "I'm going to be asking the questions."

"Whoa there!" Budge showed his hands, his magnified eyes darting between us. "What do you think you're doing? Hey, you're a professor," he said to me. "Talk some sense into her."

"I think she's about to make plenty of sense," I said. "So why don't you just settle in?"

Budge gave me a look that said, *Has the whole city gone crazy?*

"Why don't we start with Mr. Moretti?" Vega said.

"Mr. Moretti? What about him?"

"When did you start contracting him to do jobs for you?"

"The man's calling my office all the time, trying to get me to do him favors. You think I'd work with him?"

"Got a couple of his men in your yard who would probably say yes," Vega said. "If I hadn't shot them dead."

"Moretti's men?" Budge swept the hair from his brow again and leaned forward to peer out the window. When he looked back at Vega, his brow bent in confusion. He appeared at an honest loss, but then I remembered the gala and how quickly he could change his demeanor.

"Why don't we start from the beginning," Vega said. "When did you find out your wife had a daughter?"

Budge blinked his eyes. "Since before we were married."

"Yeah, right," Vega said. "When did you find out *what* she was?"

"Hey, what's this about?" Budge asked. "How do you two know so much?"

Vega glanced over at me—not the reaction she was expecting either—before pressing on. "At what point did you decide you wanted her dead? When she left school? When you found out she'd changed?"

"Wanted her dead?" Budge looked from Vega to me in horror. "What is she talking about?"

"Look," I said. "We know you hired vampire hunters to kill her. We also know you've been trying to eliminate anyone and anything that connects your wife—and you—to the creature. And that's meant contracting out work to Moretti. Makes sense. Someone running for reelection in a close race would do anything to keep a homicidal creature from being attached to his name. Can you imagine what your opponent would do with that?"

"What is this?" he asked, his neck turning red. "Some sort of blackmail job? You trying to set me up for something?"

Vega ignored the act. "Just so you know, I've given all the information we've uncovered to a third party. If anything happens to us, that information goes public. The hit on Sonny, the attempted hits on *us*, your dealings with Mr. Moretti. Even if you never see the inside of a courtroom, you're going to be slammed in the court of public opinion. You'll be done as mayor." Vega was lying about sharing the info with a third party, but damn, she was selling it well.

"If you have anything you'd like to amend," I said to the mayor. "We're all ears."

Budge looked around the room before sighing and running his hands through his hair. "All right." When he stood, Vega adjusted her aim, but he only lumbered to the fireplace. He leaned a forearm against the mantel so that he was staring into the flames. "Penny and I met at a dinner party back when I was a city commissioner. Boy, was she something. Turned every last head in the place, but for some reason she had eyes for me." Budge snorted a laugh. "So we started dating. Before we got too serious, though, I had her checked out, you know?"

"By an investigator?" Vega asked.

"And a diviner," Budge said. "An old man who lives in Chinatown. Mayor Alito swore by him." He turned toward me. "Leaders don't just use oracles in the myths, Professor. Anyway, I found out about her past at the Forty-second Street clubs. And also about her child."

"I bet that upset you," Vega said.

"Yeah, but not for the reason you might think. I came up in foster care, you see? Rough place for a kid. I couldn't stand the thought of her kid in the same system, so I made sure Alexandra was put in a good school."

"Wait." I shook my head. "*You* were Mr. Smith, her sponsor?"

He looked over at me. "Found out about that too, huh? Thought it was the least I could do."

"Did your wife know?" Vega asked.

Budge waved a hand. "Naw, she never talked about her, so I didn't either. I put Alexandra through twelve years of school and had her all set up for college without Penny ever knowing. But then I hear Alexandra's left the boarding school, and the diviner tells me that she's ... she's turned into some kind of monster, that she's killing people."

"And he advised you to destroy her," I said, trying to preserve the parts of Vega and my theory that still made sense. "To cover up any evidence that might connect Alexandra to your wife or to you."

"That's where you keep losing me," Budge said. "I didn't hire anyone to do anything like that."

"But you hired someone to do something else," I said, the truth rearranging itself and slotting into place. Vega and I had had the right theory, had found the right couple, but we'd reversed their roles. "You hired Arnaud to protect her."

A nervous tongue darted across Budge's lips. He dropped his head and nodded. "Hired him to capture her, actually. Takes a vampire to catch a vampire, you know? I wanted to get her some help."

"And you made him promise not to tell anyone," I said.

"Wait a sec." Budge's hands balled into hairy fists. "Was he the one who told you all of this?"

"No, in fact," I said, which was the truth—and no doubt at least part of the point of Arnaud's game. But what could Budge have possibly offered Arnaud in payment? The vampire was already a billionaire.

"Hold on a sec," Vega said, realization creeping over her face now. "If you hired Arnaud to protect your daughter, then—"

"His wife must be the big, bad wolf," someone finished.

273

I looked up, and there she was: the half-werewolf who wanted her daughter dead. Who wanted *us* dead. Penny Lowder strode down the staircase in a blue business skirt and jacket, her dyed-blond hair, usually fastened up, falling almost to her waist, loose and luxurious. Surgery no doubt masked her likeness to the young woman she'd once been. But with her veneer of submissiveness shed, I could feel her true nature, could see it radiating from her lupine eyes.

Vega trained her pistol on Penny, but the mayor's wife wasn't alone. Security guards flanked her, while others filled the two doorways to the sitting room. I sensed werewolf in them, too. With a Word, I reinforced the shield around Detective Vega and me, wondering how long I could hold it.

"Why don't you go upstairs, honey," Penny said to Budge. "We'll discuss your naughtiness later."

Budge nodded quickly, eyes large with fear, and hustled up the stairs and out of sight. I returned my attention to Penny, the power behind the mayoral throne. She stopped at a central landing.

"Now," she said in a growling voice. "What to do with these two?"

37

"You're the one who hired the vampire hunters and Moretti's men," I said, still not quite believing it. "You had Sonny killed. You put the hits on Vega and me and probably anyone else with information that would connect you to your daughter."

"I'm not going to confirm or deny anything," Penny said as the guards filed around her and down the steps. "But aren't we all after the same thing? Getting a killer off the streets? Keeping the citizens of New York safe?"

"Making sure your husband is reelected?" Vega said. "Keeping your hold on power?"

"What you think you know about my motives or past is inconsequential." She glanced at the guards. "Especially under the present circumstances."

"If anything happens to us—" Vega started to say.

"Ah, the threat." Penny grinned. "I heard everything you told my husband. The difference between my husband and me is that I can smell a lie." Her narrow nostrils flared out. "And you're giving off the sour odor, Detective. A good thing, because I *do* need you taken care of."

I cinched my grip on my cane as I counted the guards. At least twelve that I could see.

"Kill the intruders," Penny ordered.

The guards' snarling faces elongated, sprouting teeth and hair. Arms thickened and burst from uniform sleeves.

I created a firing line in Vega's shield as she squeezed off her first shots. A lunging werewolf seized his chest and fell forward, already reverting to his human form. Others swarmed over him, ears pinned back, jaws snapping against the shield. I had a cold flashback to Romania.

You possess magic now that you didn't then, I reminded myself.

Even so, what magic I possessed would only keep them off us for so long.

I drew my revolver and patted where my outer coat pockets would have been before realizing I had left my coat on Alexandra. No coat meant no more ammo. I released the revolver's cylinder and looked.

Three bullets.

A force jarred me, and the revolver fell from my hands. The werewolves were coordinating their attack, pulling back and then slamming into the shield at the same time, their supernatural strength rattling our protection all the way to my mental prism.

And with the beasts coming in low, Vega's shots were tearing into shoulders and heads more so than chests.

"*Respingere!*" I cried.

The shield pulsed, shoving the werewolves back, allowing me time to stoop and retrieve the revolver. But the chamber only held one bullet now. I found one of the dislodged bullets beside my shoe but couldn't see where the other one had clattered off to. *Dammit.* I pushed the silver bullet into the next slot and, with a wrist flick, snapped the chamber closed. Though Vega had dropped a couple more werewolves, the rest quickly reassembled.

"How you doing for ammo?" I shouted.

"Just reloaded," Vega replied, squinting down her gun's sights.

The werewolves rammed into the shield again, causing it to flicker.

"I'll set them up, you knock them down," I said through gritted teeth. "Like we did outside."

Vega nodded quickly.

"*Vigore!*" I cried, willing a force from the ground into one of the retreating werewolves. The force caught him under the chin, knocking him up and back, exposing his chest. Vega didn't miss. The shot blew through the werewolf's sternum, and we were down to eight.

The remaining werewolves let out savage barks, their eyes blazing yellow, bared fangs running with saliva. The deaths of their pack members seemed only to be making them more mindless, which was to our advantage.

With their next charge, I shouted another Word. The uppercut-like force bared another werewolf's chest, and Vega finished the job.

We're winning, I thought as the shield stood up to the collision of the remaining wolves. *We're going to get out of this.*

Shouting Word after Word, I flung the werewolves up, and Vega shot them dead. When the final werewolf fell and became human, I looked around for Penny. She was no longer on the staircase. I was opening my mouth to ask Vega if she'd seen where the mayor's wife had gone when the window behind us shattered. I wheeled as a massive stone planter ricocheted off the shield.

The two wolves outside aimed large-diameter hose nozzles. Water blasted through the window, spattering my shield and flooding the room. The magic I wielded fizzled and sparked. Vega leveled her firearm at the werewolves and squeezed, but no explosion followed.

"I'm out," she shouted.

"So are we," I said, taking her arm. The running water was drowning my magic, and we were down to two bullets. I pulled her into the foyer as my shield dispersed with a soggy pop. Through the blown-open front door, I could see the werewolves coming around to head us off.

"The window," Vega said, pulling me back into the sitting room.

We splashed toward the shattered window. Taking the end of a waterlogged rug, I heaved the thick fabric over the window's jagged lower frame and then lifted Vega so she was sitting on it. She wasted no time swinging her legs around and dropping the three feet into a flower bed.

I was preparing to follow when I heard snarling behind me.

The two werewolves had entered the sitting room and were running toward me. I drew my revolver and squeezed twice.

The point-blank shots nailed their chests, dropping them to the parquet floor.

Nice shooting, Tex, I thought, looking down at their melding bodies. *But you're out of ammo now.*

Meaning it was *really* time to get going. We had identified Alexandra's mother as the First Lady of New York City. More than that, we had discovered that she was the one trying to kill her daughter. Somewhere in there was the information Arnaud had wanted us to find.

"Oh, and you were so, so close," Penny said.

I turned to find her sauntering in from the foyer, dragging Detective Vega by her hair. The blood fell from my face. I jerked my leg back inside and shot to my feet, revolver raised.

"Drop her," I said, cocking the hammer on the empty weapon.

Penny jerked Vega up and around, clutching her in front of her, a human shield. "I will when you toss your weapon. Go on. Out the window."

I didn't move.

Penny dug her nails into the skin on either side of Vega's trachea. "Would you rather I tear out her throat?"

I sighed and did as she said, the revolver thumping onto the grass.

Penny deposited Vega in the same chair where the mayor had been reading. Beneath the light of the standing lamp, I caught a knot of bruising beneath Vega's right eye.

"Let her go," I said. "She has nothing to do with this."

Penny chuckled as she sat on the armrest, her fingers still clamping Vega's throat. "Such chivalry, Everson. But she has plenty to do with this. Now have a seat." She nodded toward a hard couch that had tipped over during the melee. "I'm going to ask you some questions. If you don't want to watch your partner die horribly, you're going to answer them."

"Okay, okay," I said, quickly righting the couch and lowering myself to the edge.

"And keep your feet in the water."

I looked down to where shallow waves lapped against the soles of my shoes. Water was a poor conductor of magic, and she knew it.

"Question number one," Penny said. "How did you learn that Alexandra was my daughter?"

"Good detective work," I replied.

Penny's nails dug deeper into the skin around Vega's throat. "Try again."

"Your old boss told us. Sonny."

"One more lie and she dies."

I glanced around for anything I could use as a weapon. No matter how I answered, her plan was to ultimately kill us both. My gaze fell to the bodies of the fallen werewolves. If only I hadn't expended all my damn silver.

"How did you learn Alexandra was my daughter?" she repeated.

"Why do you care?" I said. "Afraid that if you don't tie up all the loose ends you won't be able to pull your husband's strings anymore?"

Her eyes narrowed in a way that told me I was skating on paper-thin ice. But I needed time to come up with something. Penny probably only had one or two questions. The minute I handed her the answers, Vega and I were history. At the very least I needed to spare Vega that fate.

"You must not care for your partner very much," Penny said.

"Fine, I'll tell you." I blew out my breath. "It was Arnaud Thorne."

"Arnaud?" Penny sniffed for a lie.

"That's right."

A look of worry or anger deepened the lines around her eyes. I stole a glance at the hearth. The jets of water had doused the fire, but a few embers continued to glow in the ashes below the grate. I could work with that. While Penny grappled with the revelation, I shifted back on the couch and lifted my feet just above the water.

"Why?" Penny demanded. "What does he want?"

I silently summoned energy to my casting prism before shrugging. "Maybe he just doesn't like you."

Penny's eyes blazed orange, and her fingers bit into Vega's throat.

"Fuoco!" I shouted. Energy coursed through me in fits and starts, gained strength, and then opened out in the embers. A fireball roared from the hearth. Penny screamed as it swallowed her. I stood and drew my cane, shouting another Word. The force invocation sling-shot Vega from Penny's faltering grip toward my waiting arms. She was coming in too fast, though. The impact knocked the breath from my lungs and both of us to the floor.

Beyond my soaked legs, Penny was roaring and beating the flames that climbed her hair. Foul smoke filled the room. I forced myself to stand, pulling Vega up beside me. She coughed weakly.

"Are you all right?" I asked her.

"I'll live," she said hoarsely.

Good, because I could feel Thelonious licking his chops, waiting for me to exhaust myself with another high-energy spell.

With an arm wrapped around Vega's waist, she and I splashed from the sitting room. At the front door, I pushed her across the threshold but remained inside.

She staggered against the front-porch banister and squinted back at me. "Aren't you coming?"

"Find one of Arnaud's blood slaves," I said. "Tell him everything we've learned. That should get your son back." Before she could respond, I swung the door closed and sealed it with a basic locking spell.

Drawing the sword from my cane, I stalked back to the sitting room.

Time to finish this.

38

I returned to find Penny thrashing in a puddle of water on the floor. Desperate to extinguish the last of the flames licking from her hair, she snapped and yipped, eyes rolling back into her head. Though only part-werewolf, she had inherited their fear of fire. I don't think she even saw me as I stood over her and raised my sword.

I remained clueless as to why Arnaud had set us on her trail. Didn't know what he stood to gain by us finding out what he already knew. But Vega and I were marked now because of it.

Unless I eliminated the threat at the source.

I tightened my grip on the sword handle. The blade was steel, not silver, which meant I would need to decapitate her. Not an act I was relishing.

I braced a foot against her stomach. Her head reared back, exposing her throat. The muscles in my shoulders and upper back bunched...

And a shot rang out.

Something kicked me in the right chest. I dropped the sword and stumbled backwards, knocking over the couch. A pulsating numbness swallowed my right arm as I splashed seat down onto the floor. I pressed my hand to where I'd been hit and felt warm blood.

"I couldn't let you do that."

I raised my face to where Budge stood on the stairs, a pistol in hand.

"She's done some bad things," he said. "But I depend on her. I need her."

"Her daughter," I managed. "We helped her earlier this evening. She's not a monster anymore."

"Alexandra's okay?" The gun drifted down to Budge's side. "She's safe?"

I nodded my head, a gray nausea washing over me.

"Thank God," he breathed. "Where is she?"

Penny moved in front of my view of Budge, blackened scalp showing through what remained of her hair. Furious, orange eyes stared down on me. She spoke from a protruding jaw. "Yes, where is she?"

"That stopped being your business eighteen years ago," I mumbled.

She straddled me and knifed a talon-like nail into my wound. White-hot pain seared through me. I bit back a scream and seized her wrist, but my strength was no match for hers. She gouged deeper until my hands fell away. I slapped the floor to keep from passing out.

"You're sticking your nose into something you know nothing about," Penny said. "And I know what you're thinking. That your knowledge of Alexandra's whereabouts is going to keep you alive, that you can use it as a bargaining chip to finesse your way out of this. But if Arnaud told you about Sonny, I'm betting he also told you about Lady Bastet." Her lips spread into a crazy, canine smile. "Yes, that's where you took her. I can smell the fear pouring off of you."

"If she's not a monster anymore," Budge ventured from the staircase, "can't we just leave her alone, honey?"

"Silence!" Penny shouted.

I whipped my head from side to side as she gouged my wound again. The room wavered.

"Call for reinforcements," Penny told her husband. "I want one group to find and eliminate Detective Vega. The other will go to Lady Bastet's in the West Village. I'll join them when I finish with this one."

Something glinted just beyond my left hand. The silver bullet I'd dropped earlier. I stretched and closed my fingers around it.

"I'm just not sure I like the idea of offing all these people," Budge said.

"Well, *you* won't be offing them, will you?"

As I imagined Budge nodding in reluctant assent, his marital advice from the gala floated around me: *It's pretty simple, kids. Know when to agree, when to disagree, and when to agree to disagree.*

I chuckled through the haze of pain.

Penny's eyes glared down at me, then fell further to the bullet I was aiming at her chest.

"*Protezione,*" I mumbled. In the wetness, magical energy hissed and snapped through my prism and down my arm. A small orb manifested around the base of the bullet. I tightened the orb, willing it smaller. I just needed the pressure to ignite a single grain of the powder charge.

Penny laughed at my grunting and seized my throat. "Oh, you pathetic man. Trying to fire a bullet without a—"

The explosion kicked the shell from my seared fingers and blew the bullet into Penny. I caught her as she collapsed forward. Twisting, I deposited her on the floor on her back. Her eyes stared at the ceiling while blood bubbled and smoked from the wound below her chest. I had hit a large vessel, but missed her heart.

I collapsed against the couch, exhausted, my own blood soaking the arm of my jacket.

Budge hustled down the stairs and splashed into the sitting room. "Oh God," he cried, staring down at his wife. "Oh, Penny."

"She didn't give me a choice," I said.

His large eyes shifted to mine. They looked almost sad as he raised his gun.

"You don't have to do this," I said.

His silence seemed worse than any assertion he might have spoken. The gun's bore stared at my face. My magic spent, I squinted away, hoping Vega and I had done enough to fulfill Arnaud's terms.

"Stop!"

I rolled my head to find Vega standing in front of the broken window she'd climbed through, her pistol pointed at the mayor.

Though Budge's gun remained on me, his eyes wavered with uncertainty.

"A couple of ways we can play this," Vega said. "One, you shoot Everson, then I shoot you. Two, you let Everson walk, and we make a deal that you never come after either of us."

"Why would I do that?" the mayor asked.

"Because I just got off the phone with someone," Vega said. "And I told this person everything that Everson and I know. Your wife was right; I was bluffing before. But not this time." Her eyes were dead serious. "Rest assured, the information is safe with this person. But should anything happen to Everson, myself, or anyone close to us, they know what to do, who to contact. And I'm talking political opponents, media outlets, bloggers. You really will be finished."

The mayor's gaze moved between me and Vega, then fell to his bleeding wife. He lowered his gun.

"Go on," he said softly. "Get out of here."

39

Vega powered down the bollards blocking our exit and climbed back into the sedan.

"Any word from Arnaud?" I asked as she pulled from the driveway of the mayor's mansion.

"Nothing. You all right?"

I grunted as I pulled my arm from my blood-soaked jacket. "I will be. How about you?"

The bruising under her right eye had spread to include shades of pink and deep blue. She turned onto East Eighty-sixth Street and scanned the brightening sidewalks. "Where the hell are they?"

I squinted around. "Sunlight won't kill a blood slave, but it does strip their powers. They tend to avoid it."

"I'm through with this shit." At Third Avenue, Vega took a

hard left, snapped on her siren, and weaved through the growing traffic.

"Where are you going?"

"Where do you think?"

"The Financial District?"

"He has my son."

"We'll never get through the—"

"What would you have me do, Croft? We followed every one of his goddamned leads, and now he decides to go mute. Hasn't answered any of my texts or calls. I'm done playing his games."

I tented my fingers over my bullet wound and uttered a Word. With an agonizing tear, the bullet dislodged from bone and shot into my palm as though to a magnet.

"Christ," I hissed, dropping the bullet on the dashboard.

Vega glanced over. "Yeah, I know the feeling."

I touched my cane to my chest and incanted until healing energy cauterized the wound and anesthetized the shredded tissue. I sagged against the seat, the sweat that had sprung out over my body now soothing me.

"I can drop you off somewhere," Vega said.

I shook my head. "I'll go with you. But I need you to call Lady Bastet."

"Why?"

"Penny guessed where Alexandra was. She ordered her husband to send wolves down there. If I had killed Penny, I'd say Alexandra's safe, but I missed her heart. She could still pull through."

Vega drew out her phone and called.

"*Yes?*" Lady Bastet said over the speaker.

"It's Everson and Detective Vega," I shouted toward the phone while keeping myself a safe distance from the device. "Look, there's a good chance some werewolves are on their way to your store. You need to get yourself and Alexandra out of there and someplace safe."

"Do not worry, Everson. Alexandra is already someplace safe."

"What do you mean?" I asked.

"I foresaw the danger," she said. *"I also divined who was in the best position to protect her. A surprise, but she's in their care now."*

"Who?" Vega asked.

"The fewer who know, the better. Wouldn't you agree?"

I nodded at her logic. If and when Penny recovered, she would order a full-scale search for her daughter. She would squeeze the location out of whomever she could. "Well, what about you?" I asked.

"Wolves do not concern me, Everson. I will be fine."

I thought about the mystic's impressive powers as well as the protective wards I'd sensed in her store. "All right," I said. "But be careful. And thanks for your help."

One less worry anyway, I thought as the connection clicked off.

Seconds later, the phone rang. Vega checked the number and pressed the phone to her ear. "What's going on, Camilla?"

I could make out a fit of sobbing punctuated by attempts at speech.

"I can't understand you," Vega said. "Take a deep breath and try again."

There was a pause as her sitter inhaled, but her exhale turned into a sobbing wail. Amid the bawling, all I could make out was a name. An ice-cold hand closed around my heart.

"What about Tony?" Vega said.

Sobs surrounded more distorted word fragments.

"What about my son?" Vega repeated, shouting over the noise. "Are you at the apartment? Stay there, I'm on my way."

Vega hung up and stared at the road ahead, the engine rising another octave.

I pictured the beautiful, curly-haired boy in the photo Vega had given Hoffman.

God, please let him be okay.

I followed Vega as she sprinted up the stairwell of her apartment building and charged onto her floor. At her broken door, Vega stopped, firearm drawn. She pushed the door open with a foot.

"Camilla?" Vega called, stepping into the apartment.

The sobbing I'd heard on the phone returned, now emerging from Vega's bedroom. When Camilla appeared, she was holding a young boy. "He—he back, Ricki," Camilla managed amid the sobs. "They br-bring him back."

Vega holstered her weapon and rushed forward. She took her son from Camilla and held him up at arm's length. Tony blinked around blearily. Vega examined the fresh Band-Aid on the side of his neck, then looked the rest of him over. "Are you all right, honey? Are you hurt anywhere?"

When he didn't answer, Vega looked back at me.

I opened my wizard's senses until I could see the boy's aura.

"He's himself," I said after a moment. "He hasn't been turned into anything."

Vega sighed and pulled her son to her, burying her nose in his hair. Tony clamped his arms around her neck. "Thank God," she whispered, rocking him back and forth while Camilla looked on, crying more tears of relief. "You're safe, honey," Vega said. "Momma's got you."

She disappeared with her son into her bedroom.

"They bring him back," Camilla said to me, as though still trying to convince herself it had happened. "The men bring him back."

"The ones in suits?"

Camilla nodded. It appeared we had met Arnaud's terms, whatever the intentions behind them.

Ten minutes later, Vega emerged from her bedroom and closed the door softly. "He looks fine, but I'm going to take him to a doctor later this morning," she said. "Make sure he's all right."

While Camilla wrung her hands in prayerful thanks, Vega walked me to the door.

I pointed to her stomach. "Be sure to get yourself to a doctor, too."

"I will," she said stiffly.

"Look, I'm really sorry about..." I cocked my head toward the bedroom.

Though Vega nodded, her eyes remained unmoved. "I appreciate all of your help, Croft, but I meant what I said earlier. This is where our partnership ends." She shook her head when I tried to talk. "I know you didn't mean for anything to happen, but it did. I can't work with someone who would put my child at risk like that and not tell me, regardless of the circumstances."

I pressed my lips together. What could I say? She was absolutely right.

She extended her hand, but not to shake. "I need my pager back."

I pulled the iron-encased device from my pocket but hesitated before relinquishing it. "You have every right to feel the way you do," I said. "I screwed up. Badly. All I can say is that it will never happen again."

"The pager," she repeated.

I wanted to add that I would help her wherever and whenever she needed me. All she had to do was ask. But I knew my words would change nothing. I set the pager in her palm.

"I'll call you a cab," she said.

I remembered how vulnerable Vega had looked after I'd patched up her bullet wound, how I'd kissed her cheek. It was the first time I had considered her a friend, someone I cared about. "Ricki, I..."

"I'd prefer it if you waited outside."

40

I returned to my West Village apartment just before seven a.m. Instead of opening my door, I paused to lean against it, my blood-stained jacket over my cane arm, a heavy shroud over my heart. In the last twelve hours we had prevented a gang war, stopped a homicidal creature, saved a young woman, and seen the safe return of Vega's son. For all intents and purposes we had won.

And yet I felt like a colossal failure.

I had lost Caroline to the fae. I had lost Vega to her own good judgment. And I had played into Arnaud's hands somehow—I was sure of it. I was also sure that nothing good would come of the last.

I sighed and inserted the key into the top bolt and twisted. Already unlocked. My heart sped up. Ditto the other two bolts. I thought back. My last visit to the apartment had been a frantic race to collect some items before Moretti's men arrived. Had I forgotten to lock the door? No, more likely Moretti's men had picked the locks when they'd come looking for me.

But my wizard's intuition was telling me different.

I dropped my jacket and drew my cane apart, my chest hot and aching around the bullet wound. I rechecked the wards before opening the door.

The apartment was dark, the drapes drawn across the tall windows. I knew I hadn't done that. I scanned the sitting area, looking for Tabitha's glowing green eyes. Instead, I found a silhouette of the back of a head in my reading chair.

"You've had quite the night," the intruder said.

I turned on the flood lights. A white mane of hair glowed into view at the same moment I inhaled an odor of leather and musk.

"What are you doing here?" I demanded. "How did you get in?"

"You invited me," Arnaud replied calmly.

"Invited you? What in the hell are you talking about?"

I rounded the chair, staff and sword held out, until the vampire Arnaud waxed into full view. He wore a black cape over his stylish suit, one knee crossed over the other. On the right armrest, he held a glass of Scotch. Arnaud grinned as he gave the drink a light swirl.

"Yes, yesterday," he said. "I asked if you would prefer to meet at your place the next time, and you assented."

I tightened and then relaxed my grip on my weapons. The vampire had baited me into issuing an invitation, one that would temper my wards. And in the confusion of the opiate mist, I had obliged him, dammit.

"Well, I uninvite you now," I said. "Get out."

He chuckled. "The power of invitations doesn't work that way. You can only prevent me from returning."

I looked around for Tabitha.

Arnaud followed my gaze. "Your companion didn't much care for me. We had some words, I'm afraid. My, what a tongue she has." He waved a hand at my distressed look. "The feline is quite all right. Rather than tolerate my company, she elected to go out onto the ledge."

I relaxed slightly. I couldn't have handled another loss. Even Tabitha's.

"That doesn't change the fact you're not welcome here."

"I've surmised as much by the quality of your sauce." He looked down at his glass with a slight grimace. "But that is beside the point for now. Have you forgotten our blood deal?"

"Blood deal?"

"I said that if the arrangement concluded to everyone's satisfaction, I might have some information concerning your mother."

I stiffened. The deal had gotten buried beneath the desperateness of the night, one emergency after another—and the idiotic gamble I had made with Vega's son. I studied Arnaud's waxen face. *Did* he know something about my mother, or was this just another one of his games? I lowered myself onto the couch opposite him, knowing better than to appear too interested.

"I don't deal with scumbags who kidnap children for leverage," I said.

"Yes, but one cannot argue with the results, Mr. Croft. Besides, didn't you agree to the terms?"

Shame burned over my face. Instead of acknowledging his question, I asked one of my own. "What results?"

"Why don't you tell me? Let's see how much the weekend has taught you." He grinned as he sipped the whiskey.

"Mayor Lowder hired you to protect his stepdaughter," I said in a tired monotone, like a child reciting a catechism. "Which is why you deployed your blood slaves to the crime scene and ordered Vega and me to stay away from Ferguson Towers. Penny Lowder wanted her daughter dead so as not to jeopardize her husband's reelection and her own grip on power."

"Very good, Mr. Croft. And kudos for restoring dear Alexandra to her sentient form. Though you failed to follow my instructions to the letter at various junctures, I awarded you and the detective make-up points for saving the child. I understand she was placed in someone's stewardship?" He flashed a teasing smile.

I squinted at him. How would he know that? Unless Lady Bastet had made a gross error in divination.

"Alexandra was placed in *your* care?"

"You seem concerned."

"Well, gee, excuse me. I mean, why should I care that she was handed over to a cold-blooded killer?"

"Cold-blooded toward your kind, perhaps."

"But warm and cuddly toward a half-vampire?"

"Or a half-Thorne."

The fight fell out of me as I stammered silently. "She's yours?"

Arnaud watched me above his glass as he took another sip of whiskey.

"I thought Sonny Shoat was the father."

"The despicable Sonny Shoat was Penny's employer," Arnaud

said. "And the vampire fancied her, yes, but she was looking for someone more powerful. When the opportunity presented itself, she exercised her seductions on me—which I could hardly blame her for—but vampires and werewolves have an embattled history, as you likely know. It could never have worked. When her bid for my protection failed, Penny turned to the mortal world."

I remembered what Lady Bastet had said about two men of significance in Penny's life: one weak, the other strong. Mayor Lowder had been the man of weakness, Arnaud Thorne the man of strength.

"So where money fortifies you," I said, "politics now fortifies her."

"Precisely," Arnaud hissed.

"And that's what you wanted us to find out?"

"For decades, your cognitive scientists have clamored that the surest way to assimilate new information is through direct experience. While the detective correctly deduced that I was bound by an agreement, had I told you all you ultimately learned, it might have gone in one ear and out the other. And besides, it would only have been my word."

"Why, though? What does Penny pulling the mayor's strings have to do with anything?"

"As I said, the best investors cover all sides of a trade."

"Mayor Lowder promised you something in exchange for protecting his stepdaughter..." *If not money, then what?* I wondered. I thought about what vampires valued most. "Protection," I said.

"We'd come to a certain agreement," Arnaud confirmed.

"Protection from what, though?"

"From *who*, Mr. Croft. And I believe you can answer that for yourself."

"His wife?"

"Our kinds don't get along, but in rejecting her I made that enmity personal. I would have liked very much for you to have destroyed her. As I understand it, you came close. I don't know that it would have mattered, though," he added, as though to himself. "Wheels are already in motion."

"Wheels? What wheels?"

"Look around yourself, Everson. An election year, a close race, and more and more New Yorkers becoming aware that not only is their city crumbling, it's being overrun by undesirables."

I remembered the ghouls I'd seen in the East Village, digging through the garbage in the light of dusk. "So, what, the mayor's going to announce some sort of plan to combat the supernaturals?"

"In Europe they called it a *purge*."

"But Penny's one of them," I said.

"Which is precisely why she fought so hard to expunge her past."

"The deal you made with the mayor—it was that you'd be exempted from the purge, wasn't it?"

"I think you now appreciate how fragile that agreement is," he said.

Yeah, I thought with a tired snort, *probably about as fragile as the deal Vega and I struck with the mayor.* "But I thought you controlled the city's purse strings. Why not leverage your financial power?"

He smiled bitterly. "It seems the mood of the nation is shifting. There is talk of the U.S. government bailing the city out of its debt.

The country is hardly solvent itself, but more and more politicians are becoming uncomfortable with the power institutions like mine wield."

"And if the bailout goes through, City Hall won't need your money."

"You're a quick study, Mr. Croft."

"So that's what this whole thing was about, wasn't it?" I said, anger shaking my voice. "To make me an enemy of City Hall, too. That way you'd have an ally should Mayor Lowder renege and come after you."

"Oh, wipe that sourpuss look from your face, Mr. Croft. It wouldn't be the first time the interests of vampires and wizards coincided. Your grandfather certainly wasn't above joining forces when the need arose. Indeed, you're sitting here today because of it."

The foul fumes of resentment clouded over my exhaustion, leaving me feeling faint and sick. "Tell me whatever you know about my mother and get out."

"Ah, about that. I've decided to give you a choice." He reached into a coat pocket and held up the ring his blood slave had ripped from my finger the night before. The rearing dragon flashed dully in the faint light. "You can have the information on your mother, or you can have your grandfather's ring."

I automatically reached for the ring, then hesitated and pulled back.

"Very good." Arnaud's eyes sparkled as he pocketed the ring again. "About twenty years before his death, your grandfather came to see me."

"He did?"

"Yes, it was just as unexpected for me. Following our campaign in Europe, we drifted apart, pursued our own interests. While I built my empire in lower Manhattan, your grandfather worked as a common magician before settling into some sort of insurance trade. It puzzled me. I had seen him on the battlefield, and believe me when I tell you he was exceptionally powerful. On the night he came to see me, however, he was exceptionally inebriated. The poor man could barely hold himself up. His coat and hat were waterlogged, and the state of his shoes told me he'd been kicking around the filthy streets for hours. He asked for another drink, and I obliged him. 'They killed her,' he murmured into his glass. 'My God, they killed her.' "

I straightened. "My mother?"

"I can only presume. Her death announcement appeared in the paper the following day. Sudden illness."

That was what I had been told as well. "Who's *they*? Who killed her?"

"Your grandfather never said. He left shortly after his arrival."

"So why tell you?"

Arnaud gave a small shrug. "Who can say? Perhaps his drunkenness exaggerated whatever kinship he may have felt from our shared past. Or perhaps he had no one else to confide in."

I studied the tips of my own filthy shoes, feeling cold and small. I thought back to Grandpa's fury when I snuck into his locked study at thirteen. I remembered the flash of his sword, his stern admonition: *You must not be foolish, Everson. Things heard cannot be unheard. Things seen unseen. Things spoken unspoken. And it is this last that is most important for those of our blood.*

There was so much he hadn't wanted me to know—about him, about myself. That had become clear to me over the years. But was it because of what had happened to his daughter, my mother?

"Well, then," Arnaud said abruptly, placing the empty glass on an end table and pushing himself to his feet. "It seems all agreements have been satisfied. Until we meet again, remember what you've learned these last days. The city will be changing, and not for the better, I'm afraid. Not where our kind are concerned. Be alert for the signs, Mr. Croft. The changes may come quick and violent."

His black cape floated up as he paced to the door, opened it, and then shut it behind him.

I remained on the couch, not sure whether to finish healing my injuries and take a badly needed shower or to curl into a fetal position, close my eyes, and wish the rest of the world away.

They killed her. My God, they killed her.

41

I decided to save the fetal position for another time. I willed myself to the shower, where hot water soon dissolved the dirt and dried blood and sent them swirling down the drain. I treated my injuries. I fed Tabitha, forced down a bowl of cereal, and climbed into bed. The last thirty hours collapsed against my buzzing consciousness, dropping me into a dreamless abyss.

I was awakened by knocking. I opened my eyes to a night-dark apartment. I had slept through the day.

The knocking resumed. I rolled onto my other side, away from the front door, but when the knocking returned a third time, I sat up.

What now?

After a stop in the bathroom to scoop water against my face and swish some mouthwash, I cinched my robe and, cane in grip, squinted through the peephole. I quickly twisted the bolts and opened the door.

"Caroline?" I stammered, turning on the floodlights. "What are you doing here?"

"May I?" she asked, stepping past me.

I locked the door behind her and took her coat, hanging my cane beside it on the rack. Though fae power moved around her, she wore mortal attire: a white blouse and long khaki skirt, leather boots.

She turned toward me, a heaviness in her eyes.

"What is it?" I asked.

She stepped forward until it only seemed natural for me to hold her. She slipped her arms beneath mine and around my back, and nestled her head against my shoulder. She rocked me slowly, her warmth pulsating against me.

"My father's cancer is in remission," she said.

I nodded over her. "I'm glad to hear that. I really am."

"Everson..." She paused and held me tighter. "I'm still getting used to this, to being fae, but I can feel things I couldn't before. I never knew the depths of your emotions around, you know, us. I should have seen it."

"Or maybe I should have just told you."

She leaned back and studied my face. I wasn't sure what she saw, but I didn't try to hide anything. I was too spent. She kissed each of my cheeks, her lips soft against my whiskers. Healing energy whispered through me. When she looked at me again, I sensed her reluctance to pull away.

I couldn't watch her leave a second time.

Inhaling the perfume of her magic, I leaned down and pressed my lips to hers. The kiss deepened, and we moved in a dizzying slow dance. Across the living room, into my bedroom, across the bed.

I pushed everything else away. My fallout with Vega, my mother's death, Arnaud's warning about a coming purge, Caroline's marriage to a fae. I shoved them clear from the thrumming now.

When we came up for air, I looked down on her. With her golden hair fanning against the white bedspread and over the shoulders of her open blouse, her blue-green eyes gleamed up at me. I saw in them fear and at the same time a determination to hold onto her old world.

I smoothed each slender eyebrow with a finger and kissed her forehead.

"I do love you," I said. "But are you sure about this?"

She nodded and pulled me back to her.

"I'm sure," she breathed.

THE SERIES CONTINUES...

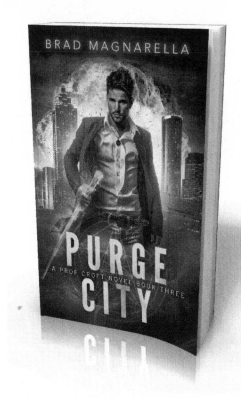

PURGE CITY (PROF CROFT, BOOK 3)

- On sale now -

About the Author

Brad Magnarella is an author of speculative fiction. His books include the *Prof Croft* novels and the young-adult superhero series, *XGeneration*. Raised in Gainesville, Florida, he now calls various cities home. He currently lives and writes in Washington, D.C.

www.bradmagnarella.com

BOOKS BY BRAD MAGNARELLA

THE PROF CROFT SERIES
Book of Souls

Demon Moon

Blood Deal

Purge City

Death Mage

THE XGENERATION SERIES
You Don't Know Me

The Watchers

Silent Generation

Pressure Drop

Cry Little Sister

Greatest Good

Dead Hand

THE PRISONER AND THE SUN
Escape

Lights and Shadows

Final Passage

Made in the USA
Middletown, DE
26 June 2017